"A VERY MODERN COMEDY THAT SKEWERS FAMILY LIFE WITH HEART AND WIT."
—*New York* magazine

"A comic look at what makes family bonds durable, which turns out to be a capacity for shared malice as much as a capacity for shared love."
—*New York Observer*

"Schine's rueful wit animates this beguiling contemporary comedy of manners."
—*Publishers Weekly*

"Schine writes dead-on dialogue that crackles with idiosyncrasies of character . . . the Brody family, still crazy, is lovable enough to read about yet again."
—*San Francisco Chronicle*

"Wild and wacky." —*Anniston Star*

"Dizzy, hilarious, authentic, original."
—*Washington Post Book World*

"As a comic writer, Cathleen Schine has a splendid voice . . . a remarkable gift for the varieties of comedic experience . . . she can write boffo one-liners . . . toss off slapstick scenes with Keystone Kops appeal . . . and balance zaniness with poignancy."
—*Newsday*

CATHLEEN SCHINE has written three other acclaimed novels: *Alice in Bed*, *Rameau's Niece* (both available in Plume editions), and most recently, *The Love Letter* (available in a Signet edition). She lives in New York City with her husband, film critic David Denby, and their two sons.

Other Books by Cathleen Schine

The Love Letter

Rameau's Niece

Alice in Bed

TO THE BIRDHOUSE

Cathleen Schine

A PLUME BOOK

PLUME
Published by the Penguin Group
Penguin Books USA Inc., 375 Hudson Street,
New York, New York 10014, U.S.A.
Penguin Books Ltd, 27 Wrights Lane, London W8 5TZ, England
Penguin Books Australia Ltd, Ringwood, Victoria, Australia
Penguin Books Canada Ltd, 10 Alcorn Avenue,
Toronto, Ontario, Canada M4V 3B2
Penguin Books (N.Z.) Ltd, 182–190 Wairau Road, Auckland 10, New Zealand

Penguin Books Ltd, Registered Offices: Harmondsworth, Middlesex, England

Published by Plume, an imprint of Dutton Signet,
a division of Penguin Books USA Inc.
This is an authorized reprint of a hardcover edition published by
Farrar, Straus and Giroux. For information address Farrar, Straus and Giroux,
19 Union Square West, New York, New York 10003.

First Plume Printing, July, 1996
10 9 8 7 6 5 4 3 2 1

(P) REGISTERED TRADEMARK—MARCA REGISTRADA

LIBRARY OF CONGRESS CATALOGING-IN-PUBLICATION DATA
Schine, Cathleen.
        To the birdhouse / Cathleen Schine.
            p.   cm.
        ISBN 0-452-27662-4
        1. Man-woman relationships—United States—Fiction.   2. Mothers
and daughters—United States—Fiction.   I. Title.
[PS3569.C497T6   1996]
813'.54—dc20   96–33688
                                                                          CIP

Printed in the United States of America
Original hardcover design by Cynthia Krupat

PUBLISHER'S NOTE
This is a work of fiction. Names, characters, places, and incidents either are
the product of the author's imagination or are used fictitiously, and any
resemblance to actual persons, living or dead, events, or locales is entirely
coincidental.

FOR DAVID AND DAD

1 / *To the Birdhouse*

Nothing sounded more inviting to her than settling down. Settling down would be like curling up; it would be like stretching out: it would be comfortable. After circling around a few times, like an Irish setter on the rug before the hearth, she would give a sigh, wag her tail, and then, in a delirious descent toward calm and stability, she would settle down. Alice Brody was getting married.

She was marrying a tall, distracted man named Peter Eiger. Alice was a generous person, in her way, and so it occurred to her that many other people should settle down and get married to tall, distracted men, too. She wanted other people to be as happy and contented as she now planned to be, and she was determined to help them and not to rest until she had succeeded. Still a little startled by her own good fortune, Alice looked around her like a farmer who's struck oil and decides to clean up the tacky little town nearby. She would build a movie theater and a new jail. There would be sidewalks.

The prime candidate for reconstruction was her

mother, who now stood buttoning Alice's wedding dress up the back and smiling for the photographer who had come in to record the preparations. When the photographer was finished, Brenda Brody looked in the mirror and saw herself, pink and smiling, with several fat, turquoise-colored curlers bobbing and swinging from her hair.

"Hmm," she said.

Alice was happy and had decided her mother must be made happy, too. But how could she be? Alice still couldn't believe, not really, that her mother had a boyfriend like Louie Scifo.

"Don't you dare invite him to my wedding," she had said.

"Of course you don't mean that, dear," her mother said mildly. "It would be too inconsiderate to me."

Alice had long since despaired of helping her father find happiness. He had, first of all, divorced her mother, but worse, he had taken it on himself to marry someone else—someone not at all like Peter.

Holding her father's arm, Alice walked down the aisle of the wood-paneled room. This was the Yale Club, her father's favorite institution, preferred by far to the university itself. Boolah, Boolah, she thought happily and looked up at Dad for an instant. They both turned their heads, trying not to giggle stupidly. She looked toward the rows of guests and saw her grandmother sniffling into a lace handkerchief. The night Alice's grandmother met Peter, she had pulled Alice into another room while everyone ate dessert, and said, "So? so?" Months later, when Alice told her she and Peter were getting married, her grandmother hugged and kissed Alice and clapped her hands and said, "Oh! Oh! I'm so happy and please God don't let him turn out like that *malekhamoves* your father he should go to hell the dirty bitch what he did to my Brenda," with a happy grin on her soft, white face.

Alice stood beside Peter and listened to the rabbi talking, without hearing what he said. The rabbi's first wife had committed suicide, she remembered. From the corner of her eye she could see Peter in profile, could see his long, narrow face and the high brow that was always just a little creased, so that Peter seemed to be permanently thinking. She had first realized she was in love with Peter when she noticed she was consistently giving him the largest portions of good things to eat.

After the ceremony, Alice stood in a row of relatives shaking hands with other relatives. Her mother was next to her, and next to her mother, her father. Alice looked at them, for a moment remembering what an uncomfortable couple they had made.

"Now you can go dance the first dance, dear," her mother said when everyone had wandered into the grand, sparkling dining room. "Go with Peter."

"It's too embarrassing," Alice said.

"You only have to dance if you want to," said her father, which almost made Alice want to. "After all, this is your day." Her father patted her hand, then made a low, strangled sound, covered his eyes suddenly, and walked away, his shoulders shaking.

Alice's mother continued to lecture her on the necessity of a first dance. She told her she was probably a repressed exhibitionist and would have to seek professional help after the reception. Brenda was a child psychologist.

"Yes, Mom," Alice said. She was watching a small, rather gaunt man who had appeared at a table near them. He placed something in the centerpiece, then dashed away to the next table, where he repeated the procedure.

Louie Scifo Lives, Alice thought. She had not noticed him before. Now she watched as he moved quickly around the room, compact and horrifyingly efficient, sweeping from table to table with wiry, vigorous force. He was not young, and his hair, which was long and luxuriant, emphasized the signs of age in his face. He kept pushing it back with both hands, like a teenage girl. His round eyes were moist, the whites not white at all, but tan, like a horse's eyes.

Alice walked over to the table and parted the flowers. She saw a small white card, a business card, tucked among the blossoms. She picked it up and read aloud: "Scifo Art Gallery Including TOP Jewels and Gems," and then Brenda's address.

"That Louie!" Brenda said. She laughed. Then she called to her son and his girlfriend, a Japanese graduate student spending a year at Columbia. "Yuki, come sit with us. Willie, tell your sister to dance."

"Why do you think he's putting his business card in all the flowers?" Peter asked. Louie was making his way around the room, from table to table.

"Is this American custom?" asked Willie's girlfriend.

Alice buried her face in her hands.

Her mother seemed not to have heard. "Dance, Alice," she said, as if she were training a puppy. "Dance."

Alice danced with Peter as best she could. She had refused to attend Westport's dance classes for young ladies and gentlemen. "And now I must pay the price," she said.

Peter had been to dancing school, and he said, "Just shuffle your feet."

Alice put her face against his shoulder, shuffled her feet, and felt content. She realized she had been smiling for over an hour. The grin just stayed on her face, stretching her mouth, and it was beginning to hurt. "Peter," she said dreamily from his shoulder, "I'd like to kill my mother."

Louie Scifo was making his way across the dance floor, and Alice could tell he was headed directly for her, like a guided missile, although he made several detours and loop-the-loops, swooping toward people with his arms outstretched.

"Good, that's good," he said reassuringly to the band, embracing the accordion player.

"Quick," Alice said, "dance over there," and Peter directed her smoothly in the direction of the buffet table.

"Behave, Alice," he said.

"Dance with your mother," Louie was saying to Alice's brother.

Alice didn't want to behave. She wanted Louie to behave, which meant, in her mind, to go home.

"That's beautiful," Louie was saying to Peter's parents, who were dancing cheek to cheek. "Just beautiful."

Louie shook hands with several people, threw his arms around an elderly man as he introduced himself, and continued his approach.

"Dance with your mother," she heard him say to someone she didn't recognize.

"Dance with your mother," he said to Peter, appearing beside him. "Allow me to cut in and hold your most lovely bride in my lonely arms. Dance with your mother."

"I think Alice is supposed to dance the second dance with her father," Peter said. "Isn't that the tradition?"

Alice looked up at him gratefully, although she suspected his motives were mixed. She had told him earlier that she would not dance with her father because he paid her mother insufficient alimony and was from Canada.

"Far be it from me," Louie was saying, holding up his hands and stepping back.

Alice glanced around the room in search of her father and spotted him carrying two glasses of champagne toward an empty table. Nearby, his new wife, Patricia, danced with a tall, skinny, bored-looking boy, her son, Charles. One of the reasons her father had married Patricia, Alice thought, was that she came complete with a nine-year-old son, who her father had not had the foresight to realize would inevitably grow up, as in fact he had done. The nine-year-old, now sixteen, sang in a rock band specializing in songs of the sixties, the same songs that had caused her father to cover his face in disgust and anger when Alice, years ago —before they became artifacts of nostalgia—had played them loudly on her record player. It gratified Alice to think of her father suffering in his easy chair as the lanky teenager banged mercilessly on his drums in the basement playroom, singing, "We *gotta* get *out*a this place." Another reason her father had married Patricia, according to Alice's theory, was that Patricia informed him that the head of state in Canada was the Queen. Alice always pictured Patricia in a tweed suit and sensible shoes, briskly walking her hounds, although Patricia had no hounds (dogs were known to shed).

Alice imagined her with hounds because she thought that's how her father imagined her, striding along, hearty and very nearly British in the gray drizzle of Vancouver, for the weather there was very British indeed. Dad's Anglophilia was accepted by Alice the way another daughter might treat a parent's senility: she gently worked around it, trying not to notice the careful combing of the stiff mustache, smiling indulgently at the proud lectures on parliamentary government or the benefits of commonwealth.

"Yup, that's certainly the tradition," Alice said to

Louie. But he was already engaged in steering Peter toward his mother. He did turn around long enough to say sternly, "Dance with your father," and summon Alan Brody with a shout and a wave.

Alice's father was broad and tall, and dancing with him, Alice could see nothing but the pinstripes of his jacket, his white shirt, and his tie, held in place at the collar with a gold pin. She could feel the small ring that had been his grandfather's on his finger. The tie he was wearing was an ugly one, which surprised her. She attributed the gold-and-green design to Canadian fashion.

"I was waiting for a waltz," he said. "I love to waltz." And then he burst into tears.

Her father was a sentimental sort. When Alice was in the hospital for so long, so many years ago, he had stood by her bedside and cried. When he divorced Brenda, he had cried on the witness stand while testifying to an untidy house. He had probably cried when he'd married Patricia Hum. He had certainly done so when he called the hospital to tell Alice about their wedding, a civil ceremony he found moving in its simplicity. If he did not always pay much attention to the sorrows of others, he certainly felt deeply everything that happened to him. And now, surrounded by his old family and his new, he was probably feeling the loss of Alice and Willie, perhaps even Brenda, and blaming himself, if not for leaving them, then for leaving when he did.

Alice began to cry, too. They stood at the edge of the dance floor while she blew her nose in her father's handkerchief. When she gave it back, a white crumpled ball, he pushed it into his jacket pocket, cleared his throat, and asked if she remembered standing on his feet to dance as a little girl. He began to weep again.

"You don't have to feel so guilty, Daddy," she said magnanimously. On this, her wedding day, she would dispense a pardon. It was only right. He was her father, she was married, and she could remember standing on his feet to dance. She could remember it clearly.

"I don't feel guilty," he said.

"Well, you *should*. You certainly should."

"But you just said—"

"Never mind, Daddy." She tried to steer him in a different direction.

"Alice, just follow."

"Well, let's dance over there, thataway," she said. "No, wait a second, what about over here?" But no matter which way she and Alan Brody went, she could see Louie Scifo, smiling, stepping lightly through the crowd, toward her.

"Alice, what's the matter with you?" her father asked. He stopped altogether and stood, puzzled, and wiped his still damp eyes.

"Nothing," Alice said. Stalked by Mom's boyfriend, that's all, Dad, she thought. A very dignified person for whom I have the greatest respect.

"Your mother's, um, friend, seems a fine chap," her father had said to her earlier.

"Yes," she had said helplessly, covering the hideous blot on her mother's reputation as best she could. "Yes."

"There's Louie's little bride," Louie was saying. "May Louie have this dance? Dance with your mother," he said to Alice's father.

"She's dead," Alice said, and her father began to cry again.

Louie Scifo held one of Alice's hands; he put his other arm around her waist; he opened his mouth in a wide smile. He wore a diamond pinkie ring that she thought was not only ugly but hot. She wondered if he would tell her to dance with her mother. She hoped so.

"Shall we dance, milady?" he said.

As Louie began patiently to lead her around the room in a waltz, Alice saw him glance at her mother, who was talking to the maître d'.

"You know, Alice, this is your wedding day, the day you become what you might call, what you might call a *woman*," Louie said. He stared at Brenda.

Alice wondered if Louie would release her in order to start noisily accusing Brenda of flirting with the help, as was his custom. And why *didn't* her mother flirt with the maître d', she wondered, a pleasant, respectable man in a tuxedo who was gainfully employed. He wasn't Jewish and he wasn't in a profession, but neither was he dressed in a baby-blue suit and brown patent-leather boots, drunk and placing his hand on Alice's bottom.

"Now, your mother," Louie said, still watching Brenda and the maître d', "she's a very warm and emotional woman. Passionate, you understand me?"

She removed Louie's hand and sighed. She wished she could get angry enough with him someday to slap his face or holler at him or spit or throw a stone. But, instead, she merely felt a drifting, enervated dismay. He just didn't seem possible. Not in her life, with her mother, at her wedding. So she never did much of anything about Louie except avoid him and, occasionally, lecture her mother about him, and then feel bad afterward. Now, dancing with Louie, Alice felt a little guilty at the unhappiness those lectures had caused her mother, although clearly it was Louie's fault for being objectionable enough to cause Alice to try to turn her mother against him in the first place.

"Thank you for the lovely vase," she told Louie.

"A lovely vase for a lovely lady," Louie said, and Alice hoped he would not put his hand back on her behind, although she knew Louie's occasional pinch or lascivious look had no real intention behind it. He had once given her a clingy nightgown, chosen by her mother, for Christmas, and a card with this message:

> To the One I love
> > Here I'm the Dirty Old Man
> I wish I was Young
> And gay to see You in this—
> You and I with your loveliness
> Body and Soul
> For you are a lovely Woman
> To have a Man
> Want you hold you and love you
> —Louie!

"He's sort of a romantic," Alice's mother remarked when she read the card.

"Sort of," said Alice.

Alice looked unhappily at Louie. He swung her around, saying, "La dolce vita, you catch my drift?" Her chin was well over the top of Louie's head as they danced, and when she grimaced, he couldn't tell. Alice grimaced at Peter, who was dancing with his mother.

"See that, see that?" Louie was saying, pointing at the couple. "That Peter, he's a good boy."

Alice thought, Yes, he is a good boy. He loomed over his mother, a tiny person whose voice could be heard in far-off provinces. "Don't neglect your triglycerides, Peter . . ."

Alice reflected on how much her feet hurt, how they throbbed inside her shoes, a condition she blamed on Louie. At my own wedding, she thought. My *own wedding*.

She did notice, however, that her own wedding was moving along in spite of her sore feet and her unspeakable dancing partner. Well, good, she thought. What they don't know won't hurt them. The band, an accordion, clarinet, and saxophone, alternated between delirious, wailing klezmer, during which people swung themselves around in a sloppy hora, and familiar wedding fox-trots and jitterbugs. Alice wondered if almost everyone her age—everyone but Willie and Peter—had skipped dancing school, for she observed that while the older couples glided and spun during these dances, their children seemed content to stand almost completely still, swaying, as if they were on the deck of a ship, or feeling ill. That was a pleasant thought—that no one else could dance, either. She looked at the table where the buffet was laid out. Most of the activity centered around a gigantic smoked salmon her father had brought with him from British Columbia. But the chafing dishes were doing a pretty brisk business as well, and Alice nodded approvingly, like an attentive shopkeeper. She looked suddenly at Louie Scifo. She had almost forgotten him.

" 'I-I-I'll be seeing you in a-a-all the o-o-old familiar places . . .' " he sang along with the band, winking at Alice's grandmother as they danced by.

Alice noticed that the Brodys' neighbor from Westport, Jack Mandell, was walking toward her.

Alice smiled at Jack. Short and solid, Jack walked in bursts—quick explosions of energy that carried him a certain distance, then left him there to stand and recoup before they carried him off again. This had always seemed to Alice to give him an air of bustling importance and power. She had been very fond of him as a child, and also a little afraid.

"May I cut in?" Jack said.

"But of course," said Louie in an exaggerated French accent.

Alice put her arms around Jack and kissed him. They danced off, starting and stopping like a cold car.

"I thought I should cut in. And then Willie said, you know, with the, with the, with Louie," he said. "With the dancing."

"Thank you," said Alice.

"I thought maybe," said Jack, who favored somewhat mysterious sentence fragments. "On account of that."

"With Louie with the dancing," Alice said. She had known Jack for as long as she could remember.

"That's what I thought," Jack said, and Alice put her head on his shoulder, comforted by this unchanging remnant of the past. She thought of all the summers she had spent hanging around the Mandells' house when their own children, who were older than Alice, were away at camp. She'd felt a happy responsibility toward Jack and Nancy, who were obviously incomplete without their kids, in need of a temporary fill-in, in need of Alice. She used to sit importantly in Jack's driveway, looking up at him on his ladder, watching his every move as he painted his house. Sometimes, on oppressively hot days, Alice would walk into the Mandells' house and settle herself into a corner, watching particles of dust drift along beams of sunlight, enthralled by the chill of the air-conditioning. She would sit there, quite still, for hours sometimes, until Jack or his wife, Nancy, came in and jumped at the unexpected sight of the silent child.

Jack was apparently thinking of the same time, because he said, "Remember? With the painting?"

"Yes, I do remember," Alice said. "Of course I remember."

Jack and Nancy still lived in Westport, in the same house, the same summer chill. They had always seemed a miraculous couple to Alice, so busy, so completely engaged in the routine of being a family. They were still busy. Every year, Jack climbed his ladder and painted his house white. After work, in the summer twilight, he mowed the lawn, up and down, hour after hour. "It's relaxing," he would say, when asked why he mowed a lawn that had been mowed by the gardener that morning. In the winter, with the first flake of snow, you could hear the scraping of Jack's snow shovel on the paved driveway, back and forth, soothing and seemingly forever. Nancy could still be found standing behind the ironing board, surrounded by piles of freshly laundered towels and shirts and sheets, pushing the iron across the smooth arm of a permanent-press blouse. "It's so relaxing," she would say. All summer long, there was ice tea and watermelon and bowls of cherries in the Mandells' refrigerator. It was a household that never ran out of anything, not even Mallomars.

A friend of Peter's, a bearded English professor who had devoted his career, as well as a large portion of his conversation, to an emotionally charged campaign to promote the reputation of Wilkie Collins, pushed through the dancers and tapped Jack's shoulder.

When Jack had sputtered off, he said, "Peter suggested I remove you from the grasp of that person. Your mother's boyfriend."

"Jack?" Alice said. She was about to explain when she

allowed herself the momentary luxury of imagining that Jack, not Louie, was her mother's boyfriend. "Yes," she finally said, "yes. Thank you."

"I've rescued the Woman in White," he said, beaming.

"Oh, good," Alice said.

When the dance was over, Alice walked among the tables, making her way over to Willie and Yuki. Willie, who had recently drifted into Ottoman Studies, had mercifully left his fez at home today. He and Yuki had met at Columbia's School of International Affairs, a name he found uproariously funny. ("Get it? Get it?")

"I sent Jack to rescue you," Willie said. "You know, Louie is a big pain. I mean, he tells me to dance with Mom, like I'm not going to dance with Mom at your wedding, I mean, he doesn't have to tell me to dance with my own mother."

"Yeah, well, now he's preoccupied, anyway," Alice said, and glanced over at Louie, who was dancing with Mom, his face buried in her chest, his hands clutching her waist. Alice was tempted to say something else—"Blech!" for example—but stopped herself.

"Willie is so very ambivalent toward his mother," Yuki said. "But this is so common ambivalence of Jewish young male. In my studies of—I have told you, Willie, you must read Roth, you must read Malamud, all you read is E. P. Thompson—in my studies this is, this is trope, absolute trope. And now, shall we dance, now?"

Alice sat down at a table with her friend Katie and Katie's husband, Mike.

"I went to Yale," Mike said.

"And now you have gone to the Yale Club," Alice said.

"There is no Florida Institute of Technology Club," Katie said sadly.

Alice walked toward the table where some of her college friends sat. There was James, a skinny giant in a baggy Italian gray silk suit, red in the face from an acrobatic hora. Her friend Cindy was there with her husband. They were in an unsuccessful rock band and shared each other's earrings. One of Alice's friends, her former roommate Caroline, now a struggling actress, had come all the way from L.A. She gleamed with studied, California good health— her smooth, tan skin; her shaggy blond hair; even her dress, which resembled a leotard. Alice hadn't seen her in years, only spoken to her on the telephone. In fact, she had not remained terribly close to any of her college friends. They had moved back to Cleveland, or they lived too far downtown. But when she and Peter decided to get married, Alice felt a surge of nostalgia for these people, and she was happy to see them now, together at a table, admiring each other and being admired. They used to dress for their cafeteria dinners.

Caroline put her arms around Alice. "A married lady!" she cried. "Soon, a washer-dryer."

"Yeah," Alice said. She wanted a washer and a dryer, actually.

"Alice," Caroline said, leaning closer, whispering, "I can't look. I don't want to look interested."

"Where?" Alice said. "Look where?"

"At that guy, Alice. Alice, who is that guy?"

"You mean Willie?" she asked, pointing. "That's my brother." He danced gracefully with Yuki, moving his large feet and towering body as if they were as light as hers. Alice felt a twinge of irritation that her parents had insisted that

Willie go to dancing school but had let her off. He'd objected less violently than she had, but still, her parents' indulgence had left her at a tremendous social disadvantage.

"Not your little brother, Alice. That *guy* in the blue suit."

"Dad?" Alice said.

"Light blue, Alice."

"Oh. Him."

"He's an agent, isn't he?" Caroline said. "The truth, Alice."

Alice sat staring at Louie Scifo. He stood nearby, talking to one of Brenda's friends. He had glanced over at Alice and Caroline, but now turned his attention back to Miriam.

Through the chatter of the guests, Alice could hear his voice. "I just wanted you to know," he was saying.

"But cancer of the spine . . . Oh, Louie! I'm so sorry," came the answer.

"Yeah," said Louie.

Louie had taken hold of Miriam's hand after she began to tremble. He patted her, gently covering, Alice noticed, her diamond bracelet. For a moment, Alice feared he would lift his fingers to reveal nothing on Miriam's wrist, that, like a conjurer, he would have made the bracelet disappear. But when he let go of Miriam to pull a pack of cigarettes from his pocket, her jewelry was still intact. Alice was a little disappointed.

Miriam stepped back from the cloud of smoke that had gathered around Louie Scifo. "Three months. Only three months," she said. "Are they absolutely sure?"

"Yeah," said Louie bravely.

"Oh dear, I don't know what to say."

"I knew you would understand," Louie said. "What with you just having the double mastectomy and all."

"Alice," Caroline was saying, "introduce me. Contacts, Alice, are very important. I could, you know, *flirt* with him."

"No," Alice said. "I can't have it on my conscience."

Caroline sighed. "He's married," she said.

"No," Alice said. "He's not married."

"Well, that's okay, then," said Caroline.

"Yes," Alice said. *"That's* okay."

Alice found her mother sitting at a table with an ancient aunt who could not see but pretended she could. Her aunt was smoking from a long cigarette holder, and with her bangs and beaded dress, she looked like a flapper, which she had once been. Alice had seen pictures of her perched in a rumble seat. She had never changed her hair—it fell around her face in a short, swingy bob. Alice suspected that her lively manner was a holdover from those days, too, a bright sophistication that was quite out of fashion.

"Why, who's that sneaking up on us girls?" cried Aunt Beverly when Alice approached the table and coughed to get her mother's attention.

"Hi, Aunt Beverly. It's me, Alice," Alice said. "The bride," she added.

"Why, Alice, you cheeky thing, sneaking around. Give your aunt a kiss. Your dress is the living end. Pizzazz!" Aunt Beverly said, staring at Brenda and blowing a smoke ring.

"Thank you," Alice said. "And you look great, too." Aunt Beverly did look great. She had eliminated the unpleasant possibility of accidently donning clothes in clashing patterns and colors by buying everything in the same becoming shade of blue, which Brenda helped her locate on quarterly shopping expeditions. "Why, it's as smart as can be, isn't it?" she would ask, holding out an orange sweater. "Blue is my color!"

"You *always* look great, Aunt Beverly. Like a teenager. Mom," Alice said, pulling at her mother's sleeve, as Aunt Beverly smiled in quiet enjoyment of the compliment. "Mommy! Louie told Miriam he has spine cancer."

"Breast cancer, dear. She had breast cancer."

"Mom," Alice said very slowly, "Louie told Miriam, a woman who has just had a mastectomy, *two* mastectomies, that he, Louie Scifo, has cancer of the *spine*."

"Tsk, tsk," said Aunt Beverly. "The poor man."

Brenda shook her head. "Well," she said after a pause, "I'm surprised he didn't say he'd had *three* mastectomies." She drummed her fingers on the table. The sound was muffled by the white tablecloth. "Louie must be upset about something," she finally said. But it was Brenda who looked upset.

"And three months to live," Alice added, encouraged by her mother's face.

"Tragic!" said Aunt Beverly, blinking.

Brenda stood up. She towered above Alice and Aunt Beverly, her red hair falling on her shoulders; she *loomed*, large and imposing, like a diva seen from the second row.

"Cancer of the spine?" she muttered, curling her lip in disgust. The only times Alice noticed any real physical resemblance between herself and her mother were those rare moments when her mother's face twisted into this expression. "Three months to live?" And she walked away.

Aunt Beverly had been gently led off by one of her daughters to have her picture taken, and Alice was left alone at the table. She sat on one chair, her feet up on another. Her voice hadn't cracked when she said, "I do." She had tried to put Peter's ring on his index finger, but after several unsuccessful thrusts and Peter's ultimate intervention, she had corrected the error and no one had noticed. She hadn't been overcome by *fou rire*, or fallen down in a mass of torn lace and snapped high heels. Everyone had been too polite to notice that she couldn't dance. And her mother seemed to be angry at Louie Scifo. Alice smiled and nodded regally at the guests.

In a rush of goodwill, she smiled at Louie Scifo himself. He had alienated himself from her mother. He was not such a terrible guy.

Louie smiled back and made a sweeping bow. He was standing by the bandleader, the chubby accordionist. Louie put his arm around the man's shoulders and pointed at Alice, then at himself. Alice supposed he was telling the bandleader that he was the judge who had married the happy couple or that he had flown Alice here in his airplane, having just rescued her from a forest fire on his two-billion-acre estate in the Himalayas. Louie's actual occupation was unknown. He seemed to have retired from a great many occupations, however. He had been, he said, a stockbroker, a doctor, a pilot. Alice was so pleased that Louie had annoyed her mother that she didn't think she would have cared if he was telling the accordionist that he was the groom and had condescended to accept Alice— even *without* a dowry.

Louie smiled at her again, a wide, white smile, and then took the microphone off its stand.

Alice's smile faded.

That's what happens when you smile at people, she thought. They sing.

Alice put her feet down on the floor, sat very straight, and studied her hands, which looked to her like someone else's, with their gleaming red nails manicured for the wedding. She looked around for someone to chat with, but the chairs around her were still empty. She stood up and began to walk to a more crowded part of the room. "I-I-I'll be seeing you," Louie sang in a liquid voice. "Yeah! In *all* the *old* familiar places." Louie was embarrassing. More embarrassing than any relative. Didn't he know any other songs? He broke off with a sob. Alice turned around to watch him.

With a great sweep of his hand, up and then down, dramatically flicking the cord of the microphone, Louie took his bow.

Good God, Alice thought. He seemed to be waiting for applause. What an absurd, nasty little man, crashing her wedding and singing and bowing.

But Louie bowed again, and Alice realized that he was bowing because people were applauding.

Peter came and stood next to her. "Bravo!" he called out. He winked at her.

"You just did that to annoy me. Bravo, indeed."

"Well, he's pretty good," Peter said.

Alice sniffed.

"Really."

"I heard him," Alice said. She wondered if Peter was drunk. "Are you drunk?" she asked.

"Well, yes, of course, a little. Aren't you?"

"Thank you, thank you all, lovely ladies and your lucky gentlemen," Louie called out, blowing kisses. "And a one, and a two, and a . . . O! sole meeee-oh . . ."

Louie finished to more applause.

"You're crazy," Alice said to Peter. "Louie's singing is completely embarrassing." She looked at Peter, expecting him to argue, but he just stood looking back, smiling happily. She had never seen him in a suit before that day, and he looked terribly handsome to her. One point of his collar had turned up over his lapel a little, and his tie was slightly twisted. She pushed the collar down and watched it spring back.

Alice loved Peter's looks. He resembled a great, gawky adolescent—all hands and feet and untied shoelaces. His skinny legs in his corduroy Levi's that had dark blue ink stains on the back pockets; the ratty, army-green T-shirt under the proper button-down Oxford shirt with the ink stain on its pocket; the large sneakers with the worn rubber toes—all these things reminded her of the boys she knew in high school. His neck stretched out in curiosity, up above the puerile clothing, and then his bony face, a craggy peak above the clouds, lofty and grownup and with the darkest brown eyes she had ever seen.

"You look handsome," Alice said, pushing the collar down again.

"I do?"

"Yes. You do. And Louie sings okay, sort of, if you like that sort of thing, which, now that we're married, I hope you will cease to do." Alice sank down happily into a chair, pleased that she had made this conciliatory gesture. Peter sat beside her and they held hands. She looked at him and marveled that this was really her husband, that she had a husband now with whom she would wake up each morning. The sparrows would chirp outside, a bus would grind its gears, and she would turn over and see this man whom she loved and admired. Then they would have breakfast, and they would not have to fight over the paper, because he always read the sports section first. Then they would do their work, then eat and gossip, then go to bed, and then wake up again. It seemed like a miracle to Alice.

"You're . . ." She suddenly became embarrassed, as

if they had just met and she were blurting out some intimate bit of information. "A great guy," she said finally.

Her brother sat down with his girlfriend. "I still say you must read Bernard Malamud, Willie," she was saying. "Yes, I think so. You have not read him. This I find so extraordinary. *Pictures of Fidelman*, even? And no Bellow, too!"

Alice's father appeared and asked if she would pose for a picture with him and his wife and his stepson, Charles. Willie was extracted from the literary admonitions of Yuki, and they all stood in a row. Alice could see Charles squirming in his suit, and her heart went out to him. Dad as a stepfather. Imagine.

"What a lovely celebration," Dad's wife, Patricia, said to Alice.

"I'm glad you're having a good time," Alice said. She's not supposed to have a good time, Alice thought, considerably annoyed. She's supposed to be uncomfortable because my mother's here, and my grandmother and all my relatives who think she's a low interloper are here shooting nasty glances her way.

Alice stood between her father and Patricia and watched the waiters clearing off tables. Her wedding was almost over. She smiled at the photographer, who, all evening, had conscientiously climbed aboard chairs or crouched on the floor to say, "That's it, that's it, that's *it!*" Behind the photographer, Alice's grandmother glared, clearly outraged at the presumption of her former son-in-law and his present wife.

"Family group, my foot," Alice heard her say loudly. Behind Grandma, Louie Scifo stood holding a waiter's arm.

"Those flowers are the property of the Brody–Eiger matrimonial party. Exclusively," he said.

"Oh, no, sir, their flowers are over there on that table if anyone wants to take them home, although there's someone's business card in most of them," the waiter answered politely. He pointed to a table of vases filled with anemones.

Louie grabbed the pot of chrysanthemums from the waiter. "Hey, you there, Cousin Sylvia—here, take this lovely arrangement, my compliments, you see?"

Alice smiled at the photographer and watched as Louie ran from waiter to waiter, reaching for all the flowers being put out for the next day's breakfast. She turned and said goodbye to Jack, her Westport neighbor, who told her, "You'll be very, very." And then to Aunt Beverly, who pushed her daughters away when they tried to lead her toward Alice. "I'm not senile," she growled, and reached out to hug Alice, who leaped across the three-foot distance between them just in time to receive her embrace.

When Alice turned back toward Louie Scifo, he was gone and the flowers seemed to have been set up on the tables where they belonged.

Alice and Peter waved goodbye to the photographer, who made them stand in the elevator, although they were planning to leave by the stairs. They walked down to the marble lobby, and she was so tired she barely noticed the snowstorm raging beyond the big doors or the man being escorted out into it by the blue-coated security guards. He clutched two pots of chrysanthemums in his arms and wore a baby-blue suit, but Alice knew it couldn't be Louie Scifo, because her mother walked right past him without so much as a glance in his direction.

🦜 /   A birding friend from Brooklyn called at seven the next morning.

"Peter, Peter, get up!" Alice said. "It's Arthur! It's a Bullock's oriole!" She shook Peter. She told him she loved him. She thanked him for not being able to leave on their honeymoon until February.

"You're welcome," he said.

Her friend had been birding in Prospect Park before breakfast and just south of the cemetery he'd seen the Bullock's oriole. The howling snowstorm the night before was the second in a week, and the oriole, which usually did not venture too far east of the Rockies, had apparently come along for the ride. Peter nodded from the depths of his pillow, then went back to sleep.

"Well, they're supposed to stop at the *Great Plains*," Alice said.

Alice got dressed, hung her binoculars and camera from her neck, slung the aluminum monopod from her shoulder, and put on Peter's parka. She hoped that if anyone noticed the bulk beneath the big coat, they would think she was heavily armed. Peter looked warm and comfortable under the covers, but Alice was excited about the Western oriole. And if she could photograph it decently, much of that month's work would be over. Alice worked as the photographer and art director of a bird magazine, which was convenient. She gave herself assignments, agreed to do them, and then accepted them.

The magazine was a slender monthly publication that had originated with a federal grant during the governmental generosity of the sixties. The grant was gone now, and *The Urban Bird* operated on some scraps of state money, some conservation-group funds, and the willingness of Alice and Martin, the editor and only other staffer, to work for practically nothing. There was no office. Alice did the layouts at home; Martin worked on a computer at his house in Westchester. They rarely saw each other, or even spoke, communicating primarily by mail and computer modem. For him, it was something of a hobby: he was a retired newspaper copy editor and a feverish birder. Alice wasn't sure how she ended up there, except that one boyfriend had once given her a camera and another boyfriend had been a birder, and taking pictures of birds at five in the morning was a pleasant way to procrastinate in graduate school. She had met Martin in the park on one of these mornings and soon left higher education behind forever. Her work was soothing and refreshing; there were no exams; occasionally, when a rare bird appeared, like today, it was even exciting.

The subway wouldn't be too bad—the Sixth Avenue IND, the D train, a fairly quick, fairly clean, fairly safe train. But the park itself was large and eerie, its enormous open fields rolling headlong in every direction, crashing rudely into crowded streets, abandoned buildings, the litter and bustle and general urban disorder of Brooklyn. The park's trees were so tall they seemed almost threatening, too wild and majestic to shade a picnic table or a jungle gym. It was dangerous to go there alone, but with a Bullock's oriole around, Alice knew she would have company. There had never before been a Bullock's oriole in Prospect Park. This was a great coup for the city, like landing a contract for a naval base.

On the train, she sat beside a young man who was loudly chewing gum. It was strawberry gum. She could smell it—the same insidious, syrupy smell that came from the pink cardboard trees taxi drivers hung from their rear-view mirrors. Perhaps this was a taxi driver, on his way to work, his entire life consumed by a destructive, antisocial chemical addiction to synthetic strawberry fumes. Alice moved to the next car.

At Fourteenth Street, a man got on carrying a thermos on a strap over his shoulder and binoculars around his neck. The thermos was red and seemed to radiate heat. Probably full of hot coffee, the milk mixed in. It had been eleven degrees when Alice left the house. She imagined snapping pictures in the park with her bared fingers.

"Hello," she said to the man, whom she had suddenly decided looked extremely familiar. She hoped there was no sugar in his coffee. "Going to see the—"

"Bullock's oriole," he said.

Alice moved next to him and they chatted over the roar of the train. He was a lawyer and an avid birder who took expensive trips to exotic lands to add to his life list. So he was a rich lawyer; in his early sixties, Alice thought. Perfect for Mom. Widowers were good marriage material. She hoped fervently that his wife had died.

"My husband wouldn't even open his eyes this morning," she said. She had a little trouble saying the words "my husband." She felt herself blushing, and at the same time she felt absurdly proud. She giggled, idiotically she knew, but she couldn't help it, and she looked at the man, hoping he would say something about his wife, that she wouldn't open her eyes either, or that she would never open them again.

"Can't blame him," the man said, not taking up the bait. "Pretty cold."

Alice sat and said nothing for a while, annoyed. She stamped her feet on the subway floor, which was covered with watery mud from the melted snow, splashing a little on her neighbor's shoes. She hoped he didn't notice. She looked at the lawyer. It was difficult to make a judgment. With his knit cap pulled low over his forehead, he looked somewhat demented, but he had shaved, which seemed an encouraging indication of wholesome habits. He turned his head and looked at her, catching her by surprise. Alice, embarrassed, smiled.

"Um, it's terrible, having a spouse who won't bird," she said finally.

She wondered if that sounded in some way obscene. But it was true. Peter's life had no room for birds who flew off-course; it was devoted to producing rational, numerical descriptions of a game. Peter was a statistical analyst of baseball. He wrote books and a monthly newsletter and sometimes gave lectures. He was tireless in his pursuit of baseball reason. Every step, every windup, every swing, every error had some meaning in his world; they were fragments, and he was there with his computer and mathematical formulae to make something whole from them. Birds, on the other hand, did things because they were hungry or genetically programmed or blown by the wind. Their lives did not add up to anything. They lacked intellectual depth.

"They fly from Peru to Greenland. And back," Alice had once said to him. "What more do you want from them?"

The man in the subway continued to look at Alice curiously. Alice forced another smile. When would he offer her some coffee? It would have been much easier if Brenda Brody had been there herself, cheerful and glamorous in a somewhat overweight sort of way. Alice would have to start bringing her mother with her on birding expeditions. The man's eyes moved from her face over the bulky coat, down to her rubber boots and back up. He looked her in the eyes.

Alice stopped smiling. She realized the man thought she was trying to pick him up. For herself.

"But my husband and I go to a lot of baseball games," she said quickly. "Lots. I love baseball. Do you like baseball? My husband knows everything about baseball. Baseball's great, just great."

"I don't care for baseball," the man said, and pulled a rolled-up newspaper from his pocket.

Alice had moved a little farther away from him, but she realized now that it wasn't necessary: she had been rejected.

I have been rejected by an old lawyer who doesn't even know if his wife is dead or alive, she thought. She glared at him. And now there would be no date for Mom. And no coffee.

"I just got married," she said after a while. "Yesterday."

"Congratulations," said the man.

"To my husband," Alice said.

Alice walked into the park with the man but soon saw several people she recognized wandering around, people she often saw bird-watching in Central Park, and she ditched her unappreciative would-be suitor/stepfather and his thermos.

The sun was out, but it was still quite windy, and stinging clouds of snow blew across the park. Alice stopped to take a picture of a black-capped chickadee perched beneath an icicle, probably thirsty and waiting for the icicle to drip. But it was too cold for drips, even with the bright sun. Alice headed for the woods, where the oriole had last been seen, and she welcomed the gloomy shade from the snow-covered branches. She walked quietly, up one little hill, down another, passing the tracks of other birders, occasionally seeing one and stopping to exchange information.

It took her a while to find the Bullock's oriole, but when she did find it, it seemed to be posing for her. A female, it stood on the lower branch of an elm, the sun streaming in through the trees to illuminate its olive-colored back, its yellow breast, and, to Alice's great satisfaction, the whitish belly that clearly distinguished it from the female orioles that one was supposed to see in the East.

Alice watched the bird for some time. It hardly moved and she was able to step a little closer. She not only had her big 400-mm lens, she'd also brought an extension tube, and so the bird stood, gigantic and clear, in her sights. Resting after its unscheduled cross-continental flight, it blinked, but did not stir. Alice shot several rolls of film, then just stood and looked at the oriole. A sleepy exotic, camped on a snowy branch. A few other birders, people she didn't know, had gathered, also looking up, silent and respectful, like tourists in a church. Otherwise, the park was empty, blanketed with the quiet of the snowfall. Alice wondered how the bird would survive here. No flock. No family. No mate. Everybody it knew and cared about back in Mexico feasting on winter strawberries. Bullock's orioles fiercely defended their nests against marauding avian neighbors—she had briefly read up on the bird before leaving the house. But this Bullock's would have no nest to defend.

Alice blew on her fingers, feeling intrusive and melancholy. She was exploiting a desolate creature's misfortune.

She looked at the bird sparkling in the sun. Its eyes blinked. The wind howled beyond the stand of pine trees. But it's just a stupid bird, she thought. This is not Vietnam. I am not Weegee.

Then Alice remembered that, where their ranges overlapped in the Great Plains, the Bullock's oriole and the Baltimore oriole interbred. That's okay then, Alice thought, and she snapped some more pictures. The lost Bullock's would find a local mate and build a silvery hanging nest and chase wrens and catbirds away. Male Baltimore orioles were more beautiful than Bullock's anyway, brighter orange and richer black; they had a baseball team; and their songs were far more melodious. So, that's fine, then, Alice thought, much relieved. The stray female Bullock's oriole would make an excellent match and find happiness in Brooklyn.

✖ / Alice and Peter lived together like two animals in a cave, both working at home, prowling around each other. Alice liked Peter's apartment, a large dark shabby place full of corridors and doors. The doors all seemed to open into each other and were forever colliding, rattling their glass panes until their loose brass knobs dropped heavily, like fruit, to the floor. On the street below, the traffic swept by in blustery waves. After a brief but violent squall of garbage trucks and dragging mufflers, there would be sudden quiet, and Alice would hear the tiny jingle of dog tags, the whir of a coasting bicycle, the bright chirp of a sparrow.

In the mornings, they chatted and drank coffee and interrupted each other to read aloud from the paper, then slowly retreated to their work, Peter to his desk, Alice to her darkroom in the extra bathroom. Alice felt comfortable, mildly productive, and grateful. Sometimes, lonesome for Peter, she would walk into the bedroom he used as an office and sit on his lap.

Outside, the traffic light swayed, back and forth, a giant

bauble in the wind. In the hall, the smoke detector, which needed a new battery, beeped intermittently. Black Coat, Alice's cat, stood beneath it, growling. Alice kissed Peter and smoothed his hair.

"What is that noise?" Peter said.

Alice listened but heard only familiar sounds.

"Something hit the window," Peter said. He pushed her off his lap.

Together, they went and pressed their foreheads against the cold windowpane to look down. A young man stood below with a girl. He was tossing up a penny.

"What is that idiot . . . Oh, it's Willie," Peter said. He gave a disgusted sigh, shook his head, and went back to work.

When Willie came upstairs, Alice looked at him sternly. "We're working," she said.

He shrugged and smiled. "Surprise!" he said. "Alice, this is Lulu."

Willie's new girlfriend had wavy black hair that fell to her shoulders and a black dress that fell off them. Circled in kohl, her eyes looked even larger and more sultry than they were. Willie wore a plastic case for pens and pencils in the breast pocket of his jacket. Alice wondered how anyone who wore such a thing could have so many girlfriends, and such beautiful ones. "I think they feel sorry for me," Willie had once said.

The real reason was that Willie was so beautiful himself and had never realized it. He was tall and broad-shouldered, with large, perfect features and long eyelashes that gave his face an austerely romantic look—until he smiled. Then all the strong lines of his face dissolved into general, goofy happiness. The combination of Willie's good looks, his happy, deranged smile, and the complete absence of vanity was irresistible. Even Alice, who had grown up feeling the constant, needling anger an older sister feels toward a younger brother, found it difficult to work herself into any proper kind of rage at him these days.

Her brother seemed to be adrift, though, floating from girl to girl, always welcome initially, but then infuriating them by drifting still. He was always in love with them, but just as he did not think all that much about himself, he tended not to think all that much about them. They were pretty and friendly and interesting and sexy, and that was all there was to it. He never fought with them, never discussed their relationship, never demanded anything; he got on their nerves. The girls began their invariable retreat from him with sulks and pouts and accusations of betrayal or neglect, then began storming out of restaurants, finally hurling things at him. (Willie had so provoked Yuki, his last girlfriend, that she had let fly her extensive library of the post-war urban Jewish novel.) Willie would watch in dismay, wondering what they were so angry about, and patiently wait for whatever it was to blow over, certain that it would. He was perfectly satisfied, and so he believed they must be, too. When the girl, rather than the problem, blew over, Willie would mope, inconsolable, until the next girl turned up, which was generally a matter of days.

It annoyed Alice that Willie meandered from girl to girl. For one thing, she became attached to his girlfriends. And, now, she wanted to impose her new ideas about stability and matrimony on everyone, especially her own brother. Willie's roving love life gaped, a blank in her attractive design for universal domestic bliss.

"So! The sis-*tayr* of my Willie," Lulu was saying. "I am enchanting!" The radiant Lulu kissed Alice like an aunt, a French aunt, leaving lipstick marks on both cheeks.

"Yes, I guess you are," Alice said.

"So!" Willie said.

"My Willie has told me so much about you. You take photography of the bird, yes? We have so much in common. I stuff the bird. We coincide."

"Lulu is a, um, taxidermist."

"Oh, Willie, my darling boy." Lulu looked modestly down. "Not yet."

"That is, she is a *student* of taxidermy. In exile," Willie said. "She's from Beirut."

Lulu wore a cross around her neck and spoke in an impossibly French French accent; she was a curling, fanciful rococo chip from the crumbled edifice of French Beirut. Willie had told Alice nothing about Lulu before this meeting, except to say that she would make an ideal deposed dictator's wife.

"There is nothing for me there, in my city of Beirut. All the discotheques, everything, gone, phht!" Lulu said. Then she began gently waving her arms, as if to diffuse the memory of the bombed-out city, or the reality, or perhaps both. Her pretty face looked so sad that Alice felt sorry for her, in the same way she had felt a little sorry for AT&T after Ma Bell had fallen to deregulation. Then Lulu smiled, and Alice could see why Willie liked her. It was a delighted smile aimed right at Alice, and it seemed to say: Yes, in spite of everything, the world is a marvelous place, and it is you, Alice, who makes it so. When Lulu turned her smile to Willie, it was he who made the sun shine and the flowers grow. Even when she looked at Black Coat, the cat, Lulu's smile seemed to bestow some kind of cat grace on his bulky, black, hairy being. She was glamorously dressed, mostly in leather, and her earrings were made of feathers and fur, as if she were one of her own creations, the ultimate object of her training in taxidermy.

"I love what is your face, Alice. The shape, yes? So much to work with."

Alice eyed the student of taxidermy suspiciously.

"Come," said Lulu, taking Alice's hand.

Alice put her other hand unhappily to her face.

"Show me please, you have tweezers? I am so at home here. I am fixing your eyebrows, yes? Then, when you look beautiful, I have for you a gift."

Lulu saw the darkroom sink through the open door and walked in, pushing bottles of chemicals aside, searching for a tweezers. Plastic pans bounced onto the floor.

"The other bathroom," Willie told her, steering her in the right direction. "Lulu is flying back to Idaho tomorrow morning," he said to Alice, as if to reassure her.

"I study there, in Idaho. Idaho." Lulu sighed, but just for a moment. Then her smile returned and she brought her face close to Alice's, squinting at Alice's eyebrows. "I have my work," she said. "When I am done, Cousin Adnon buys for me the lab in California. This is a place for taxidermy, yes? Hollywood? Ahh! *Mon petit* kitty-cat, you follow me. *Bonjour*, kitty-cat. I give to you a big *bisou*, how I would like to take you to Idaho, you are so grand and black."

Black Coat lay down on the bathroom floor and purred. A large dramatic mass of long, black fur, the cat had been obtained at the ASPCA several years before. Alice had accompanied a friend who wanted an orange kitten, and she had seen the black grown cat, snarling and wailing in its miserable confinement, too large and too disagreeable to be adopted. To Alice's dismay, she had been overtaken by a

shiver of sympathy for the miserable cat and found herself
carrying the enormous, unpleasant pet home. The regis-
tration card had listed the cat's name as Black Coat, and
though she suspected there had been a mistake, that a de-
scription of the cat had been entered on the wrong line of
the form, she did not want to confuse the creature if Black
Coat was indeed its name.

Black Coat bit, with great force, and with Peter as a
frequent victim. And, each night, the cat howled into the
darkness. It meowed incessantly at any human being lying
motionless on a bed. (Alice theorized that Black Coat's
former owner had died, alone and unnoticed, except by the
cat, who had meowed for days and days, helpless and hungry.) Later, in the silence of the dawn, Alice would hear
the *scrape, scrape* as the cat gently pawed fragile wedding
presents to the edges of tables and shelves, and then the
crash as they hit the floor. But Alice was fond of him. He
was her responsibility; this bond endeared him to her.

Lulu wants to stuff you, you stupid cat, Alice thought.

"Willie, you do not like it when I mention Cousin
Adnon. You burn with jealousy."

Willie looked surprised. "I *do*?" he said.

"He is of the family, you comprehend? Distant, yes.
But, Alice, sometimes I see such anger in your brother. I
love jealousy in a man."

Alice looked at Willie, curious to see him burn with
jealousy. He was sitting on the edge of the tub, tying his
sneakers. He looked up at Alice and smiled. "So, what's for
dinner, Sis?"

There was nothing for dinner, and Lulu's gift to Alice
was a stuffed mouse.

"I don't know what to say," Alice said. "Peter, do you
know what to say?"

"Thank you?" Peter said. He was standing by the front door, his hand on the knob. He smiled at his guests, tilting his head encouragingly at the exit. He had deserted his office after Willie appeared there, demanding to know the human population of Idaho, the animal population, the animals per capita in Hollywood, and what this meant for taxidermy in general and Lulu's future as a taxidermist in particular. "That's what statisticians do, right?" Willie had said, pulling a chair up next to Peter's in front of the computer.

"*Thank* you," Alice said. "*That's* it. Thank you, Lulu. What a thoughtful gift. But listen, about dinner . . ."

"Ah, but of course, you must not worry—you will teach to me the American cuisine, yes? The potato cooked in the metal paper . . ."

The doorbell rang, and Peter, in position, answered it.

"Brenda!" he said.

"Mom?" Alice said.

"What a surprise," Peter was saying. "The *whole family.*"

Alice held the mouse in its mauve wrapping paper. For this, she thought, Willie had left Yuki, or had allowed her to leave him, a perfectly lovely, attractive intellectual from a good family who had given Alice a copy of Irving Howe's autobiography for a Christmas present. She looked at the mouse's whiskers: they were symmetrical, three on each side. The whole family, Alice thought. Welcome to the family, little rodent.

"Well, I was three blocks away, and I realized that my five-o'clock patient lives in this neighborhood," Alice's mother said. "And so I had an inspiration. I thought, why should the little fellow have to drag himself all the way over to my office, when I can use *Peter's* office, right here!"

Brenda beamed with pride. She stressed informality in her work.

Peter paced silently.

The doorbell rang again.

"Your patient," Alice said with a sigh.

"Oh, no, Alice," Brenda said, as if Alice had suggested something terribly stupid. "The boy is not coming for half an hour. That's *Grandma*. I called and asked her to meet me here. We're having dinner later. Hello, Mother," she said, letting her in. "Now!" And Brenda began to take off her coat. She looked down at a bag she was holding. "What's this?"

Alice looked inside. "A chicken," she said.

"A chicken? When did I buy *this*? What do I need a chicken for? I need a *notebook*. Peter, find me a nice fresh notebook, dear. Here, Alice, do something with this chicken, sweetheart."

Brenda held the chicken by its legs and handed it to Alice, who turned to Willie and Lulu. "Chicken for dinner," she said, and she went off to put the uninvited chicken in the oven for her uninvited guests.

While the chicken was cooking, Alice made herself a cup of tea and sat down at the kitchen table. She could hear Grandma and Lulu talking in the living room.

"Your coat is so lovely. I have never worked with mink. It is an ambition with me."

"You're a furrier? So young and pretty? Now, look what those filthy hangers they give you, they should drop off the face of the earth, did to my beautiful coat, poor thing . . ."

Alice could hear the murmur of her mother talking to Peter in the study. The television had been turned on in the bedroom, presumably by her brother. The house rasped and sputtered with relatives. They had made their nests in the corners, suddenly, without warning, like insects.

"*There's* my patient!" Brenda called as the doorbell rang.

When Alice answered the door, a small boy ran past her into the house. Black Coat ran past her out of the house. When she lunged after him, Alice heard the door slam shut behind her.

She stood at her own door, ringing the bell, the cat hissing in her arms.

Brenda's patient opened the door.

"Who are you?" he asked.

"Never mind," Alice said.

Alice led the child to Peter's office, passing through the living room, where Grandma and Lulu were still deep in a discussion of pelts, then looked in on her brother in the bedroom. He was stretched out on the bed, asleep. He looked comfortable, and Alice lay down on the other side of the bed to watch a documentary from the Margaret Mead Film Festival. She must have fallen asleep, too, because the cat was crouched at their feet, yowling. She turned off the TV and went back to the kitchen. Peter was sitting at the table, drinking her cold tea.

"Peter, I'm sorry about all this commotion. My family is not what you'd call real considerate about privacy. Not high on our list."

An even-tempered, only child, Peter had lived all alone until he married Alice, and he was not accustomed to family noise and friction. No one had ever interfered with Peter, not his parents, not his friends. No one had urged him to become a doctor or to get married, and it had been a principle of his life, one easily maintained because it suited him, to be left alone and leave people alone in turn. He had told Alice how he fondly remembered standing behind the apartment building he grew up in, on the quiet dead-end street that led to the river, a pink rubber ball in his hand. In front of him, painted on the red brick wall, was a white square. He didn't know how it got there or what its original purpose might have been, but he did know that it corresponded, almost exactly in position and size, to the strike zone. Every afternoon, he would stand there and hurl the spaldeen at the white square. He could still remember the feeling of the ball, smooth and a little spongy, as he held it. He would bring his arm back, drop his shoulder down, and then bring his arm up in an arc, whipping the ball toward an imaginary home plate, blowing it by an imaginary batter. Even now, he said, he could hear the rubber ball slapping against the wall, and bouncing off the irregular bricks, to be fielded by the pitcher turned outfielder. When Peter told Alice about this solitary game, she had said, "Poor Peter," and told him he should have had brothers and sisters.

He'd had to explain to her that it was a pleasant memory.

"I'm sorry about Mom and Willie," Alice said now. "And Grandma and Little Lulu, too, of course. And Black Coat?" she added, hoping to make him laugh. She remembered how Peter had shuddered when she proposed siblings for him; and now, the newlywed grace period apparently over, her family had come lurching in, making itself at home. She closed the door to the kitchen, as if to reestablish the hazy solitude of the early part of the day. "I'll talk to them, I promise. They're just not used to my being married."

She wasn't used to it yet, either. And she did not even want to think what effect so many in-laws and their retainers would have on her quiet, somewhat introverted husband. Peter was an obligingly preoccupied person, too busy with his box scores to pay much attention to what went on in the house. But even he must notice the occupation of his office by an eight-year-old.

"Okay, Peter? I'll reform them."

"It's fine. Don't worry about it. I don't mind."

"You don't?" He certainly didn't look as if he minded. He was tapping his pencil on the table and humming, a sure sign of high spirits.

"No," Peter said.

"Why *not*?"

"Well, actually, I was having a horrible, frustrating day. I mean work, of course," he said, patting her. "Nothing came out right. And then your brother didn't help much, to tell you the truth. But when your mom came over, she was all fired up over some article she'd read, in *Smithsonian* or something, and she started asking me questions about things I haven't bothered to think about in years, and it was so, I don't know, bracing, and then this little kid comes in and he's a computer nut and starts programming the thing to answer "I just want to help the team, Ralph," no matter what you punch in. It was, to quote your mother, fun. Your mom said I could show the kid some of my work on the computer at the end of the session. He gets my newsletter! Obviously an intelligent, well-adjusted child. Asked for my *autograph*." Peter beamed. He handed Alice the empty cup, embraced her, tucked his pencil behind his ear, and left.

Alice sat holding the teacup, relieved but somehow dissatisfied. It would be difficult, as well as pointless, to reform her family if no one objected to them. Peter did not, at the moment, object, and neither did she, not really. So that was that. She regretted the lost opportunity to correct her relatives and to attempt to impose her will on them. But perhaps it was better this way, in the long run.

From the kitchen window, she could see into the window of the spare bedroom Peter used as an office. She watched the little boy move a fat crayon across a sheet of paper, his head bent over his work, while her mother paced back and forth behind him, her mouth moving constantly. Once a white dove with a banded leg had landed on the kitchen sill, pecking with great determination at the window, staring at Alice with its beady eyes, an emissary from the sooty sky. Black Coat had pawed at the window, his claws scratching noisily on the glass. Alice had been almost as excited as the cat. The existence of birds in New York was hardly a surprise. She photographed them all the time. But every time she actually saw a bird, its wiry feet clamped firmly on the branch of a scrawny tree, it seemed almost a miracle to her. It *looked* so miraculous—all those delicate little feathers among the huge brick towers. And then the shrill, piping voice rising above the taxi horns and clatter of trucks.

Alice had taken the white dove's picture, but then she'd remembered something and shooed the bird away. She had remembered how as a child she had once looked up and noticed a beautiful model of a cardinal that sat on a high shelf in a bookcase. She had thought how skilled her little brother had become, how neatly the bird was painted, with no globs of glue showing on the plastic seams. But then the model cardinal had blinked one of its bright, jeweled eyes and flown wildly around the room, unable to find its way out. She had been terrified.

"Oh, Alice, I am so enjoying it here!" cried Lulu, pushing open the kitchen door, her heels clicking on the tile floor. "You are all so kind. I make my mind. I stay.

Bon. I cancel my flight. I stay here, in your house. I have chosen."

Lulu stayed for over a week. Alice realized the exquisitely sly and preposterously feminine Lulu was trying to make Willie jealous by preferring to stay with his sister; and that she was trying at the same time to win Willie by winning his family. Willie was oblivious to both maneuvers and simply moved in with Lulu. They slept on the convertible couch. Peter seemed barely to notice them, except, having squeezed by them one morning in one of the narrow hallways, to remark cheerfully that he felt as if he were in an ant farm.

Each morning, Lulu would examine Alice, then drag her into the bathroom to apply creams and lotions and paints to her face, pencils and brushes to her eyes, gels and mousses and combs to her hair. Then she would release Alice to the day. With sunlight streaming through the window, Alice would stand at the mirror, as sparkling and iridescent as one of the birds in her pictures.

"Aren't you missing an awful lot of classes?" Alice asked her.

"I go on independent study," she replied.

Willie was helpful and neat, volunteering for the least desirable household chores. Alice pretended he was an au pair, and she was content. But Lulu clearly was not. She turned the glittering beam of her smile less and less on Willie. Alice sometimes heard them squabbling at night, Lulu's voice angrier and angrier, while Willie answered in his usual placid, agreeable way. And then one morning, with the words "Thank you so much. I long for Idaho. I wish to kill your brother. I depart," she was gone.

Lulu left her makeup as a gift for Alice. Alice was

touched, but it was Lulu's earlier gift that won her deeper gratitude, for immediately following Lulu's departure, Black Coat gave up his nightly prowling in search of vulnerable bowls and pitchers. He now spent his evenings quietly gnawing the little stuffed mouse, something he had never even attempted with Irving Howe's autobiography.

April 14
Prospect Park

Today the ruby-crowned kinglets were
overwhelming, everywhere, their crowns
visible and bright. Singing and chanting.
They hung from the branches in bunches.

1. 12 mallards
2. 4 herring gulls
3. 2 laughing gulls
4. 1 mourning dove
5. 20 pigeons
6. 1 kingfisher
7. 36 flickers
8. 2 yellow-bellied sapsuckers
9. 1 red-bellied woodpecker, male
10. 12 downy woodpeckers, courting, drumming
    (they keep the same mate up to 4 years—
    it's romantic)
11. 3 phoebes
12. 6 tree swallows
13. 1 crow

14. 1 blue jay
15. 6 chickadees
16. 6 tufted titmice
17. 1 white-breasted nuthatch
18. 1 red-breasted nuthatch
19. 16 brown creepers
20. 24 ruby-crowned kinglets
21. 4 golden-crowned kinglets
22. 1 hermit thrush
23. 6 robins
24. 8 myrtle warblers
25. 12 pine warblers
26. 15 palm warblers
27. 2 red-winged blackbirds
28. 10 grackles
29. 15 starlings
30. 28 house sparrows
31. 22 juncos
32. 2 cardinals, male and female
33. 6 house finches
34. 6 white-throated sparrows
35. 1 field sparrow
36. 1 swamp sparrow
37. 2 song sparrows

❧ / Alice spent the spring and summer in a happy, overheated daze. The weather was unusually warm, and she would often have to stand on a sun-baked street corner waiting hours for the return of a rare bird that supposedly had passed there the day before. But, more than that, she was excited all the time. Each morning she woke up with a start, ready to pop out of bed, as if every day held a big event that she did not want to miss. When she was a little girl, she used to wake up like that on the day of a horse show. She and Peter had gone on a honeymoon—to the Dominican Republic, where she watched birds and he watched winter ball—but the sultry summer felt more like a honeymoon to Alice.

She would sit up and listen for a moment to the house finches courting in the trees outside the window. Then she would hear the whirring of the automatic coffee maker. It was a wedding gift, and you could set it the night before. It would grind the beans, then make the coffee, so that by the time Alice came into the kitchen, a steaming pot would be waiting for her.

"It's romantic," she said to Peter.

Everything seemed romantic to her. The elevator man collected baseball cards. The next-door neighbors had not yet removed their kid's sled from the hall. The mailman whistled as he sorted the mail, called her Mrs. Eiger, and appeared one night on *Dr. Ruth*. Even that seemed romantic.

Peter had been astoundingly good-natured about all the family interruptions; but Alice soon came to realize that Peter possessed an almost universal tolerance. It was a little unnerving sometimes. She could admit to him that she had never read *Anna Karenina* but had seen it on *Masterpiece Theatre*.

"I can be stupid, and you don't mind," she said. "It's very romantic."

Music, classical music, was the one thing that Peter took as seriously as he did baseball. He would flood the living room with music from the radio, and then, like someone in a trance, like a somnambulist with no place to go, he would begin to pace. He knew what he was listening to on the radio, what orchestra it was, who was conducting, and that it was a listless and pedestrian performance or a stormy, unconventional one, long before the honey-voiced DJ with the Continental accent said anything at all. Sometimes Peter would stand facing the speakers, waving his arms, using a pencil as a baton. His eyes closed, his lips moving, emitting an occasional "bum *bum*," he seemed to her a miracle of earnest concentration and joy. And she would blurt out something about the music, something she knew was probably wrong, just to have the pleasure of watching him not mind.

"What is this music? It sounds like premenstrual syndrome."

"Schönberg. Twelve-tone music has been criticized a lot because of that—people said it could express angst but not much else."

"So, what was that? Mozart? Haydn?" she would ask, and Peter would say no, it was Beethoven, but early Beethoven, and heavily influenced by Haydn. When she thought Mahler was Wagner, he told her that Wagner was Mahler's god.

She became bolder and asked why *Die Frau ohne Schatten* didn't have any waltzes in it. He explained to her about the different Strausses. Once, when Peter asked her if she wanted to hear *Les Troyens* by Berlioz, she said, Oh, yes, she would like that because she liked that thing about the oyster catchers that the three men sing in that other Berlioz opera. And Peter just shook his head and said, No, no, that was the duet from *The Pearl Fishers*, and it was by Bizet, not Berlioz.

"Oops!" she said. But Peter was delighted that she remembered the Bizet duet at all, and had already put it on the turntable.

In March, he'd spent hours with her, watching baseball games taped from last season, explaining why there couldn't be a left-handed shortstop, why you shouldn't risk making the first or third out on a stolen base, what a slider was, why little skinny guys lead off instead of big power hitters. He would sit for weeks at his computer and she would ask him what he was doing and he would tell her he was analyzing the effectiveness of some outfielder's throwing arm in preventing runs, and then patiently explain the statistical method he was using.

They began going to games in April, and by May, the height of spring migration, Alice was spending the days birding, trying to find a warbler who would stand still long enough for her to take its picture, and the evenings at Shea Stadium. Each time she stepped off the subway and onto the ramp high above the stadium, she felt the same sense of pleasant confusion. The field was so bright below, the green so rich and unlikely, the diamond perfect and far away. When they were late, they would hear roars from the crowd, a giant, heavy noise that somehow drifted lightly on the warm breeze. When they got inside, Alice would glance longingly at the souvenir stands, too embarrassed to stop and buy anything, while Peter hurried on his long legs toward the seats. A man in an orange jumpsuit sometimes wiped the seats off with a cloth, a gesture without practical value since the seats were neither dirty nor wet, a residual behavior, Alice thought, from an earlier, more polite era. That was one of her favorite parts of going to a game. Birds had behaviors like that, movements that had once been meaningful and had now become ritualized. "Like preening during courtship," she told Peter. "Ducks start wiping their bills. Not to clean them. It's part of a display."

And, then, on those days when she decided to stay home and do nothing, even then she felt excited. There was no one around to bother them, for a change. Her brother had gone to Turkey on an archaeological dig. Her mother had gone to Westport. Louie Scifo seemed to commute between Westport, when he was in favor, and his sister's house in Florida, when he was not. Only Alice's grandmother was left in New York, and rarely dropped by, although she did call several times a day.

"Honey, I need a chiropodist. It's an emergency," she would say.

"Well, what is a chiropodist, anyway?"

"Oh. It can wait."

Once she called to ask about a new box of Cream of

Wheat she had just bought. "I can't read the date on it. Is it safe?"

Another time she called about a bowl of Jell-O. She had made it the night before, then left it on the counter to cool before putting it in the refrigerator. But she had forgotten about it, fallen asleep, and left it out all night. "I don't know, what do you think, is it safe?"

Alice told her to throw it out. She always told her to throw questionable food out, because she knew her grandmother would anyway. "Throw it out. Why take a chance?"

Then Alice would lie on the couch and listen to records. She spent much of August, a slow time for birds, spread out there, wishing she still smoked cigarettes, listening to Wagner. Looking out the window at the hot heavy sky above the brownstone roofs across the street, she would feel the sweat trickling down the sides of her face as she listened to the "Liebestod" from *Tristan and Isolde*.

"It's decadent to listen to Wagner in this heat," Peter said.

"It's . . ."

"Romantic?"

"Sexy," Alice said. "Shh! The 'passion swelling' part is coming."

"Flagstad," Peter murmured happily, and he closed his eyes and began conducting.

September 15
Jamaica Bay Wildlife Refuge

The shorebirds are still migrating: swarms,
crowds, Vs and spirals, flotillas, entire
fleets, whole displaced flying villages,
nations, empires. I saw a Eurasian wigeon, a
life bird! I saw 4 Hudsonian godwits feeding,
jabbing their bills into the water, up past
their eyeballs, then raising their heads to
swallow their mucky fodder, then jabbing them
down again. I crawled up to them, but they
didn't care. Every other bird flapped off in
alarm, but the godwits stayed, oblivious,
obtuse, blind to me, bumping into each other,
squeaking and eating and squeaking.

1. 2 pied—billed grebes
2. 14 double—crested cormorants
3. 2 great blue herons
4. 50, perhaps, great egrets
5. 30 or so snowy egrets

6. 24 glossy ibises
7. 50 Canada geese
8. 1 snow goose
9. 48 mallards
10. 6 black ducks
11. 44 blue-winged teals
12. American wigeon, common
13. Eurasian wigeon*
14. 40 shovelers
15. 1 lesser scaup
16. 18 ruddy ducks
17. 2 sharp-shinned hawks
18. 2 marsh hawks
19. 1 osprey
20. 1 pheasant, female
21. 1 bobwhite
22. 1 common gallinule
23. 36 coots
24. 2 killdeers
25. 4 Hudsonian godwits
26. 12 greater yellowlegs
27. 8 lesser yellowlegs
28. 1 spotted sandpiper
29. 12 short-billed dowitchers (I identified
    them by their calls, because the physical
    differences between short- and long-
    billed still escape me)
30. 12 semipalmated sandpipers
31. 3 pectoral sandpipers
32. 25 herring gulls
33. 16 ring-billed gulls
34. 8 laughing gulls
35. 32 black skimmers

36. 26 pigeons
37. 2 mourning doves
38. 1 belted kingfisher
39. 28 flickers (migrating flock, obviously
    in for the day, visiting this uncustomary
    habitat, the water's edge)
40. 12 tree swallows
41. 5 American crows
42. 1 marsh wren
43. 1 mockingbird
44. 1 catbird
45. 1 golden-crowned kinglet
46. 6 starlings
47. 32 myrtle warblers
48. 16 house sparrows
49. 13 red-winged blackbirds (1 male among
    them)
50. 1 goldfinch
51. 2 towhees
52. 1 song sparrow
53. 3 black-bellied plovers (from the car on
    my way in, then no more)

🦅 / It had been six months since Brenda
first sent Louie to Florida, or since he first insisted on going
there. Alice was never quite sure which it was, and didn't
much care. Louie had gone. This, she thought, would give
her mother a chance to behave, and it would relieve Alice
of Louie's occasional but unwelcome company.

But, since then, Brenda and Louie had come together
and split apart and come together again almost seasonally.
Louie would migrate south, then utter piercing calls of
loneliness and contrition until Brenda flew down to join
him. Louie was like a large bird in full courtship plumage,
but instead of bright mating feathers and an aggressive,
jaunty dance, Louie's courtship display was sad and skulk-
ing, a ritual of hapless need.

Maybe I should just let her be, Alice thought as she
drove from Jamaica Bay to the airport. She was tired and
content, cans of exposed film rolling on the seat beside her,
the light growing dim and peaceful. Just pick them up and

shut up. Who cares? She'd seen fifty-three kinds of birds and not one of them cared.

Alice wished she didn't care, either. She wished sometimes that she lived in another city and twice a year held her breath, saw her mother, disapproved silently, then went home and forgot about it. But she didn't live in another city and her mother's situation annoyed her, not a great deal, but with a certain nagging consistency, like the sight of a roommate's pile of old magazines or stray socks.

Alice believed in propriety. Life was full of horrors, unexpected ones, unlikely ones, like going to the hospital and spending a year there. Alice had gone to the hospital and spent a year there. She didn't blame anyone for that year (although she would have liked to) because she could not determine with any precision whose fault it had been— it had just happened. And it turned out to be not the experience of being in pain or in the hospital that had stayed with her, but precisely this inability to assign guilt, this imprecision. Behaving properly was no defense against this, but it was a kind of defiance. If the world would not be orderly, then at least she would be. And anyone around her whom she could convince to join her cause. Brenda's life, Willie's, even Peter's, spread out before her like steaming swamps waiting to be drained, to be claimed for cultivation, acre after acre of misjudgment, lethargy, and frivolity.

"Let her be. Hmmph," Alice said.

Inside the terminal, Alice saw a crowd of passengers in summery clothes intently watching a conveyer belt that carried luggage around and around, out of sight through a rubber curtain, then back in through another. She could see Brenda, tall and rather stately, her head above most of the other passengers'. Her mother was wearing sunglasses, and Alice did not know if Brenda had spotted her. Louie was not visible, but Alice could hear what she thought was Louie's voice.

"Yeah? Well, *you* belong in an institution, that's who," said the voice.

Alice walked through the crowd toward her mother, whom she saw dragging a suitcase off the conveyer. When Brenda turned toward her, Alice saw her own face, muddy and rather pink from her day's exertions, reflected in each large lens of her mother's sunglasses.

"So horrible I'm just about ready to kill him," Brenda said.

Alice smiled. "Hi, Mom."

A small woman wearing a navy-blue suit had followed Brenda from the crowd waiting for luggage. "He drinka too much," she said, shaking her head. She patted Brenda's hand and moved on, dragging a great suitcase on wheels like a large dog on a leash.

"He does drinka too much," Brenda said.

"Had fun, huh?"

"Hmmph," snorted Brenda.

Alice began whistling to herself, glad now that she had driven to the airport, rewarded for her trouble. She took one handle of her mother's bag. If she didn't ask where Louie was, perhaps he wouldn't be anywhere.

But as they walked toward the large glass doors, she heard him calling, "You! You there!"

Brenda stopped.

"Let's ditch him," Alice said.

"Let's shut up and behave and not antagonize our mother."

Louie was approaching, carrying his suitcase, stopping periodically to deliver short, swift kicks to its brown canvas side.

"Well, why don't I go get the car?" Alice said when Louie and his suitcase finally arrived.

"Now, don't worry about that, little lady. I'll get it, no problem, you understand?" Louie said. He put his arm around Alice's shoulders, then noticed the caked mud on her jacket, and drew back. Alice smelled alcohol and cologne.

"That's okay, Louie, you don't know where it's parked and—"

"Let's get something straightened out, you see?" Louie said. Louie was pointing at her, wagging his index finger back and forth like a pendulum, closer and closer to her face. It's like a horror movie, Alice thought. A cheapo horror movie. She could almost hear the sound track, dah-dah dah-dah. He was whispering, but whispering loudly. "What's wrong, Alice, you don't have trust for me?"

"Yeah," Alice said. "That's right." Dah-dah dah-dah. She was rather excited. She had never answered Louie directly like that.

"Alice, Alice, Alice," Louie said.

She could think of nothing to reply to this, nothing that would live up to "Yeah, that's right." She considered repeating it.

"Yeah, that's right," she said, deciding it was a powerful phrase. "Yeah," she added, for emphasis.

"All I ask is a little respect, Alice," Louie said. He took one of her hands in both of his. She pulled it back. "A little respect, that's all, that's all that I ask." Louie's words were slurred. The off-white around his dark pupils had turned a milky pink. "Exactly," Louie whispered.

Alice looked at her mother, but Brenda had suddenly become preoccupied with cleaning her sunglasses. She polished them carefully with a Kleenex, leaving bits of white fuzz, then polished again.

Louie smiled. "That's what I say to you, you understand? I say, 'Little lady, give Louie the keys.' "

"Well, ta-ta, I'm off," Alice said. "Anyone want a lift?"

"Bootan," said Louie.

Alice said, "It's pronounced *putana*."

"Alice studied in Florence, you know," Brenda said.

"Thank you, Mom."

People filed past, their faces brown and radiant, their arms full of plastic net bags packed with oranges and rosy grapefruits, and they did not seem to notice that Louie Scifo had taken hold of Alice's chin, like a menacing grandmother. He glared up at her, and Alice wondered if the passersby were embarrassed and pretending not to see, or just didn't notice.

"Louie," Brenda said. Her voice was firm but gentle, the voice of a schoolteacher disciplining her pet student. "Stop it this instant or we're leaving you here. Do you hear me?" *Putana*, not bootan, five hundred times on the blackboard, young man.

Louie kicked his suitcase and made it clear that he would die before riding in the same car with a bootan—two bootans who had no trust in him—and that, as a matter of fact, he preferred never to set eyes on any of the company of bootans again, in his entire life, which would probably not last too much longer anyway, considering what he had to take from so many bootans.

Brenda began to laugh and then asked for that in writing.

"Typical request from a greedy Jew bootan with no respect, not an ounce," Louie said.

"Well, that's it," Brenda said. She had stopped laughing.

Alice waited, hoping Louie would say it again. Greedy Jew. She repeated it over and over to herself. It was like music.

Alice wondered why she had never thought of this strategy before. She had long ago noticed that the slightest hint of anti-Semitism could suddenly inspire her assimilated, apathetic family to near-hysteria, to ominous head-shaking and cries of "Never again!" She could provoke such remarks, surely. She would have to pay more attention, watch for opportunities.

"You," Brenda said slowly, magisterially, to Louie Scifo, "are disgusting." She lifted her suitcase. With her free hand she took Alice's and said, "Come."

Alice turned around once to look. Louie had not moved. A spiral of smoke from his cigarette climbed through the air and hung, a dark cartoon cloud, above his head.

／ Alice wrinkled her nose at the smell of tomato sauce that wafted through the room. She hated tomato sauce when she was at her mother's. She hated garlic and onions and cheese and spaghetti and espresso. They were symbols of Louie's occupation, foreign flags waving over town hall. When she visited her father in Vancouver, she hated roast beef.

Alice began to remove piles of laundry from the dining-room table. Her mother had recently begun doing her ironing there, the result of seeing a dining-room table used as an ironing board in an Italian movie. A different Italian movie had inspired Brenda to use thick, squat orange-juice glasses for wine. Alice put some out on the table when she set it.

It was not clear to Alice whether this dinner, to which she and Peter and Willie had been invited, along with Jack and Nancy from Westport, was a celebration, an experiment, or just a dinner. Louie Scifo, at any rate, was conspicuously absent. Two days had passed since Brenda's return from Florida, but Brenda had not mentioned the incident at the airport. Alice hadn't brought it up, either, although she was curious. Perhaps Louie had been so emotionally shattered that he had taken the next plane out of town. He'd joined the Foreign Legion. Or the Mujahedeen. Her mother gave no clue. As they ate their spaghetti, Brenda chatted about Florida, about how Mediterranean it was, not unlike Sicily, even though there were no mountains or rocks and it was much damper and the food was vile and it was full of highways and malls. "But there's something about it."

"The air?" Alice asked.

"Oh, no. Not like Sicily's air at all. The air in Florida is so wet. And polluted."

"The water?"

"The water. No. Dirty and cold."

"Cold, with the man, the fish—man-of-war," said Jack. And they began to talk about a trip the two families had taken to Florida twenty years before, driving all day and all night in the blue Pontiac station wagon, the children camped out in the back on a foam mattress. Alice remembered the trip vividly. She had a pair of toy handcuffs and they had become entangled in her hair.

Alice drank her wine from the fat glass and felt increasingly drowsy. The last time she ate dinner at her mother's had been in the spring. "Now, Alice," her mother had said, "I wanted to tell you, about Louie telling Miriam he was sick at your wedding, Louie has a very deep-seated fear of death. It started after his plane crash during the war, and he can become overly *empathetic* at times . . ."

Alice's mother had an arsenal of excuses for Louie Scifo. If Louie picked a fight with a parking-garage attendant, it was because he was insecure. When he burned fifty-dollar bills in a restaurant, yelling, "You think I care about money? *This* is how much I care about money!" it was because he had been rich and was no longer. When he snapped his fingers at waiters and called them "boy," it was because he had been *poor* as a child.

"Hey!" Jack was saying to Alice. "Paesan! A *bisl* cheese?"

Alice took the Parmesan. Jack had been poor as a child, she thought. And *he* never snapped his fingers, not even to music.

Alice's mother seemed to understand that Louie had several unpleasant characteristics. She never actually said as much, but whenever he behaved particularly badly, she began recounting his troubled childhood, his difficult marriage, his financial worries. But instead of driving her away from him, Louie's faults had always seemed to draw her closer. They were weaknesses, and so Louie must be weak—fragile and in need of help. Alice thought Louie never told the truth, even about everyday things, like the weather. To Alice, he seemed shifty and mean, a noisy, snarling cur. To Alice's mother, he was man's best friend, abandoned and injured on the highway. Of course, she had to pull over.

Alice almost admired her for her generosity. "But you know," she told Peter, "she's like that guy who gave soup to Frankenstein—blind like that guy."

"But the blind man was the only one who saw the monster's sweet soul," Peter said.

"Oh yeah? But you know what I mean."

Brenda thought the world had been hard on Louie and so he was bitter. Alice thought he was bitter and bad-spirited to begin with, and so the world had turned on him. Even his parents disliked Louie. They lived in a brick house in Queens, not far from the maze of entrance ramps leading to Kennedy Airport. Alice's mother had taken her there to sip dark, sweet sherry among the lace doilies and the roar of the planes. "Isn't it exciting?" she said in the car, pointing heavenward at a landing aircraft.

Louie's parents, two tiny, kindly old people who looked a little like lace doilies themselves, served the sherry with a tray of cookies. They looked disapprovingly out the parlor window.

"No peace," said Mrs. Scifo.

"Since the planes came, no peace," Mr. Scifo said.

"Poor Louie." Mrs. Scifo sighed, shaking her head at a jumbo jet. She wore an apron even though she was not cooking.

"Always," her husband said, a little too loud, for the plane had already passed over, and the room was suddenly very quiet.

Mrs. Scifo once told Mrs. Brody that Louie was a victim not only of excessive air traffic but also of the army. After he was wounded (in the Korean War, he said; Alice suspected he lied about his age and that it was World War I), a steel plate was put in his head. "And then the blood," Mrs. Scifo said. "They took it out, they put some back, but what they put back"—she shook her finger—"bad blood."

"Mom, even his own mother thinks he's a little off," Alice once said. But her mother just laughed. Sometimes Louie would drink too much and boast that he had a gun. Alice's mother said it was because he was shy.

When they stood up from the table, there was a pink ring around Willie's mouth from the spaghetti sauce. All through dinner, as Alice thought of Louie Scifo in his absence, her dislike of him had flourished, like a potted plant taken outside into the sun. In a sudden desire to share this luxurious feeling, Alice grabbed Peter's arm and led him away.

"Look," she said, pointing to the maid's room. "He lives there. Like a bug."

"I know," Peter said.

The narrow maid's room was crammed full of things— buggy-looking things. An old sagging cot, unmade, the sheets yellowed. A small TV with a wire hanger dangling from its antenna and a ball of aluminum foil attached to that. Nearly half the room was occupied by radios, televisions, and tape recorders in boxes piled almost to the ceiling. Leaning against this brown cardboard edifice was one small oil painting of a clown with very large eyes, each sporting a shiny tear.

"Ah. He's become an art dealer," Alice said.

A yellow window shade was drawn three-quarters of the way down. Red taillights and white headlights were shining on the street below, bright, faraway, framed by the gray walls and yellow shade.

"It's not a very cheerful room, is it?" Peter said.

"It's cozy," Brenda had once explained to Alice. "This is Louie's little lair. A place he can escape to."

Alice thought the room looked more like a place to escape from. There were battered metal ashtrays brimming with cigarette butts and silvery ashes. An extensive array of after-shave and cologne sat on the glass shelf above the small, cracked sink in the corner.

"Looks a little like a jail," Peter said.

"So he feels more at home," Alice said.

"Alice!" Brenda said. She was standing at the door of the maid's room. "This is Louie's office. Now show a little respect."

Brenda often asked her children to show some respect. It was a phrase Alice associated with movies about the Mafia. She pointed this out to her mother.

Brenda said, "Show some respect!"

One time, when Alice made some comment about Louie, her mother had said, "You're too old to be jealous of your mother's boyfriend."

"I'm not jealous," Alice said, and then she'd wondered if she was. She liked her mother's company and resented Louie's presence, which either deprived her of being with her mother or forced her to spend time with him.

"Maybe I'm jealous because every time I see you, or almost every time, that little person is here stalking around," Alice said.

"He doesn't stalk."

"He creeps," Alice had said. "He creeps, then."

"You like Mommy's ring?" he would say. "You like Louie's taste? In other words, from a friend. He fixed it for me, you follow?"

This indistinct, aimless muttering seemed to have completely reordered her mother's world, diminished it, until Brenda became small and fragile, fussing and careful.

At Brenda Brody's fiftieth birthday party, Louie Scifo gave her fifty one-hundred-dollar bills, gift-wrapped in a box. The wrapping paper had hearts and bare-bottomed cupids on it. When Brenda tore it off and lifted the lid of the box, Louie insisted she count the bills.

"Not now, dear," she said with the tight, forced smile she had begun to display in his company.

"For the people," Louie said. "To show the people."

"He didn't mean anything," her mother said when Alice remarked on the episode after the party. "He just doesn't understand certain things. And, anyway, he took the money back."

"You *gave the money back?*"

Alice had been disgusted. Clearly, Louie had known that her mother would not keep the money, which was why he had been able to bring himself to part with it in the first place. When she suggested this to her mother, Brenda said, "It was very generous of him. Not in the best of taste, I admit, but Louie is from a different culture."

"Louie is a-cultural," Alice said, but then her mother looked as if she might cry, and Alice was forced to hold her peace. It was galling that Brenda's vulnerability constantly prevented Alice from protecting her.

The dinner party moved into the living room for coffee, and Alice sat, sleepy and a little drunk, soothed by the conversation of people who didn't care if she paid attention, and thought of Louie as she had seen him before his last trip to Florida, standing beside her mother. His hard leathery face with its swimmy eyes and cloud of soft, juvenile hair; one arm was around her waist. Brenda had just invited Alice to stay for dinner.

"Oh, but Mother's tired, dear," Louie quickly interjected. He opened his mouth in a stiff, frightful smile. "Another night, you understand? Not that you aren't welcome like you're our own flesh and blood."

"Louie," Alice's mother said. "She is my flesh and blood."

"Now, don't feel bad that Alice won't stay. We understand she's got things to do. No time for dinner with Mommy. It's generational, you see what I'm getting at here?"

Alice's mother had taken her aside and said, "Alice, I'm sorry. I don't want to start anything. I'm not in the mood. Another night, okay?"

One day her mother had been Mrs. Alan Brody, a housewife considered industrious because she was studying for a Ph.D. in psychology; the next day, she was a middle-aged divorcée with no job, no experience, one of those part-time students who hadn't even gotten her degree yet, at her age.

"I was so tired," Brenda once told her.

Alice looked at her and realized for the first time that her mother was getting old.

"I didn't know how to do anything, I didn't know anything. And there was Louie, busy like a bug, doing everything."

Alice never doubted that Louie was devoted to her mother, but Louie's devotion was not reassuring to her.

Louie had a habit of discovering potential disasters and then rescuing everyone from them. There were sudden gaping cracks in the ceiling, gas leaks from the stove; in the car, mufflers would drag, distributor caps disappear, brake fluid drain to the pavement. Louie was always the first to spot the cracks or sniff the gas. And having detected the problem, he would somehow solve it, improvising with great energy, making his elaborate repairs with bits of this and other bits of that he'd gotten here and picked up cheap over there.

"What would we do without him?" Brenda would say.

But Alice thought they had done rather well without him. No ceilings had crushed them, no gas had choked them, their brakes had not failed. Alice was convinced that Louie had created these crises—that he snuck around swinging sledgehammers into ceilings and gas pipes—so that he could later come upon the damage and repair it. Not for any personal glory, but because he wanted to serve Brenda, to protect her, and he believed that breaking something and then fixing it was just as good as fixing something that had broken of its own accord. It was better, even; it was noble, for it required more effort, more thought, more care. For Louie, this was neither dishonesty nor sleight of hand: it was gallantry.

When the Brodys' divorce had gone through, the house in Westport was sold and Brenda moved to New York to finish her dissertation (which consisted of constructing weird toys out of weird household detritus, playing with the weird toys with wide-eyed children, and then producing hundreds of graphs and charts and pages of footnotes surrounding a smattering of text). As Brenda was fond of noting, Louie was there, always there, throughout the writing of the dissertation and then the eventual opening of her practice as a therapist who made and played with weird toys. Alice was initially surprised at how very much he was there. He didn't get up to go to the office every morning like most men. He didn't get up to go to the office on any morning. He didn't go home to his own apartment to water the plants or feed the cats. He didn't seem to have an apartment.

It was not clear where Louie had lived before Brenda moved into the city. When Alice was in the hospital, Brenda would walk from her hotel to visit her every day and she would pass Louie sitting on the stoop of a fancy East Side brownstone. That was how they met. Louie claimed to own the house at the time, but it turned out to belong to an elderly lady who explained to Brenda that she and Louie had once been "very close." She allowed him to use a corner of her basement as an office, she said, and he sometimes stayed in one of the apartments when it wasn't rented. Louie explained the discrepancies in the two stories by saying this lady had tricked him out of his share of the building, which he had designed and constructed with his own two hands, and as soon as he could move his office into Brenda's new apartment, he added, he would sue his former partner.

Alice was not sure whether or not he had sued the woman. He often talked about his lawsuits, but there were several of them, and as Alice never encouraged a conversation with her mother's boyfriend, she had been unable to distinguish much among his cases. She did know that there was a case against the city for physical and emotional stress caused by a beer bottle that struck his head while he watched the Puerto Rican Day Parade. Louie had shown her the bottle, Miller Lite, which he referred to as "the evidence." There was also a suit for damages resulting from a car accident: he wanted several million dollars to compensate him for the loss of the use of his legs, a loss he often bemoaned as he scampered and sprang across the roof of the Brodys' barn in Westport. (After the divorce, Brenda had used the money from the sale of her half of the house to buy out Alan Brody's share in the barn, and Louie, despite his infirmity, insisted on remodeling it.)

Louie did, as promised, move into Brenda's apartment, there to sue his enemies and woo . . . *my mother*, Alice thought. Why her? Why not some other buxom, indiscriminate gal, like Elizabeth Taylor, for example. Brenda had suffered from a bad case of empty-nest syndrome—in which she had been forced to leave the nest along with everyone else. And now here was Louie, a loyal new bird among the twigs of the new nest, to which he constantly contributed his bits of string and candy wrappers. Louie Scifo found all sorts of things on the sidewalk, with special attention to old eyeglasses.

"Oh, thank you, Louie," Alice's mother said when battered spectacles were presented to her. "I can always use an extra pair. Always losing mine. The prescription is not too far off, you know that?"

Alice sank back into her chair and looked at Nancy and Jack, wondering what it would have been like to have them as parents. Her own mother and father had earned their divorce, since all they did was fight; but then they had immediately tied themselves down to people even worse than each other, with whom they couldn't possibly get along, and got along with them. But there were Nancy and Jack, the same cheerful, friendly couple. Small and neat and appealing, they matched, complemented each other like two porcelain figurines. Still, Alice thought, if they'd been my parents I would have had to go to one of those Jewish summer camps where you have teams and your team loses and everyone blames you.

"Brenda, this couch is so comfortable," Nancy said, and she took off her shoes and pulled her feet up under her until she was as curled and compact as a cat.

The couch had come from the Long Island house of Louie Scifo's dead wife. It was extraordinarily long, the most prominent example of Mrs. Scifo's unwitting bequest. But there were also matching dressers painted bone-white with gold accents. And, of course, the round, glass coffee table, with the bronzed base shaped like a sheaf of wheat, which fell over if anything was placed on one side of it with nothing placed on the other for balance.

First of all, he drove his wife insane and plagued her

until she had a heart attack and died, Alice thought. (Brenda had told her that Louie's wife became paranoid, suspicious of Louie, even calling the police toward the end, saying he was following her, spying on her, stealing her jewelry and selling it.) Second, Alice thought, the furniture is ugly.

Alice moved to the couch and sat beside Nancy. In Florida, on that trip, Nancy had squeezed Sea & Ski from the green plastic bottle onto Alice's back. Every morning, beside the pool. Alice remembered the cold shiver of the cream as Nancy rubbed it in, describing the pictures it was forming—a beach umbrella, a birthday cake, a pelican.

Jack was smoking his pipe and the smell of it made Alice dizzy. She lay down with her head on Nancy's lap. Sometimes she wished she was like Nancy. She wished she was decorous and busy and relaxed all at the same time. Jack began to cough. Alice looked up and saw his face get redder and redder. Alice's brother was, for some reason, reciting the Turkish alphabet. Peter put his drink down on the glass coffee table that had been a gift from Louie Scifo.

Alice watched as the table tilted, slowly, dreamily, and the thick glass of red wine spilled, languid and inevitable, onto the floor.

✦ / Aunt Frieda died that month, and Alice cried and wondered why she always forgot Aunt Frieda's name. Aunt Frieda was one of Grandma's sisters, a tall blonde with a smooth, flat face and placid blue eyes. When they saw each other, she was fun, in a brisk, adept way, but more often they spoke on the phone.

"Hello?"

"Do you know who this is?" Aunt Frieda would say.

"Hi!" Alice had only to hear Aunt Frieda's voice to forget Aunt Frieda's name.

"So," Aunt Frieda would say suspiciously after Alice had said Hi several more times. "It's your Aunt Frieda."

"I know."

"Have you spoken to your grandmother? Have you spoken to your mother? Has your mother spoken to your grandmother? Has your brother spoken to your mother and your grandmother? This is your Aunt Frieda."

Aunt Frieda was the arbiter of family phoning. Grandma often called Alice to say, "I talked to Frieda today," her voice high-pitched and anxious. That was the sole content of the call, the reason behind it, a sisterly command carried through. Grandma affectionately called her Frieda the Policeman.

"Who's this?" Aunt Frieda said the last time they spoke, stretching out the final word in a challenging singsong. "Who's thi-is?"

"Alice," Alice said.

"No, I mean who's *this*?"

"Oh, *this*."

Aunt Frieda was satisfied and moved on to the secondary reason for her call—an invitation to dinner. Alice loved dinner at Aunt Frieda's. Aunt Frieda and Uncle Abe lived in an Art Deco apartment in New Jersey. It was perfect in every detail, a museum of black-and-white tiles, of dusty pink-and-green velvet, of silver cigarette cases on chunky, lacquered tables. Her aunt and uncle were not fastidious collectors; they had just never changed a thing from the time they moved into the apartment fifty years ago.

Alice liked having a great-aunt and great-uncle she could visit in an Art Deco apartment. They were not intimate relatives. They never hugged her or squeezed her cheeks, the way her grandmother did. But they accepted her unequivocally, they loved her without ever thinking why, and she loved them, too. Alice and her aunt and uncle had nothing in common; they had nothing specifically to give to or take from each other. The relationship just existed, independent of all the things that comprise a relationship.

But now Aunt Frieda was dead and Alice cried in the small chapel. It was windowless and paneled in mahogany, just like the coffin, Alice thought. From the murmur of sad voices, a loud laugh would occasionally break out.

Uncle Abe kissed Alice and squeezed her hand. Alice

felt sorry and sad and a little frightened. She mumbled, squeezed his hand back, walked away.

"Darling," Aunt Beverly the flapper said, opening her eyes in a coquettish gaze. "Do you know who I am?"

Oh God, Alice thought. They will take on Frieda's personality as a sign of veneration. There are four of them left. Then she realized that Aunt Beverly, blind as ever, was probably just trying to figure out who Alice was.

"Aunt Beverly, really," she said and wagged a reprimanding finger that her aunt could not see.

"Oh, hello, Alice," Aunt Beverly said and began to sob. Alice patted her hand, trying to think of something soothing to say.

"I like your dress, Aunt Beverly." That usually worked, and for a moment Aunt Beverly's face perked up. But only for a moment. "I got it at Loehmann's," she said, the tears streaming down her face. "Frieda loved Loehmann's so."

Willie, wearing a puckered blue polyester yarmulke, came over and hugged the small, weeping woman. He wrinkled his nose as a feather protruding from Aunt Beverly's hat brushed against it.

"There, there. Hello, Aunt Beverly," he said.

"Do you know who I am?" she said fiercely.

Alice wished Peter had come. He had met Aunt Frieda at the wedding, but he couldn't remember her, which seemed sad to Alice, though she wasn't sure why. She had told him not to come.

Alice said a silent prayer during the moment of silence, and just at the point when Aunt Frieda's name should have come up, she forgot Aunt Frieda's name.

She burst into tears.

"We'll all miss her very much," Alice's mother whispered, putting her arm around Alice comfortingly.

"Who?" Alice wanted to say, but she just nodded her head.

"And who's this?" Aunt Selma said, coming up to kiss her.

Alice looked up quickly, then realized it was just a greeting.

"Alice," she said, anyway.

Aunt Selma laughed, then began to cry.

Alice wondered whether to say I like your dress again. "We'll all miss her," she said instead.

"Who?" her Aunt Selma said.

"Her," Alice said, horrified. "*Her*," she said pointing to the coffin.

"*Who* will miss her? That's what I want to know," Aunt Selma was saying. "That good-for-nothing daughter of hers, three thousand miles away? California, California, everything California. The East Coast isn't good enough for her. Not one city along the entire Eastern Seaboard, not one . . ."

Alice backed away, nodding politely, like a retreating courtier.

"It's disgusting to grow old," she heard Aunt Selma saying as she turned and walked out to the parking lot.

"Let's go," the funeral director said. He was quiet but efficient, like a skilled sheepdog, nipping gently at the mourners' hooves. "This way, this way."

Alice walked outside. The funeral home's driver paced beside the hearse, waving people toward their cars.

"Come on, Aunt Gert, you come with me," Cousin Sid the furrier said to the youngest of the four remaining sisters. Cousin Sid owned a black Cadillac and a red jeep. Today he had driven from his house in Great Neck in the jeep. Why? Alice wondered. The Cadillac, gliding smoothly along, was too like the hearse, perhaps. Jewish parents were not supposed to name their children after themselves because when the angel of death came for Mom or Dad he might mistakenly pluck up little Junior instead. Maybe Cousin Sid thought this carried over to cars.

Aunt Gert looked at the open jeep with its huge wheels and thick roll bar. She was plagued by phobias; she was afraid to fly, to drive; she required psychopharmaceuticals before crossing a busy street. She stared at the open jeep with a detached, quizzical expression, as if it had materialized on TV as she flipped through the channels.

"Whee!" she cried, her eyes wide and glazed, her bony hands reaching for the dashboard, as Cousin Sid lifted her into the high seat.

"My Harry," Grandma moaned at the sight of Brenda's car, a large Buick that had belonged to Alice's grandfather. Willie still wore his yarmulke. It perched on his head, looking precarious but clinging there just the same. Willie and the blue yarmulke towered above Grandma as he opened the car door for her, and Alice thought of the tree outside her bedroom window in the city, from which a gray-and-red sweat sock had dangled for months.

Brenda lifted her bag onto the seat and began snapping and zipping and rooting around. "Where are they?" she said. "They're not here, they're not here, they are not here."

"Come on, Mom," Alice said.

"I left the car keys in New York."

"Mom!" Alice did not point out that they could not have driven to New Jersey if the keys had been left in New York. This was sheer showing off on her mother's part.

"I left them in New York, right on the table in the hall."

Willie reached over from the back seat and pointed to the keys dangling from the ignition.

The cars lined up behind the hearse in the parking lot, a train of dressed-up people weeping behind their sunglasses. Directly in front of the Buick, Aunt Gert and Cousin Sid bounced into line in the jeep.

"Poor thing," Grandma said.

"We'll all miss her," Alice said.

"Her," Grandma said, pointing to Aunt Gert's wildly jouncing head.

"Don't lose them, Mom," Alice said, also pointing, but to the hearse, which rolled, rather quickly, Alice thought, out of the driveway onto the street.

"They're in the ignition, Alice. Honestly."

It was a beautiful day. The sunlight was clear and rich. The lawns and the sky and the large old houses sparkled in the cool air. The hearse, ostentatiously black in the bright suburban neighborhood, roared to the top of the next hill, then through a yellow light.

Left behind at the red light, the mourners waited. Alice could see the hearse ahead, stopped at the next light. The lights changed together and the wheels of the hearse screeched, leaving black tire tracks on the pavement. In the left lane of the highway now, it passed a Jaguar, then cut into the middle lane to roar past a red Maserati.

With her foot to the floor, her hands clamped tightly on the wheel, Brenda hunched forward, squinting in concentration.

"Cabbie, follow that hearse!" Willie said.

Cars with their lights on raced beside them. The grim and orderly funeral procession had scattered across the three lanes of the highway, the drivers warily eyeing each other like teenagers in a drag race.

"I'm going seventy-five miles an hour," Brenda said. "Eighty!"

"Rush, rush, rush. This modern era," Grandma said. "Always chasing a buck."

"We're chasing a car, Mother."

"Ah, the thrill of the hunt," Alice said. "The poor birds have only two kinds of chase, neither of which involves automobiles—chasing something because you want to catch it and eat it, chasing something because you want it to go away."

"We are not birds," Brenda said, swerving sharply into the left lane to pass a bus.

As they rounded the bus, Alice could see the hearse far ahead, sparkling for a moment in a blazing, silvery reflection of the afternoon sun, before it pulled over the horizon and disappeared.

"Where is the goddamn hearse?" Brenda said.

"The dirty thieves," said Grandma.

Brenda was crying. She had been very close to Aunt Frieda in the last few years, visiting her weekly after she got sick.

"Where *is* she?" Brenda said, wiping the tears from her eyes and shaking her fist at the driver of a tractor-trailer as she passed him.

"Well, I don't believe in heaven," Grandma said. "Although you'd think, after this hideous world, it would only be fair."

They pulled off at an exit and stopped at a gas station. Brenda took a deep breath. "That was exciting," she said.

Alice saw her mother's bright eyes and realized she meant it.

While Brenda asked the attendant for directions to the

cemetery, Cousin Sid's jeep and a few other family vehicles pulled up behind them. Brenda wrote everything down on the back of an envelope and the diminished cortege proceeded out of the gas station back onto the road.

"We're off!" Brenda said.

They cruised onto another thruway, realized they were lost, stopped at another gas station, and finally ended up at Our Lady of the Sacred Heart Cemetery.

"Nope," Willie said.

They hit two Episcopal cemeteries and a Greek Orthodox one as the afternoon progressed. Brenda had stopped crying completely and insisted on driving through the various graveyards, pointing to especially pretty headstones, remarking on the interesting names and the marvelous diversity of American society. Grandma muttered something in the back which meant "one hundred years" in Yiddish and referred, Alice supposed, to the time when Grandma might first consider joining any of these ethnic gatherings.

Only the jeep was still with them.

"Gert, Gert, come with us, Gert, why are you in that truck?" Grandma said when they pulled over to ask directions of a boy on a bicycle. Aunt Gert stared ahead and smiled slightly. She did not answer.

"My poor sister," Grandma said.

"Which one?" Alice said.

"Let's find a lovely place to eat!" Brenda said. "An adventure!"

It was after four, and they had not had lunch, but the town they found themselves in did not look promising. There was not a restaurant in sight, only tall white houses with ancient elms and their dark shadows on the lawns.

"What a beautiful town," Brenda said. "Maybe we should move here."

"There!" Alice cried. They were approaching the back of a large Victorian house with a parking lot filled with cars. "Look, they're from everywhere. From Ohio, Delaware—it's an inn."

"An inn!" Brenda said.

"Mmm," Willie said. "New Jersey Buttered Fluorocarbon Biscuits . . ."

"Never mind," Alice said. They had lost their quarry, but that did not mean they had to starve.

"I can't eat restaurant poison," Grandma muttered as she inched her way slowly out of the car. "Oy. An inn yet." She looked around for the jeep carrying her sister Gert, but it was no longer with them.

It was a rather formal lobby with red carpeting and crystal chandeliers. There were a few people standing around and they looked formal, too, dressed up and dignified.

"Are you with the McDonald party?" the man behind the desk asked. The word McDonald made Alice even more hungry.

"No," Brenda said. "We were just driving by."

"I see," said the man.

"Good thing I'm wearing a tie," Willie said, looking around.

"I mean, you're open now, right?" Alice asked. It was almost 4:30.

"Well, yes."

"Maybe a roll," Grandma was saying. "Tea."

Alice tapped her fingers on the man's polished desktop. "Are you serving dinner now? Or lunch? Or anything?" He had been watching her with a troubled expression and she wondered if she had lipstick on her cheek or something.

"Madam," he began.

"Do you have rooms, too?" Brenda asked.

"I'm not staying in this spooky place," Willie said.

"We're staying overnight? I haven't got my medicinals!" Grandma began searching through her bag for pills.

The man at the desk was saying, "Madam, please . . ."

"It's not spooky at all," Brenda politely reassured him. "It's *Victorian*."

Maybe the inn was full, Alice thought. No room at the inn. They should have a sign. A blinking one, like motels in the Catskills: NO VACANCY, and the NO part could be turned off when necessary. Then embarrassing moments like this would be avoided.

"Please, please, Madam . . ." the man continued.

It was something about the way he said Madam, or that he said it at all. It wasn't inn-like, somehow. Madam. And the people standing in small hushed groups were non-inn, too. The men were in dark suits. The women looked as if they were going to church.

"Madam, this is . . ."

"Not an inn!" Alice said.

"No."

"Mom, this is a funeral parlor!"

"Home," said the man.

"What a coincidence!" said Brenda.

"So, they're not serving?" Grandma said.

They got back in the car, and Alice read out the directions she had gotten from the man. "The cemetery's just a few blocks away."

"Cast bread upon the waters," Grandma said.

They drove the few blocks and there at last was the elusive cemetery. The hearse was long gone, the coffin lowered into the grave, the border piles of freshly dug dirt shoveled over it. They got out of the car and stood quietly around the grave. Alice thought, I'm sorry that you died and I'll miss you and I hope you are resting in peace or whatever it is people do when they're dead that is best.

🦋 / "What kind of normal family has mothers, amiable, pretty mothers, who call their children for protection from menacing boyfriends?" Peter said.

"Mine," said Alice.

It was just a few weeks after the dinner party at Brenda's house. Aunt Frieda's death had caused a frenzy of family phoning, usually about nothing at all—a posthumous tribute. But tonight Brenda called to say that she had broken up with Louie, she really meant it this time, but that he was oblivious to this turn of events. He refused to leave her apartment. He was frightening her.

"My parents live *in Florida*," Peter said.

They were standing in the hall, outside Brenda Brody's door, and they could already hear the argument.

"It's over," Brenda was saying. "O-V-E-R. Finished. The end."

"Don't threaten me, missy. Is that a threat? Or something?"

"Louie, I mean it. I've had enough."

"Meaning what? 'Enough' meaning what?"

Peter put his hand out to ring the doorbell, but Alice grabbed his arm. "Shhh," she whispered.

Louie was saying, "Kindly return my goods. The ring, for example. It's my ring, you understand?"

"Here," Brenda said.

"This ring? It's mine, you understand? Sentimental value, you see?"

"Okay."

"Just like that? You return something I gave to you, a gift from the heart, and you return it coldly to me? Keep it. It has no meaning to me."

Brenda said in an almost friendly voice, "Good. Thank you. I like this ring."

"Hand it over!"

The hall had recently been painted a creamy yellow color, the doors brown. Alice could still smell the paint. She sneezed. The nameplate said Dr. Brenda Brody. Peter nudged Alice, pointed to the doorbell, and said loudly, "Well, here we are, Alice, dear," and pressed the bell. They heard it buzz shrilly inside.

When Brenda answered the door, she was twisting a big diamond ring off her finger. Her normally round cheery face seemed all angles; it was hard and set. She rolled her eyes as they heard Louie's voice from the kitchen: "No way do you keep a ring I gave you as tokens of deep feeling, a present from my heart to your heart. No way. It's the sentimental value, you understand? Mm-hmm. Three and a half carats."

The ring was a large and valuable diamond that Louie gave Brenda after her own diamond ring, somewhat smaller but more valuable, had been stolen.

"By Louie," Alice said when it happened, marveling at how he had contrived to look generous and make a small profit at the same time. "Someone breaks into the house on the one night my mother isn't there, and the one night the ring is there instead of in the vault, and Louie is the only one who knows, and he disappears that night and whoever steals the ring goes right to the jewelry box, in exactly the right drawer, without searching through the house, and when Mom and Louie go out to Westport the next day, Louie keeps saying, Gee, you better check your jewelry, and, Gee, I better check the downstairs door and make sure no one has broken in and stolen your jewelry, which you better check in case someone has stolen it after breaking in through the downstairs door which I better go check. Gee, I wonder who stole Mom's ring. Can't imagine. Beats the hell out of me."

Brenda laughed at Alice's conclusion. She didn't know people who stole rings. She did know Louie. Therefore, Louie did not steal rings.

"That's a false syllogism, Mom. Or is it a tautology? I think that's a syllogism."

"Really, Alice, you're so melodramatic. And why would Louie steal a ring, anyway, when he's always picking up such bargains at the Jewelry Exchange?"

Now Brenda was saying, "Here, here, take it. God knows where you got it in the first place."

"Hi, Louie," Alice said.

"Why do you hate me, Alice? Why?" Louie said. He was wearing a tan, three-quarter-length coat that Alice recognized. It had been hers in high school. As he spoke, he held out his hands in a gesture of despair, as if he were begging for coins.

"Because—"

"Come on, Alice, let's sit in the living room," Peter said quickly, and he pulled Alice away as Louie carefully placed the large diamond ring in his pants pocket while telling Brenda she was not herself.

"No, actually, Louie, I'm myself for the first time in years."

Louie said no, she wasn't.

"Well, never mind," Brenda said.

"Brenda, what can I do?" Louie said.

Alice felt a faint pang of pity for Louie. He sounded genuinely upset. And confused. What had he done, after all, that he hadn't always done?

"What can I say, what, what?"

"Nothing," said Brenda. "I'm worn out. What do you want from me?"

"You're with somebody. A bootan to be with someone else, you bootan—"

"Louie! Show a little respect," Brenda said.

"I worship you like a madonna," Louie said.

Peter, sitting on the sofa, had begun to tap his feet, first one, then the other, then the first again. He sat forward on the sofa, staring down: one foot was on the wood floor, one on the rug. He was wearing sneakers. Only the foot on the floor made a noise. A skipped beat. "Alice," he whispered desperately.

Alice held her finger to her lips to silence him. She smiled. She was enjoying herself. There was something queasy about listening to someone else's quarrel, particularly one's mother's, but, on the other hand, this was a moment of triumph.

"Stop gloating," Peter said. "And I'm bored. And embarrassed."

Brenda had begun spelling "over" to Louie again.

"I wonder if sitting in on a series of arguments and recording the number of times Louie uses the word 'bootan' would allow me to predict the number of 'bootans' to be used in subsequent arguments," Peter said.

"Goodbye, Louie," Brenda said.

"You want me to *leave*?" Louie said.

Alice made a disgusted cluck with her tongue. Peter stood up and began to pace. "The number of 'bootans' into the number of arguments over x times the number of other epithets squared with y being greater than . . ." The apartment was too hot, baked by the banging, choking radiator, while bits of intimate but inconclusive conversation drifted through the room.

"Goodbye, Louie," Brenda was saying.

Louie Scifo said, "I don't understand."

Alice realized that Brenda had begun to cry, and she stood up and began pacing with Peter. "Get out, get out, why don't you get out," Brenda kept saying.

"Do you want me to go do something?" Peter said. "Say something? Go in the kitchen and punch him out? Make toast? Why am I here? I hate your family."

Louie said, "He's dead. Your lover boy is dead, a dead man, you see?" He banged open the swinging door and stood at the entrance to the living room. "He's dead," Louie said to Alice and Peter, then went back to the kitchen. "So, I'm not good enough for you, Madam Princess of the World from Westport," Alice could hear him saying. "You and all your hoi-polloi friends—"

" 'Hoi polloi' doesn't mean that," Alice shouted.

"You see? You see that? But remember this, Brenda Big Shot . . ."

A siren screamed outside. Alice looked over toward the window and saw Peter standing there. A woman across the street watered her potted plants, then hurriedly drew the curtains as she spotted Peter.

"Alice, a woman across the street thinks I'm a voyeur, I think," he said.

"Well, you're not," Alice said loyally.

The orange tail of Brenda's cat protruded from the slipcover skirts of Louie Scifo's dead wife's sofa, flicking back and forth, then disappeared.

"Alice, I think it's time to go home now," Peter said.

"I know," Alice said. But she didn't move.

Brenda and Louie were again discussing whether anything Louie could say or do would change Brenda's mind. Brenda was of the opinion that it could not, while Louie was of the opinion that it could if only Brenda would stop being of the opinion that it could not.

"In my own personal views," Louie said after the discussion had circled around several times, "I have nothing further to say. Do you see? Goodbye and may God bless you, you follow?"

A door slammed. God bless you, too, Alice thought.

They listened. Alice could hear only the pipes rattling and the cat growling beneath the couch. And then the piercing whistle of a kettle.

Peter and Alice pushed open the kitchen door to find Brenda fixing herself a cup of tea. She stood between the stove and a table that, although tiny, was far too large for the narrow kitchen, jutting out to leave just enough room for the oven door to be opened. Brenda sat down, squeezed between the table and the window behind her, a favorite spot. She held the dripping tea bag over her cup.

"Mom," Alice said, "congratulations. What a relief."

As she spoke, the back door suddenly sprang open. Standing behind two green plastic garbage cans, partly hidden, his hands clasped together on his chest, was Louie. His frozen posture vividly reminded Alice of a possum she had once startled on the back steps, its spindly legs just withdrawn from the dog's tin dish. For a moment, she expected to see Louie's eyes glittering red, like the possum's, in the gloom.

"Aha!" Louie said.

Alice ushered Peter back into the living room. This second act was anticlimactic, she admitted. Louie's arguments were becoming increasingly irrelevant, delivered in shorter and shorter bursts, until they could hear only a blur of staccato oaths and fist-pounding; while Brenda sounded ever more calm, her words drifting along as unhurried and rhythmic as a prayer memorized in childhood. Alice wondered what she could do to liven things up. "I've been thinking a lot about the infield-fly rule," she said.

Peter leaned back into the sofa with a sigh. His head touched the cushion, which suddenly moved, then reached out to scratch his cheek.

"Peter, don't tease that poor old cat," Alice said.

"Aha!" Louie said, stepping into view, then ducking into the dining room.

"I'm going into the kitchen to see your mother now," Peter said. "Then I'm going home. Period."

"Okay, okay," Alice said, and she went with him.

Her mother smiled absently up at them, sipped her tea, and said nothing.

"So!" Alice said. Why had they come in here? To tell Brenda to hurry things along? To ask to be excused, please, we're quite finished, Peter is embarrassed and I'm impatient? Alice tried to think of something to say, something bracing, before they left. Louie was her mother's nuisance, after all, not hers. She had made her contribution. Now she was bored. It was time to go home.

Peter was tapping his foot again and she looked down. On the floor, by his foot, a small mouse wriggled in a mousetrap.

"Oh God, Mom, there's a mouse here."

"I know. Poor little thing. The cat won't touch them, you know. Could you pick him up, Peter dear, and throw him away or something?"

"Brenda, I'm not really—"

"Yes, you're right. We'll have to ask Louie. I would rather not be in his debt, but . . ."

Alice wondered how deep in Louie's debt Brenda would stand after the disposal of a dying mouse. She considered Lulu, the taxidermy princess, and wished she had already opened her salon. She looked at Brenda, who sat wedged at the little table, her cheeks flushed, pink even for Brenda as she pushed a teaspoon back and forth in the cup, not so much stirring as clanking. Alice listened to the faint clink, clink. She heard the mouse squeak.

"God, this family," Peter said, moving away from the mouse.

"Peter," Brenda said, very quietly. "Please do something." She clanked the spoon, back and forth, in the teacup, which Alice realized from the sound was empty. Brenda began to cry.

"It's not *dead* yet," Peter said.

"Just talk to him or something. Anything. Get Louie out of here."

There were noises from the maid's room—rummaging, drawers banging. Perhaps Louie was packing.

"Okay, Brenda," Peter said. "Okay, Louie," he said more loudly.

Louie darted out of the maid's room into the kitchen.

"I've got a gun!" he said. He was out of breath, standing in the gloomy little hall, nearly invisible in the darkness, panting loudly.

They stood stiff and still. The mouse squeaked again.

"Somewhere, anyway." Louie sighed and returned to his search.

Peter glared at Alice.

"It's not my fault," she said. She peered into Louie's room and saw him emptying the drawers of his desk, as if he'd been fired, which he has, Alice thought.

Peter pushed past into the narrow room. "Look, Louie . . ." he began, trying to find a place to stand among the boxes and piles of clothing on the floor. From one drawer, Louie carefully removed a few ballpoint pens, a pencil stub, some pieces of broken jewelry, a black-and-white photo of himself in a bombardier jacket, and another of himself in an Indian headdress.

"I was in pictures, you know," he said to Peter, showing him the photographs. "The cinema."

"Louie, it's time for you to leave."

Alice stepped back from the doorway, trying to be inconspicuous, but she didn't want to miss anything, either. She could tell Peter was angry. He rarely got angry, and she was always impressed. He became so quiet. He didn't stutter or cry the way she did. He just spoke, quietly, logically, in a low, tight, unfriendly monotone, until he had made his point.

Louie looked at him, his big eyes narrowed, his head tilted to one side. He was wearing a baseball cap he had probably found in one of the emptied drawers. A Yankee cap.

"You're going now," Peter continued. "If you don't

leave, I will have to call the police, which would be ridiculous, wouldn't it?"

"Would it?" Louie said. He sat on the bed and lit a cigarette. "I was leaving anyways, you understand?"

"Fine," Peter said.

Louie picked up a flight bag and put the photos and broken jewelry in it, stood up and put the strap over his shoulder. "This is my personal private property," he said, pointing to the piles on the floor and the bed.

"Fine," Peter said again.

"I've got claims," Louie said. "Rights."

Alice stood aside as Louie and then Peter left the little room. She followed them to the kitchen, where Louie glanced at the kitchen table. Alice looked, too. Brenda was not there.

Peter opened the door for Louie, who ceremoniously shook Peter's hand, gave Alice an exaggerated cold shoulder, and then walked to the elevator. When Louie had gotten in and the doors had closed behind him, Peter slammed Brenda's door shut and locked it.

"Alice, I'm going to find Louie's gun and kill you," he said to his wife in the living room. "And you, too," he said to Brenda.

"You were great, wasn't he, Mom?"

He sat down, checking the cushion to make sure it was free of cats, and then leaned back and closed his eyes.

"Can I have a drink?" he said. "Please?"

"What are we going to do about the mouse?" Brenda said.

Alice poured Peter a scotch and thought of the mouse. The tortured mouse in its horrifying trap.

"There have to be other ways of getting rid of mice," Peter said. "Efficient, sanitary, civilized methods."

"Maybe we should call Louie back," Brenda said. "Just for a minute," she added, when Peter jerked his head up to look at her.

Peter leaped up, staring at his mother-in-law, and bolted into the kitchen. Alice followed him. Swiftly, but gingerly, Peter lifted the small gray mouse by its long gray tail. He carried it, trap and all, in the direction of the incinerator.

◆ / "Now we are going to socialize," Alice told her mother. "With nice people."

"I like nice people," Brenda said.

Every other Tuesday evening, bird-watchers would gather in the bowels of the Museum of Natural History for a meeting of the Linnaean Society. Alice wanted her mother to accompany her to these gatherings, to watch the slide shows and listen to the lectures—it would be a cleansing experience, a soothing first step back to civilization. "And there are lots of lovely widowers. Probably."

Alice and Brenda met at the south entrance. As they walked through the museum, their footsteps boomed, as loud as drums, in the empty halls. It was dark, and the dioramas hid behind the glass, mysterious suggestions of shapes that Alice knew but could not see. Dusty model apples and their dusty model worms, stuffed dodoes and little sailing ships. Occasionally, light filtered in from intersecting hallways, and they would be able to make out Eskimos or fish vertebrae. Grave Indians in buckskins, carrying big spears, would stare at them, rather fiercely, Alice thought, dolls watching from the darkness.

"Spooky," Brenda said.

"The exhibits' revenge."

And then, suddenly, at the end of a dim corridor, the meeting room was in front of them, filled with bright light and comfortable hubbub. Alice introduced her mother to those she recognized, although none was a widower, as far as she knew, and she realized she must not ask. Still, her mother looked happy. "Will there be a movie?" she asked Alice excitedly, and Alice felt she had done a good deed.

There was no movie. There was instead a slide show about grouse delivered by a strapping young professor of ornithology with bouncing blond curls.

"Grouse?" Brenda whispered. She sounded disappointed.

"Oh well, what's the difference?"

"They're not even birds, not really. They're, you know, prey."

The professor began with a slide showing a mother grouse and her young standing in a field. In the fall, he said, grouse families break up. (Click. Mother grouse alone.) Some young grouse, grown now and unhappy at being crowded, aggressively drive their brothers and sisters away (Grouse aggressively driving away other grouse), something called the fall shuffle. Sometimes, the lecturer continued, if one of these birds is continuously chased by another and hasn't found its own fall territory yet, it cracks up (Lone grouse flapping wings in a blur).

Alice yawned and stretched her legs out into the aisle. She had been up before dawn, searching for straggling fall migrants in Central Park. In the spring, the pretty, brightly colored warblers in the green treetops sparkled like precious ornaments, sang like a sacred choir. In the autumn, those same birds, now gray and brown and laconic, provided an academic challenge—was that a juvenile mourning warbler or a Connecticut warbler, a female black-throated blue or a Philadelphia vireo?—but the mood was far less inspired. Alice had never liked fall that much. Her depression over its imminent arrival usually began just after the Fourth of July.

The bird starts out skittish, the professor was saying, then gets more and more agitated until it breaks into directionless, patternless flight, far away from its coverts, banging into buildings (Slide of grouse banging into church spire). This behavior is called crazy flight.

The lights went on and Alice yawned again. She turned to her mother to tell her that yes, perhaps grouse were best shot after all, but stopped herself. Brenda was sniffling with emotion.

"Thank you, Alice, for bringing me here," Brenda said, dabbing at her eyes.

When they left the museum, Brenda offered to drive Alice home. "Wasn't I lucky to find a space?" she said proudly. Driving the short distance from Brenda's apartment to the museum was ridiculous, and the even shorter distance to Alice's apartment more ridiculous, but Brenda drove almost everywhere. Alice thought it was to lessen the shock of the city, a nostalgic attachment to a suburban memory. "I parked right around the corner here, right up here, right along here somewhere. I'm sure it was this side of the street, right here, in the middle of the block, definitely along here . . ."

They walked farther up the block. They stopped for a minute to look in the windows of a school cafeteria, usually dark at this hour but now filled with the blue, washed-out color of fluorescent light, as well as the earnest sounds of the school band, the loud rhythmic thumping of a bass drum in particular. Alice smiled indulgently. They're trying so hard, she thought. They puffed and banged behind the large glass windows, and to Alice they looked like the dioramas in the museum, as unaware, as unreal, as exotic. A little farther on, about fifty girls were lined up in the playground, each holding a white triangular flag. Illuminated only by streetlamps, they stood in an oddly calm quiet, no giggling or chitchat, just the muted strains of the cafeteria's marching music and the flapping of the tiny flags in the breeze.

The girls suddenly, in unison, waved their flags to the left. Then to the right. They all, together, lifted off the ground in a soundless jump. Alice began walking again. She preferred teenagers behind glass. With their oddly regulated behavior, their uniform white banners, the girls might have been training for a teenage supremacist vigilante group.

"Where is your car?" Alice asked. "Let's get out of here."

"Isn't this interesting? I don't know, Alice. I left it here somewhere. Not somewhere. I left it right here, right exactly here. This is where I left it."

"It's not here."

"It's gone."

The girls, bidden by some silent sign, had rushed to the middle of the playground, where they were noiselessly climbing up on each other's backs to form a pyramid, their banners left behind in a pale, neat pile. The band began to play the "Under the Double Eagle" march.

"My car has been stolen."

Brenda walked with Alice toward Alice's apartment. They didn't say much. Brenda was clearly miserable.

"Maybe it was towed," Alice said finally. But they both knew it hadn't been towed. The space was not only legal, it was good for two days, a great parking space, a coup, a wonder.

"But I guess it doesn't do me much good without the car," Brenda remarked thoughtfully.

"No," Alice said.

They stopped at the curb to wait for a red light, and Alice turned around to look back, as if the car might have slipped in behind them.

"Hey, look, Mom, there's Louie, I think," she said. "Look, going into that restaurant."

"Oh, so it is. What a coincidence. Good, he doesn't see us. That's all I need."

They stopped at the corner Korean market to get some milk, and Alice bought her mother a brownie to cheer her up.

"There were two bags of newspapers to be recycled," Brenda said sorrowfully. "In the trunk."

"Well, frankly, Mom, that car was kind of a pain in the ass. It was so big."

"And a bag of empty bottles."

"It was insured."

"And cans."

Alice was beginning to feel terrible. Her mother's car had been stolen. Alice had forced her mother to attend a boring meeting, and now Mom had no car. She would never buy a new one—it was like a dog in the city. If you are already stuck with one, you keep it. You walk it and spend hundreds of dollars at the vet and vacuum its hairs off the couch until it dies. But you don't buy a new one. Brenda's life had been largely regulated by her car; she scheduled her life—her patients, her appointments, her classes—around alternate-side-of-the-street parking. She knew which streets had no parking on Tuesday and Thursdays, which on Monday, Wednesday, and Friday, which parts of the city demanded you move your car from eight to eleven or eleven to two, and she visited them accordingly. Mom without a car was inconceivable.

"This is awful. And it's all my fault, sort of," Alice said. "If I hadn't made you come with me, you wouldn't have parked it there and they would have taken whatever other car was in that space and you would still have your space. I mean, your car."

"Well, the grouse were very moving, Alice."

They turned onto Alice's block. The leaves on the ginkgo trees had turned yellow. There was one small red maple a few doors down and it glistened beneath the streetlight. Alice liked the little trees on her street, some of them in the courtyards of brownstones, some surrounded by white picket fences with hand-painted signs asking dog owners to take their pets elsewhere. But best of all were two squares that had once held trees but were now overgrown with clumps of tall, swaying grass, small spontaneous meadows just a few doors down from Alice's own front door. She looked at them now as the wind blew through the grass and she smiled. Oh, and look at that, she thought. A car the same color as the Buick. And what a coincidence, it's a Buick, too, with Connecticut plates.

"Oh, look, Alice," Brenda was saying. "*There* it is. This is where I parked, dear, not over by the museum. I guess. Now isn't this convenient. Well, goodbye, sweetheart," she continued as she unlocked the car door. "What a lovely walk we had."

Alice, unsure whether to be relieved or even more concerned on Brenda's behalf, stared unhappily at her mother. "Drive carefully," she said as Brenda waved and gave the horn a gay toot.

⚓ / Alice sat on the bed eating potato chips. She was supposed to be watching the World Series. The TV set was on in front of her, and everyone else in the room was intently staring at it. Alice, too, was intently staring at it, but sometimes when she watched baseball she seemed not to take it in at all. She would be watching and watching and suddenly there would be two men on base and she would have no idea how they got there, no memory of it. At other times, she would see a hit and cry out, "All right!" only to realize that the wrong team was up.

"All right!" she said now, seeing a ball bounce past a diving second-baseman. Then she noticed that the second-baseman was wearing a Dodgers uniform, and she was rooting for them.

"Well, it's past my bedtime," she said when the others turned to look at her. And my bed has people on it, she didn't say. Alice had mixed feelings about social encounters in the evening. She approved in principle, but because she got up so early, she was often too tired to actually participate. Still, these were close friends. Not much was expected of her. Peter's college buddy, Richard the Wilkie Collins re-visionist, was there. He had brought his baseball glove for good luck and kept slamming his hand into it, making a popping noise. He remarked that Wilkie Collins would have made a great manager, and Peter said, "In the minors?" to annoy him. Alice's friend Katie had come, too, and her husband, Mike, who said, "Yeah, well, Wilkie Collins wouldn't've been half as good as Alf Landon."

Alice stood up and looked out the window. She wished it would snow. If it had to be cold and miserable for the next six months, then it might as well begin now and there might as well be snow. Two white sanitation trucks, as big as elephants, passed each other, one going north, the other south. "You asshole," a man called out to a car as it ran a red light. "You apple!" cried a child excitedly from its stroller.

Alice returned to the bed and the game. Alice watched the pitches carefully. She could distinguish a curve ball from other pitches, but that was all. Was that a split-fingered fastball or a slurve?

When the doorbell rang, Peter looked at Alice in surprise.

"Well, don't look at me," she said. "I don't know who it is."

It was Willie. With him was a pretty girl with red hair. On her back was a backpack with a baby in it.

"Hello," Alice said, shaking the girl's hand. Alice had asked Willie to come by, but he'd said he had a date.

"I'm Mary," the redheaded girl said in a heavy Irish accent. "I've always wanted to see a baseball match, and that's the truth."

The baby looked at Alice, peering over Mary's curls. It said nothing.

"Yeah, a baseball match," Alice said.

"Do you have anything to eat?" Willie asked.

They went into the bedroom and Peter said, "Oh, hi, I thought you had a date."

"I do, this is Mary, but she had to work, so I wasn't sure what we were doing, but she wanted to come here."

"Well, that's good you got off work," Alice said, helping extricate the baby from the pack. Where does one put a baby? It might fall off the bed if she put it there, or get sat on. On the floor, it would be stepped on. She realized she didn't know any babies. It seemed terribly heavy for something so small.

"No, no, I am working, you see. This is my job, aren't you, little Alice," she said to the baby still in Alice's arms. "And look, here's a big Alice. See? See? Say hello."

Little Alice looked at Big Alice and smiled. She had no teeth. She had no hair. Alice smiled back. Nice baby, she thought. Now go away.

"Mary's a nanny," Willie said.

Mary held Little Alice on her lap and together they watched the baseball match. "Well, will you look at that?" Mary said now and then, tenderly, to the little girl, who within minutes had fallen asleep.

During the seventh-inning stretch, the doorbell rang again.

"It's only me," Brenda said when Alice opened the door. "I knew you were having company, so I dropped by. Hello, Willie, dear."

Willie had followed Alice out of the bedroom on his way to the refrigerator. "Oh, yeah, Alice, I forgot to tell you, Mom is coming."

"It's perfect, Alice, just what I need."

Alice thought, Well, if Mom needs to get out of the

house, I guess I should be supportive. But her mother had no interest in baseball. It seemed an odd evening to visit.

"Just wanted some company, Mom?" she said, giving her mother a kiss.

"Alice, would I barge in on you and your friends for company?"

Alice took a deep breath.

"I came," Brenda continued, "for the population."

She began digging in a canvas book bag, extracting a large leather box and a bag from a sporting-goods store. "Now, here are my vials. My vile vials," she said and chuckled happily. "And here are my clickers. They, of course, are for a different project. That one will take several months, but we can certainly begin tonight. And then we'll get to Yik and Vom."

Brenda went into the bedroom. "Oh, look at the little baby. What a beautiful child. Whose is it?" She beckoned to Katie. "Come. You will be my first subject," she said.

"Subject of what?" Katie asked, but Brenda just led her out of the room into the kitchen. There, she opened the case to reveal hundreds of vials packed in like cigars in a canister.

"These are smells," Brenda said. "You smell them and then you rate them, you see. I'm writing a paper."

"I thought you got your doctorate already, Brenda."

"I did."

"This is just for fun," Alice said.

"Alice, really. This is post-doctoral work. Now, Katie, smell, go ahead, smell."

Katie began sniffing the vials, now screwing up her face in disgust, now raising her eyebrows in surprised pleasure, finally gasping, "This is the worst, the worst smell, categorically, ever."

"Civet," Brenda said. "They use it in perfume. Isn't this fun?"

"I told you," Alice said.

Brenda left Katie to finish sniffing the vials and marking down her ratings. "Because I must get to Yik and Vom. I don't want to waste time, I mean, since everyone is here, is kind enough to be here." And she went into the bedroom and asked Mary to use the words Yik and Vom in a sentence. "Yik is the noun," she said. "Vom is the verb."

"Lord, but it's vomming with yik tonight," Mary said obligingly, and Alice thought it must be all her practice with the baby. In fact, Alice was rather jealous of this sentence. With Mary's velvety accent, it sounded almost poetical, an old, obscure Irish proverb. All she could think of was, "The yiks are not vomming this year," which she tried to change to "The yiks are vomming late this year," but her mother wouldn't let her.

The Dodgers lost the game, which freed Brenda's population to concentrate on their tasks. "Yik vommed only twelve times last year," Peter said. Then Brenda began handing out what looked like watches but were really golf-scoring devices. When you pushed a button, the watch recorded it—the face would say "1." If you pushed it a second time, it would say "2," and so on. The watches were to be worn for two months. Brenda gave two to each person. They were to pick a behavior they wanted to change, click each time they wanted to do it and click on the other watch each time they actually did it. "Then I make a graph. You'll see." Brenda was wearing one watch herself. The behavior she wanted to change was forgetting things, and since she forgot to click so much of the time, indeed had forgotten to wear the second watch, she felt she had definitely chosen the right behavior to try to modify.

Mike and Katie happily donned their watches, sniffed the vials, wrote out their sentences. They were endlessly curious people, equally curious about the interesting and the banal, the type of people who read *The New England Journal of Medicine*, *Consumer Reports*, *Commentary*, and *Cricket*—anything they could lay their hands on. They had theories about everything, based on scientific and sociological models. They discussed new technology in fire-fighting equipment, the comparative merits of New York's and Philadelphia's water supply, the deforestation of Tibet, the economic value and risks of a higher minimum wage, and the fate of the black-footed ferret. They were quite comfortable wearing the watches, ready to quantify and conquer.

Richard was less enthusiastic at first, until Alice suggested he use the clicking watches to monitor the times he secretly thought about Dickens when he knew he ought to be thinking about Someone Else.

Alice declined to participate in the smell test, claiming she was 4F on account of allergies, but her mother just laughed pleasantly and held each vial under her nose, like smelling salts.

"Mom, it's so late, go home. Take your potions. You're like a witch with all this junk. Go away," Alice said when offered the civet vial.

"What time is it? Just smell it, Alice. Don't be a baby. The worst? Okay, okay, I'm writing it down."

Peter was clicking his watches, testing them out, unable to decide on a behavior to modify. Little Alice began to cry, and Willie suggested they give her two watches, too, to help her control these outbursts.

"Don't listen to him, little Alice," Mary said as she stuck a pacifier in the baby's mouth. She put the baby back into the pack and Willie hoisted the thing up onto his own shoulders. "Well, goodbye then, and thanks," Mary said, and they left, the baby hanging on to Willie's hair as if it were a pony's flying mane.

"Now," Brenda said. "I've got a wonderful new machine that I must test out."

"Mom, enough."

"No, no, my new answering machine." She picked up the phone in the kitchen and dialed her number, then her new answering-machine code number, which she had written on a Post-it stuck to her wallet.

"Oh, goody," she said after a considerable time. "So many messages. I love getting messages. It makes me feel important! Of course, they *are* all from Louie." She paused. "Still," she said, and smiling happily, she packed up her vials and left.

＊ / The cat was curled in Alice's lap, under the table. The apartment was quite dark as the rain came down hard outside, the rushing sound of cars even louder than usual. With lights on so early in the day, it felt like winter to Alice. Peter was marking up a pile of paper, computer printout paper. Black Coat stood up, stretched, and climbed laboriously onto the table.

The cat lumbered closer to Peter and began to pull at the little holes along either side of the sheets of his computer paper.

"Glue factory," Peter said under his breath.

Black Coat growled, baring his teeth like a dog.

"Black Coat, stop it," Alice said, and swept him off the table.

Peter looked up, surprised.

"Peter, I love you. You're a wonderful husband. You're a wonderful human being," Alice said.

"Can we put the cat to sleep?"

"Would you like to come birding with me tomorrow? I'm going to Breezy Point. A red-throated loon!"

"Naah. I have to watch a tape of an old spring-training game."

Alice wondered if he was joking, but she did not question him, just in case he wasn't. He had been even more tolerant than usual recently, even agreeing to the absurd dinner Brenda had arranged for tonight. It was her birthday dinner. Louie Scifo would be one of the guests.

"Alice, you have to come and sit and stare and be unpleasant and contemptuous," said Brenda. "The way you always are. I must get him to understand. We'll go to a restaurant. Impersonal environment. That will help, won't it? And Peter. And Willie."

"Mother, I forbid this."

But her mother just told her it was her duty and that they would all have fun.

Alice sat moping for a while, until she had an idea that cheered her up. She would invite Yuki to the breaking-up party. Yuki's dissertation was some sort of sociological-literary study of Jewish-American family life and romance. This would be wonderful material for her. Yuki's presence would annoy Willie at first, pressing home the fact that he had no girlfriend at the moment (Mary having left him and little Alice for a mountain-climbing trek in New Zealand), an idea that would then suggest to him that he should never have let Yuki go, until, finally, his love for Yuki would be reignited, stronger even than before, leading him to propose on the spot. And at the same time, with an outside observer threatening to record her appalling little get-together, Brenda would suddenly realize how bizarre her behavior had become, and how unfair to her children. She would be mortified, and would stand up Louie and stay home.

Yuki was delighted with the invitation, "even if your

foolish brother must attend as well," and Peter and Alice picked her up in a cab. Yuki carried a clipboard.

They met at Brenda's. Willie had arrived before them, and to Alice's disappointment he did not appear at all distressed by Yuki's presence and Yuki was businesslike and pleasant. They were both horribly insensitive young people, Alice decided, but she still hoped the other half of her plan, the mortification of Brenda, would be successful.

"Now!" said Brenda, coming from the bedroom. She was dressed in black pants and a white sweater with a long scarf attached that was meant to be wrapped around the neck several times. She looked better than she had in years, although the scarf dragged behind her like a tail. "Oh, hello, Yuki, dear. I'm glad you could come. Yes, this is a good subject for your paper. Why didn't I think of that?" She looked around her, smiling. "This is sort of fun!" she said.

"Mom," Alice said.

As they walked to the elevator, Alice picked up the end of her mother's white fuzzy train and held it. Yuki watched her carefully, then took out a pencil and scratched something on the clipboard. Alice peered over Yuki's shoulder, curious to see what sociological interpretation her gesture had inspired. But Yuki had written in Japanese.

"Alice, why are you holding my scarf, dear? It goes around my neck," Brenda said in the elevator. "Sometimes you don't think."

Willie said, "What restaurant are we going to, Mom?"

Wrapping the scarf around her, Brenda poked her elbow into Alice's face, then Peter's neck, then Alice's face again. "We're going to the coffee shop. I know it's dreary, but it seemed best. Does that seem best? Quickest. Did I do the right thing? Are you disappointed? I hope you're not disappointed . . ."

"Mom, Mom, I'm just asking. I don't care where we eat. We're here to provide moral support, right? Take it easy."

"But it's a party. The coffee shop is not a very festive place for a party. I'm sorry, children. I just wasn't thinking. I want it to be fun for you . . ."

Alice said, "Mother, we'll have banana splits, okay?"

Mrs. Brody smiled. "Yes," she said. "Good."

They sat at a booth and looked at pictures of fried chicken and pancakes on the menu, waiting for Louie Scifo.

"Everything is sort of the same color, isn't it?" Willie said.

"This really isn't a very good birthday party for you children, is it?" Mrs. Brody said. "Even *with* banana splits."

"It's not our birthday, Mom," Alice said. "It's your birthday. We've already had our birthdays. We don't mind being here. We aren't disappointed. We don't want to have fun."

Yuki wrote something down. Uh-oh, Alice thought.

Brenda, looking hurt, said, "Well, still."

When Louie came into the coffee shop, Alice almost didn't recognize him. He stood at the door, grinning at them over a bouquet of what appeared to be white-chocolate roses.

"Candy!" Brenda said.

"What happened to his tooth?" Alice whispered to Peter. "What happened to his eye?"

A large black space replaced what once had been one of Louie's shiny front teeth; a white eye patch was taped over his right eye.

"Ah," Yuki said, looking at Louie, then at Alice. She licked the tip of her pencil like a secretary in a movie.

Alice wished that this girlfriend had withstood Willie's

annoying, unruffled contentment a little longer and remained his girlfriend. Then Alice would not have been inspired to ask her to this morbid gathering, and Yuki would not be there in the coffee shop, recording Alice's every utterance like a court stenographer. Willie really ought to pull himself together and settle down, Alice thought. Look what follies his irresponsible behavior led to.

She turned back to Louie, who winked at her. Why had it taken her mother so many years to break up with him? It was unnatural. Would he now say, "My mother was a saint," like President Nixon in his gray, sweating speech on the morning of his resignation? Alice wished a helicopter would sweep down and take Louie Scifo to California, leaving a nice decent soul with a square head to be sworn in as the new Boyfriend.

"He's got his cane," Peter whispered to Alice.

Alice looked at the cane, an ebony one with a handle of bone shaped like a dog's head.

"My cane," Alice said. "From when I was sick."

"His hair turned gray," Brenda said.

"Probably dyed it gray. On top of the old black dye," Alice said. "I can't believe you gave him my cane." She looked at Yuki to see if she'd said something else noteworthy, but Yuki was sharpening her pencil with a red plastic sharpener.

Brenda got up. "Oh, I don't know what kind of birthday party this is," she murmured. She went over to Louie, accepted the chocolate flowers, then led him to an empty booth.

Peter punched keys on his pocket calculator. Yuki scribbled in her notebook. Willie ordered yellow pancakes. Louie was pointing to his eye patch. Alice thought she heard him say, "For you, Brenda. I did it for you. With a BiC."

The waiter put down four glasses of water, pushed together in the middle of the table. He slid an oval plate of pancakes toward Willie. Willie began to devour them with as much enthusiasm as if he were on a camping trip.

Louie came over to the booth and said, "Join us, my treat. Entirely."

"Treat," Yuki said thoughtfully, and she wrote something down.

Alice wondered if she should accept. Her mother had instructed her to be disapproving. Perhaps this was her chance. She could speed things up a little, too. But it was too embarrassing. She could look disapproving from afar. "No, thank you," she said.

Yuki was clearly disappointed. She scribbled disconsolately on her pad.

"Speak now or forever hold your peace!" Louie said. "And my treat just the same. That's right." He leaned on the cane and smiled.

Alice stared, fascinated by the gap in his grin. She had at first assumed he had simply blacked out the tooth, the way actors do. Now she saw that one of his caps had fallen out. She noticed the eye patch was taped on with Scotch tape.

Alice looked at him and she felt almost sympathetic. It wasn't the limp or the eye patch as much as Louie's trust in them. The clownish playacting seemed more desperate than any conventional show of grief. For a moment, Alice wondered if Louie did love her mother. He had walked away and sat now across from Brenda, his face a shade paler than the white eye patch, his uncovered eye wild and staring.

"He's sort of pitiful," Alice said.

"He is, isn't he?" Willie said. "It's sad."

"On the other hand," Alice said, "life is sad, isn't it? There are many things, a multitude of them, far sadder than Louie ostentatiously gimping around with my cane. I mean, he's not one of Jerry's kids, *is* he? Pretending to poke out his own eye!"

"Oh, Alice," Peter said.

"Can you believe it took Mom so long to break up with him?"

"Breaking up is hard to do," said Yuki. "Correct?"

"I'll be blind in a week!" Louie was shouting. "A *week*!"

Louie followed them home, back to Brenda's. He walked about ten paces behind and now and then called out, "Woe is me!" or "I'll make her sorry!"

Yuki said, "Thank you for inviting me to fascinating Italo–Jewish ritual dinner. Yes, this will give me A. This dinner is success." She said goodbye, bowing slightly and shaking hands with them all, including Willie. Then she left, turning once, not to look wistfully at Willie, as Alice first hoped, but to gaze gratefully at Louie Scifo.

Brenda, still carrying the roses, said nothing, but at the entrance to her building she told the doorman not to let Mr. Scifo up anymore, please, for he had moved out. Then she stood in the elevator and said, "Humiliating."

Once in the apartment, Alice looked out the living-room window. There was Louie, staring up. He waved.

November 18
Great Kills Park, Staten Island

The cupboard was pretty bare—ruddy turn-
stones, buffleheads, scaups, grebes.
Beautiful flock of purple sandpipers, so
dark, a dozen or so, and one old squaw in
winter plumage swimming in the bay, all
alone. AND—object of the trip:

1. azure gallinule* (In beachside cottage
    back yard. First appearance in North Amer-
    ica, ever. Dead. Cat suspected.)

▨ / Books and papers and brightly colored blocks were piled against the walls of Brenda's office. Several globes rested on the floor like abandoned beach balls. Measuring cups, a doll's head, bits of yarn, and some seashells sat in a huge Plexiglas salad bowl. An entire corner of the room was devoted to empty boxes—oatmeal cylinders, blue Tiffany boxes, amaretto tins, cigar boxes, brown cardboard in every shape and size.

Brenda sat at her desk, humming and placing coffee scoops in orderly rows according to color: blue, red, then yellow. The light filtered through the lace curtains, falling across the marmalade cat sprawled on the rug by the radiator. The radiator hissed.

"There!" Brenda said, looking at the scoops. "Now." And she began roaming through the apartment in quest of her glasses, then her phone book, then her other phone book. "It's exercise!" she said. Then she picked up the phone and dialed. "Hello? Yes, I'd like to report a peeping Tom."

Alice looked up. She had taken a cab over when her mother called, hysterically demanding that Alice remove some boxes of clothes and papers left there since college days.

"They blend right in," Alice had said.

"It's an emergency!" Brenda had screamed back at her.

"Oh, good," Brenda said now into the phone. "The vice squad."

"Well, he has binoculars," she added by way of identification.

Alice was looking through the boxes that had been piled in the closet. She found nothing worth saving—absurdly skinny blue jeans and term papers about monks who argued over whether they should be allowed to own one itchy brown dress or two—and she packed it all back up and told her mother she was saving it for her children. "Don't *ever* throw these boxes away, Mom." Then she pulled aside a corner of a curtain. Across the street, sitting on the hood of his car, Louie Scifo stared up, binoculars to his eyes.

"How did he find a parking space?" Alice said.

Alice watched Louie watch the apartment. She wondered if Louie could see her, could see her eyes looking out over the windowsill. Every once in a while, Louie would aim his glasses at people passing on the street. He apparently spoke to them, too: Alice could see their swift, startled glances as they moved by him.

What am I doing watching this voyeur, Alice thought. He's crumpling up a pack of cigarettes and throwing it on the sidewalk. He's opening a new pack. So what? But Alice could not take her eyes off Louie Scifo as Louie lit a cigarette, blew on the match, and then, the cigarette hanging from his lips, lifted the glasses back to his eyes and tilted his head back to face the fifth-story window and Alice, who crouched behind it.

Alice watched Louie intently even while Louie did not

move. Black jacket. Sunglasses. Cigarette—one lit from the end of another. Chewing gum, too. Dentyne. She watched from a kind of irrelevant, prurient fascination. Louie dangled his keys from one finger. Louie drummed his heels against the car's chrome grill. Louie waved his arms, flapped his mouth, yelling, shooing someone away. Shooing away a girl who was holding a clipboard.

"Yuki!" Alice said. "It's Yuki!"

There she was with her clipboard, circling around Louie, sucking her pencil thoughtfully, taking occasional notes as her subject danced in rage like an unwilling aborigine in a nineteenth-century ethnographic study.

"Yuki is downstairs, Mom. With Louie."

"Is she?" Brenda peeked out the window and nodded her approval. "A dissertation is a long and lonely road," she said as Louie climbed into his car, slammed the door, shook his fist at Yuki through the open window, and roared away.

"He's gone," Alice said.

"It's just as well," Brenda said, going to answer the doorbell. "I don't really want poor Louie to go to jail."

The phone rang and Alice picked it up and heard street noises. A pay phone. A voice said, "I'll be with you always."

"It's for you, Mom," Alice called, but poor Louie had already hung up.

Three big, burly policemen stood close together in the hall, shoving each other gently in an effort to get through the door. Once inside, they seemed to expand even more, until they were far too large for the foyer, their nightsticks clicking together in the dark blue crush, the worn black leather of their holsters scraping against chairs, against other nightsticks, against hanging flashlights, against more black leather holsters.

"Oh, excuse me," they said to each other as they adjusted themselves. "Pardon me. I'm sorry."

"Vice!" Brenda said happily.

"Morals," the biggest officer said.

"This is my daughter, Alice," Brenda said. "She's a witness, aren't you, dear?"

The policemen accepted Brenda's offer of tea and they all sat down in the living room, the three massive cops arranged like blue granite blocks on the couch. They discussed the psychological implications of voyeurism, sipped their tea, apologized for the inconvenience the peeping Tom had imposed on Mrs. Brody, took down some information in notebooks covered in black leather, complimented Alice on her perception and memory as a witness as well as on her hospitable and gracious mother, and left, quiet emissaries of law and order, the one in front stepping politely aside to let the other two pass.

Alice sighed. The sight of the big blue cops had pleased her. Big blue useless cops. They had reassured her. I would be a terrible anarchist, Alice thought. I would have attended the anarchists' convention, the one in Rome that never got off the ground because no one could agree on where and when everything should be held; I would have gone anyway, and sat there patiently, waiting to be told what room to go to, waiting for my stick-on badge that said, "Hello. My Name Is . . . Alice."

"Voilà!" Brenda said with a contented smile when the police had gone.

✹ / 1   For most of Alice's life, Thanksgiving had been spent at her grandparents' house in Scranton, Pennsylvania. Every year, her grandfather would cut into an enormous turkey and say, "Honey, it's the best bird you've ever made." They would eat and eat, and then lie on the floor (Alice's grandmother did not like them to crumple the silk upholstery), too full to move. Now Alice's grandfather was dead, of a heart attack. "My Harry was the *picture* of health," Alice's grandmother would say. "Except for that dirty, rotten pump."

Grandma had moved to New York, and this year the whole family was going to Westport for Thanksgiving. Alice's mother bought Bar-B-Q'd turkey on Eighty-sixth Street, and they all drove up in the Buick: Brenda, Grandma, Willie, Alice and Peter, Black Coat, and Brenda's old cat, Spotnose.

Louie Scifo, in a fedora and large sunglasses, followed in a blue Pinto.

"He's right behind us," Brenda said, looking into the rear-view mirror. "I wonder where he's going."

"That dirty bitch," Grandma said, turning around to see him. "Oh, what I've lived to see. Well, as long as I have my health. Oo, phoo, get off of me, filthy cat," she cried, as Black Coat curled up in her lap. Spotnose wailed from the cat carrier on the floor.

"Why doesn't he go to his parents' house for Thanksgiving?" Alice said.

"He's not getting any of my pie. The most delicate, difficult thing to make. A gourmet pie," Grandma said.

"Aren't Pintos dangerous?" Peter said.

"Yes," Alice said, perking up. "The gas tanks blow up." And she twisted around to watch hopefully from the rear window.

But just before the Willis Avenue Bridge, Louie, still safe and sound, turned off and left them.

When the Buick pulled onto the road to the Brodys' house, Alice said, "It used to be so pretty here before the school was built." She always said that, every time they drove up the road.

But this time Peter looked around him and said, "What school?"

And Alice realized the school was not there. It had not been an attractive school: modern in a boxy sort of way, one-story, a twisting, angular arrangement of blocks, its walls gray and metallic, its doors bright and colorful. But it had looked nice enough to her as a child, accessible and airy.

"It's gone," Alice said.

The driveway was still there. A yellow diamond-shaped sign said BUSES ONLY. Swings hung from frames in the playground. Alice pointed to lines painted on the blacktop, outlining boxes for four-square.

"There!" she said. But the school was still gone.

"They tore it down because there are no kids left in Westport," Willie said.

"Filthy politicians. Crooks. They all belong in jail," said Grandma. "Peter, darling, do you like apple pie? Of course, you've never tasted apple pie until you've tasted my *ex*-quisite apple pie . . ."

"It's sort of a park now," Willie said.

"After you've tasted my apple pie, well! It's out of this world. You will be incapable of eating that poison garbage they serve at restaurants. This is the worst era in history. In the *his*-tory of the world . . ."

Alice remembered the line of flowering cherry trees and the lush, tossing forsythia that separated Jack and Nancy Mandell's lawn from the Brodys' old house. Jack's lawn was crisp and unruffled, its only irregularity the lines left by the lawn mower. Jack's driveway was paved with smooth black tarmac, like the playground at school. The Brodys' driveway had once been covered with pebbles, but was soon worn down to bare dirt. Their lawn was neglected and shaggy, and Alice would lie there and wait for garter snakes to pass by. She sometimes found a blue plastic soldier or a bow-legged cowboy, dropped the year before and forgotten. Once she discovered a rusty horseshoe nail. Along the front of the house, rhododendron and azalea bushes sprawled, jostling the windows. Her dog slept beneath these bushes when it was very hot. Sometimes she followed him there and sat beside him, against the cool wall, on the hard packed mud.

The school was gone and the dog had died. The house had been sold, and its new owners had trimmed the rhododendrons mercilessly. I wouldn't fit behind them now anyway, Alice thought. And there were no new children to take her place, to squeeze in, the large dark leaves brushing their cheeks. We are extinct, Alice thought sadly. And look at all those trees. They don't even have any leaves. Their leaves are all brown and dry, lying on the ground.

When they got out of the car, Alice stood for a moment and looked around her while the cats ran by, into the woods. Above, the bare branches clicked and bobbed against each other, a deranged umbrella, all ribs. It always felt odd, coming to visit this place: as if Alice had never lived there at all and as if she'd never been away.

"It's pretty here," Peter said.

Alice had never thought it pretty when she lived there. It had been some sort of pathetic bourgeois compromise— neither the country nor the city, but a halfway house for people who were unable to face either of those two realities. But recently, when she'd visited Westport, her mother's little plot of land seemed to rise up and greet her, green and heroic, a scraggly, poorly manicured paradise hidden among the colonial tract houses.

"It is pretty," she said.

"And you used to be one of those suburban girls, the tall skinny ones, riding around on your horse with hair in your face?"

"Yeah."

"Very exotic, this Westport," Peter said.

In the field behind their old house was the barn Alice's mother had remodeled. She lived in her own back yard. When Louie insisted on acting as contractor for the job, he explained that after giving up his seat on the stock exchange, he had taken up building houses to fill his spare time. "It's what you might call amusing," he said. And so he had begun, putting up an addition of his own design that turned out to be so lopsided, sticking up crazily at one end of the house, that it charmed Brenda, and even Alice liked it. Leading up to the house, there was a narrow circular driveway, also of Louie's design, its circle too tight for a car to turn around in. A small irregular patch in front had been made into a neat lawn, but surrounding the barn on every other side was a bristly field of bushes, stalks, and brambles. A border of desiccated stems was on display beneath the front windows, the remains of pink impatiens that had been planted there to mask a sort of sidewalk of cement extending, for some reason, from one end of the house to the other, like the walk in front of a motel. When cars were parked in front, all lined up, the haphazard, wood-shingled barn did look a little like a motel, a motel for traveling gnomes.

"Peter, carry that pie with special care," Grandma said. "That's a treasure, and, Brenda, don't you invite any of your friends for dessert. My pies are not for strangers. Only blood eats Grandma's pie."

Inside, the smell of mildew greeted them. Alice could hear the bees that lived in the wall buzzing. The floor, squares of dark wood, had buckled and rippled, like rows of little angular waves.

"They left it pretty filthy, those tenants," Brenda said. "And the new tenants are coming next week. You guys better help me clean this place up."

Willie carried the greasy aluminum pan of Bar-B-Q'd turkey, Alice the pan of sweet potatoes and miniature marshmallows that had come with it.

"I, of course, with my delicate stomach, cannot touch that commercial poison," Grandma said as they set the pans down on the kitchen counter.

At some time in the course of every night that Alice had ever spent in the same house with her, Grandma would awake and announce that she should know better, that she simply *could not eat anything*, ever. "Oh, oh," she would wail. Then she would plunk two Alka-Seltzers into a glass of water, drink down the hissing liquid, eat a bowl of Dolly Madison vanilla ice cream "to calm her stomach," and go back to bed. Alice's grandmother was as pale as powder. She had been a redhead as a girl. As she got older, she began to dye her presumably gray hair red, then switched to an elegant ginger-colored wig. On the day Alice's grandfather died, her grandmother took off the wig and never put it on again. Brenda heard, through a complicated network of elderly Jewish gossip that stretched from Scranton to Miami to Bridgeport, that her mother's hair had turned white overnight with grief.

"*I* will have pie," Grandma said.

Alice went upstairs, opened the windows in her mother's room, and breathed in the damp smell of the outside. Her mother's huge, puffed-up feather quilt was spread out on the bed, and Alice could not resist lying down. She got under the quilt, pulling it up to her chin. The bees buzzed in the wall behind her head. At one time her mother had tried to drive them out: an exterminator came and sprayed foul-smelling poison into the hole that led to their nest. But the bees had buzzed mightily and batted their wings until they fanned the fumes away, back out the hole. Alice's mother never spoke of an exterminator again, even when the house was rented to a man severely allergic to bees. There had been a plan to have a bee farmer come and transport the hive, but at the last minute Brenda called it off. She had become fond of the noisy creatures. "They were so brave," she told Alice. "So noble, protecting their little eggs like that." The bees came every year now, welcome guests, and news of Brenda Brody's hospitality seemed to have spread throughout the insect world, for now there were boring bees, too, grinding perfect round tunnels into the walls.

The buzzing in the wall behind Alice was weak—most of the bees died by November—but the sound was regular and soothing. The sky was gray, but bright, and Brenda's pretty bedroom was bathed in soft, filmy light. Stuck in the frame of the mirror facing the bed there was an old black-and-white snapshot of Alice in a bathing suit and a straw coolie hat. She remembered the bathing suit. Red. She had worn it until it was far too small. She had been about seven years old. Above that, there was a picture of Willie grinning at his junior prom, his hair dangling down to the satin lapels of his rented tuxedo. Above that, in the top left-hand corner of the mirror, Louie Scifo showed his teeth, his eyes sparkling red from the camera's flash.

It was a terrifying picture of Louie. His face looked dark, almost green, over a yellow turtleneck. His lips, curled back from his huge white teeth, had been caught in that moment of a smile, before it actually opens up, that resembles a snarl. The photo wasn't supposed to be there. It hadn't been there when the Brodys had last been in the house. It was kept in a folder with all the snapshots Brenda took with her Polaroid camera, pictures of the remodeled barn, of Louie in front of the remodeled barn, of Louie blowing kisses at the photographer.

Alice kicked aside the billowing quilt. A feather floated into the air. Something black crawled laboriously out from under the pillow. Alice stood up and walked out to the living room.

"Mom," she said, "there's an ugly snapshot of Louie on your mirror and a poisonous spider under your pillow."

They stood in the bedroom. The sun had broken through, and light streamed in the windows. Brenda and Grandma and Willie and Alice and Peter stood and watched the spider, its bent legs carrying it slowly across the king-size bed.

"That's it!" Grandma said. "I lived through this family, this barnyard, with the horses and dogs and cats, the mice and the toads. And now bugs in the beds. At my age. I'm going to faint, that's all. Oh, oh!" But she didn't.

"It's a black widow," said Willie.

"We know that, Willie," said his older sister.

"They're venomous," Willie said.

"We know that, too," Alice said. "Put it in a bottle, you know, with aluminum foil with little holes in it."

"That's for grasshoppers, Alice."

"I'm going to faint now. I'm far, far too delicate for spiders," said Grandma.

"You're the one who used to have all those pet reptiles," Alice said to Willie. She could remember Iggy the Iguana, his bright green face smiling and toothless, looking out suddenly from beneath the sofa, blinking, then disappearing. He escaped periodically when Willie took him out of his cage in order to clean it, prowling the house like a fugitive, terrifying guests, annoying the maid, worrying Willie, somehow avoiding the cat and the dog for weeks, sometimes months, then appearing docilely in front of the glass aquarium, where he would wait to be put back in.

"Iguanas are not insects. They're not venomous insects," Willie said.

"We know that, Willie," Alice said irritably.

The spider had stopped in the middle of the bed. Alice wondered if it was looking at them. Maybe it would spin out a message the way Charlotte did in her web: "Bootan!"

"I got rid of the mouse," Peter said.

"All right," Willie said. "All right." And he put a glass jar over the spider, then slid a piece of cardboard beneath the jar and turned it over. "Okay. Big deal. Now what? Where do you want her, Mom?"

But Brenda was no longer looking at the spider, or at the mirror, with its photo in the upper left corner, Louie grinning down maniacally. She was staring at the doors that led to the porch, glass doors behind long curtains. She pointed toward the floor in front of them. It was covered with broken glass.

"Louie's been here. Look." And she pulled aside the curtain, revealing a shattered door, a crowbar, and several bits of black metal that had been the door's handle and lock.

Her mother was clearly upset, and Alice did not like the look of the broken door much, herself. The shattered glass lay on the polished wood floor, harsh and undeniable. Still, Alice hated to see her mother frightened by Louie Scifo. "Oh, so, the little fiend broke some glass and pasted up his picture. Pain in the ass," Alice said. "He put a bug in your bed. Never mind. Maybe it crawled in by itself."

"This is ridiculous," Peter said. "There are laws and Louie has broken one of them. It's very simple." He spoke slowly and enunciated each word, as if they were foreigners or deaf people who had to read lips to understand. "Call the po-leece."

Grandma said, "He should hang, the filthy crook. I'm an old woman."

"You people are lucky nothing's been taken. The perpetrators must have gotten scared off," the policeman said. He was young and had a strawberry-blond mustache and hair curling out from his cap like a baseball player's. "Well, here's your spider. Bye now." And he began to walk off.

"Bye," Alice said. She liked the policeman. He was young and smiling, like the policeman in a child's picture book, with his rosy round cheeks and shiny black shoes.

"But Louie?" Peter said. "The guy, the, you know, perpetrator?"

"This could have been perpetrated by any perpetrator," the policeman said.

"You think a burglar broke in here," Peter said, "didn't steal anything, didn't even touch anything, fished through an envelope until he found a particularly unattractive photograph of Mrs. Brody's former boyfriend, taped it to the mirror facing her bed, stuck a tarantula under her pillow, then left?"

"I don't know," said the policeman. He scratched his head thoughtfully as he walked to the car, waved, then drove off.

"Hello, little spider," Willie was saying, running his finger up and down the side of the jar. "Are you hungry?" He dropped in a tiny piece of Grandma's pie.

Alice walked up the road in the early, autumn shadows. Louie was absurd. All that melodrama and desperation. Alice didn't believe in desperation. It was embarrassing and a waste of time. Her mother seemed strangely susceptible to it, though. At least she had been, attributing a certain nobility and loyalty to the gloomy hysteria Louie had exhibited while they were going out together. And Brenda had said, just the other day, that Louie was so singleminded, so dedicated; that perhaps she should be flattered. But finally she decided it was not flattering to be tracked like an enemy submarine. It was . . .

"Sordid," Alice suggested helpfully.

Stopping for a moment, Alice pulled off her sweater and tied it around her waist. It was warm for November, almost as warm as a summer day. Oh, well, she thought.

If Louie has nothing better to do, who was she to deny him the pleasure of sitting in a parked car all day and night gazing up at windows with drawn blinds? She stepped to the side of the road onto some moss, bright and green even in the shade. A huge black dog with three legs galloped past her, chasing a yellow Toyota. Alice pushed herself up onto a stone wall. Her head touched the curled, skeletal branches of a dead fir tree, which scraped her scalp like a comb. She sat on the wall and let the breeze gently, indistinctly wash across her face. The leaves on the ground whispered and rattled. The branches overhead swayed. A warbler looked down, small and obscure in its drab brown plumage. Alice watched it lazily. Nice bird, Alice thought. Who cares what you are? A myrtle or a palm or an orange-crowned warbler? Who cares if you have a streaky breast or a plain one?

On the top branch of a tall, naked tree, Alice saw an enormous crow. She had never realized crows were that large. Or that grand. As she stared up at the black silhouette, squinting against the sun, the crow flapped its wings and flew in two directions at once, because it really was two crows pressed up close against each other.

The leaves lying all around her rustled a little. A honeysuckle bush, no longer fragrant, no longer even green, shivered in the gentle breeze. When it shook again, more violently, Alice thought there must be something behind it, a pheasant, perhaps. She had heard one honking earlier. Or a rabbit. And then she saw something stir, just slightly, something dun-colored, and her heart leaped because surely it was a deer. She'd seen a deer once in Westport, when she was in high school. She'd been at the beach at dawn, sitting on the lifeguard stand in front of her boyfriend's house, waiting for him to wake up so she could continue a fight that had been interrupted by bedtime, and she'd seen a deer swim by, its nose in the air, then clamber out on some rocks, over a fence, and into the woods.

Now Alice sat very still on the cool stone wall, hardly breathing, when suddenly the deer emerged from the tangle of bushes and stared at her, startled, with its large, liquid brown eyes.

"Alice!" the deer cried and then began to run, its patent-leather boots clattering along the asphalt, its beige Nehru jacket fluttering in the breeze.

It rained that night, and the wind howled as the Brodys ate their turkey. Peter was disgusted with the policeman, who had failed to perform the simplest logical deduction. Alice defended him as a pleasant youth.

"Here we are, rain all around us. It's like being on a boat," Brenda said, looking up at the skylight, trying to be cheerful. But Alice suspected she was thinking guiltily of Louie, who sat in his car in the driveway of the former school.

"Maybe we should bring him a drumstick," Alice said.

"Would you, Alice?" Brenda said.

"But no pie," Grandma said, looking pointedly at Willie and then at the jarred spider. "Hideous," she added.

"Mom, I was only kidding."

"Oh."

It rained all night, and when the lightning flared in the sky, they could see the school flagpole, the red barn on the hill across the way, and Louie Scifo's Pinto through the bare trees. Alice lay in bed and thought how different a storm was here. In the city, even the hardest rain was simply an inconvenience, a deterrence to finding a cab. A storm was thought of only as its damp, muddy consequences. But here, with the wind hurtling through the trees, and the black sky suddenly lit up white, the storm was an immediate, wild presence, a wave of energy and noise. The sound of the wind in the trees was loud and imposing; branches thumped hollowly against the house; the rain crashed against the cement walk outside the window. Sometimes a slash of lightning would, for a moment, give the room an unnatural glow. Then Alice huddled against Peter, waiting for the thunder.

Alice had left the curtains open in order to watch the storm, and she lay there, more and more caught up in its excitement and unpredictability. The quick, distant glimpses of Louie's car were unfortunate, she thought, although perhaps they were in character for the stormy night. What was he doing out there? What did he *think* he was doing? Did he see himself as a courtly soldier of love and devotion, a loyal knight poised in his bucket seat?

"He's just trying to scare us," Alice said to Peter. "Right?"

They sat up, staring out the window. During each flash of lightning, Alice found herself glancing at Louie's ghostly car. For a while, she tried to anticipate the lightning, to time the cracks of thunder that followed, but they caught her by surprise each time, startling her.

They heard, in the distance, the unnerving high-pitched whooping of Jack and Nancy's burglar alarm.

"The wind set it off," Alice said. "Right?"

And then, in the whining gale, Alice thought she heard voices. She was sure she heard footsteps on the wet gravel. Once, in the sudden white light, she threw her arms around Peter, convinced she'd seen a figure approaching the window.

"It's nothing," she said to him. "Right?"

"Right," Peter said. "Now, why don't I just close the curtains?"

"A lovely thunderstorm like this? You have absolutely no appreciation of nature, Peter." She pulled the covers over her head, clutched him, and eventually fell asleep.

❧ / Alice watched the cat sitting on the windowsill, silhouetted against the lurid green of the city sky. He was facing out between two wedding presents: a bowl and a ceramic pot.

Carefully, Black Coat pushed the bowl onto the floor. It landed unharmed on the rug. He had gnawed his stuffed mouse to oblivion and then returned to his old habits. Peter had told Alice that morning that her pet was the Louie Scifo of cats, and she was still annoyed. "Nice kitty," she said.

Black Coat purred luxuriously from the windowsill.

"Look at that cat," she heard someone say on the street below.

Her father had called a little while ago to say that his plane had landed safely. He would take a cab and be there in an hour.

Alice had seen him once in the year since her wedding—on Passover. She could imagine him getting out of the cab, both feet poised above the sidewalk as if he were considering the merits of actually putting them down on such a surface or somehow just holding them up for the duration of his stay. He hated New York, so why was he here, anyway? It wasn't Yom Kippur. Normally, only the Jewish holidays could bring Dad home to sit in the front pew of their smooth, Swedish-modern temple in Connecticut, flanked by his new wife and her towheaded son.

For years he had been bringing his devoutly Presbyterian but devoted wife to participate in the Brodys' celebration of various religious holidays. Alice found her enthusiasm suspect and unnatural: holiday dinners at Grandpa Brody's were noisy, interminable, the prayers and rituals considered an inescapable and mildly irritating delay before the food could be served. Then the thirty-five relatives would sit at a long table (which was actually several bridge tables pushed together and covered by white linen cloths) and call for an aunt who had once been a kindergarten teacher to play "The Hokey Pokey" on the piano. On New Year's, energetic infants dripped honey; during the Seder, they hurled soggy sacramental parsley. Alice's grandfather would doze peacefully at the head of the table. "No, no," her father would cry. "We're still on page 12."

"Your religious rituals are so deeply oriented toward the Jewish family roots," Patricia told Alice on one occasion. "Aren't they?"

Yeah, you home-wrecker, Alice thought. That's right. But she smiled and said nothing.

"Roots . . ." Patricia continued thoughtfully. "I know! Let's attempt a trace of the Brody roots. What an exciting project for a young person!"

The bell rang and Alice prepared herself for the elaborately phrased pleasantries her stepmother favored.

"Have you enjoyed your recently completed summer holiday?" Patricia would ask.

"Oh, yes," Alice would respond.

"It's a pity you've not been able to get away this year on some sort of excursion. Well, we'll keep our fingers crossed for a letup in your busy schedules, and then off to a lovely vacation spot to take advantage of the leisure activity of your choice."

Alice, furious at her stepmother's geniality and interpreting it as concealed hostility, would say, "Oh, yes," again.

Alice had some difficulty hiding her feelings about Dad's second marriage. When Patricia and her father arrived at her grandfather's house in Connecticut for a holiday dinner, Alice always stood directly beneath the elegant wedding portrait of her radiant mother, which her grandfather had neglected to take down, to welcome them each with a polite kiss.

But today, when Alice answered the door, she saw that not only had her father come East when there was no Jewish holiday, he had come alone.

Patricia must have something to do in Vancouver, Alice thought.

Like what? She was sure there was nothing at all to do in Vancouver. It was a city inhabited exclusively by trees.

Perhaps Patricia was coming later, a few days after Dad. But then surely her father would have mentioned it. And he would have put Patricia on the phone for a polite chat, a ritual he rigorously endorsed as evidence of friendly relations.

So. Dad was here. And Patricia was not. Patricia was not coming. Alice was sure of that. And Patricia had nothing better to do in Vancouver. Alice was sure of that, too.

Patricia and Alice's father were splitting up. Alice

looked at her father and she could feel it in her bones. Finally, one of her parents was behaving responsibly.

Dad stood there, his cashmere scarf tucked into his tweed jacket, his handsome face cold and red. He looked, she admitted, fine. In fact, he looked so good that at first glance she almost didn't recognize him. He'd lost a lot of weight, a lot of bulk. He was wearing glasses, too. Little half glasses, like Teddy Kennedy's. But what else? She knew there was something, something drastic. She carefully scrutinized his face. His hair, a little longish, but pretty much the same sandy-brown. He still had the same eyebrows, the same gray eyes, slight shadows beneath them. What was it? she wondered. And then she knew. It was his mustache. He'd shaved his huge, waxed mustache! And his whole face was changed—it looked longer, thinner, younger.

Alice admitted to herself that her father looked great, but she was not pleased by his appearance. She had discovered that, without much effort, she could object even to something like this. Alice could never look at his Irish sweaters or his gleaming custom-made shoes without feeling the snub to her mother.

"So, how's Patricia?" she asked.

"Oh!" said her father, looking at the floor.

Alice smiled. Something was obviously wrong.

"Is everything okay?" she asked. She put her hand comfortingly on her father's arm. Come on, Dad, she thought, spit it out.

Her father still stared at the floor.

Poor Dad, she thought. This must be so difficult for him.

"Maybe you'd like a drink," she said in a voice that sounded rather more eager than concerned. "Scotch, water, no ice. Right?" He had learned to leave out the ice on a trip to England, as well as to drink his beer warm.

"Alice," her father said.

He sighed.

"Alice," he began again, "there's something I want to tell you."

Well, she could have told them how it would be.

When Alice was about twelve, her father had decided to buy a great stone house on a hill. Dark and baronial, with a barn three times the size of the house they already lived in, the place was both wonderful and ridiculous. Of course, they never did move there. But Alice could still see her father standing beside the real-estate agent, in front of the monstrous fireplace, his hands behind his back, his legs spread, pretending. With Patricia in that absurd place, in a suburb of a city that looked like a suburb, he was pretending still, Alice thought. Pretending to live in a great stone house with a stable full of horses and contentedly munching cows. But one day he would wake up, look around him, and wonder where all the munching livestock was. That day, she realized, had finally come.

Her father sat down on the low couch and looked large and uncomfortable. His beautiful shoes were hidden by the coffee table. Alice tried to contain her enthusiasm for the impending announcement of his impending divorce.

"Alice," he said softly, "you're going to be a sibling."

Alice already was a sibling, she was sure. Her brother had not yet arrived at her apartment, it was true, but even so their relationship would not normally be described in the future tense. *Alice, you are a sibling* or *Alice, you have been a sibling* would be better phrasing. Even *Alice, you are being a sibling,* while somewhat inelegant, seemed much more to the point.

"Alice, you're going to be a sibling," her father said, "again."

The past tense, of course, was unthinkable. *Alice, you were a sibling* was a sentence she hoped never to hear. It implied death, and Alice loved her brother. Besides, she had lived so long with a brother that not having a brother seemed impossible.

Her father smiled nervously.

The future tense, on the other hand, implied nothing at all. Except perhaps birth. But that was silly. Her father was almost sixty. And Alice had lived so long with only one brother that the idea of another brother was . . .

"It's going to be a girl," her father said.

Alice knew she wasn't jealous. She was much too old to be jealous of a new baby in the house, particularly when it wasn't actually going to be in her house. It was just the idea of the thing. Almost thirty years older than a little half-sibling. It was so inappropriate, so ungainly. And it was a little girl.

"A little half-sister!" Alice said, in what she hoped was a warm and cheerful voice, though she was unable to leave off the word "half" and actually stressed it a bit. "Wow!"

And her father, to her horror, beamed.

When Willie arrived, Alice watched her father repeat his announcement.

"Ahem," he said.

Then he said, "Willie, I have something to tell you."

Then he sighed, then blushed.

Then he said, "Willie, you're going to be a sibling."

Willie looked so confused that Alice wondered whether

he didn't understand what Dad had just said, or had in fact understood it very well.

Willie glanced at her desperately. "*Alice?*" he said.

When Peter came home, Alice waited for Dad to tell him he was going to be a sibling-in-law.

"Patricia and I are going to have a baby," he said instead.

Alice sighed. Now Peter would think she had made the whole thing up.

"So, Mom?" Alice said later, on the phone to her mother. "Dad's having a baby."

"Oh, Alice, congratulations! When did you and Peter find out? Oh, Alice, I can hardly believe it. It seems like only yesterday that Daddy and I—"

"Mom, Dad's having a baby. Not me. Dad."

Alice waited. Her mother would now say something to annoy her, something kind and forgiving and utterly unrealistic, like, "Isn't that wonderful. Your father loves children so!"

But her mother said nothing.

"Mom?"

"That's very weird," her mother said finally.

Alice's mother believed that the reason there were thunderstorms was to keep the grass rich and green for picnics. Or she would have believed that if she had not liked thunderstorms so much for themselves, if she had not thought them so pretty or believed that they made staying inside so cozy. She regularly bought packages of cream-colored stationery to encourage Alice and Willie to send nice notes to their father. She was sure life was pleasant, and so had determined to experience it that way.

But now she was saying that Dad's having a baby was weird. God, Alice thought. It really must be weird.

"Let's see, this makes me what?" her mother said. "A deposed stepmother manqué? Don't you feel weird?"

"Yes, I do," Alice said. Would it really be related to her? Would that make her related to Patricia? She wondered if her father's baby would be like Little Alice, the bald and toothless child who came to watch the World Series. She hoped not, because she liked Little Alice.

"It seems like it will be such an old baby," her mother said. "Do you know what I mean?"

Alice knew just what she meant. A middle-aged, Canadian baby.

"But of course it won't," her mother continued, which seemed to cheer her up a bit, because she then said, in a lighter voice, "Imagine! Well, your father loves children so!"

Mr. Brody was leafing through a pile of Alice's photographs.

"Pleasant," he said. "But of course this isn't a proper robin, is it?"

"New World robin, Dad. Of course, we *live* in the New World . . ."

"A kind of thrush, actually. Resembles the English robin a bit. Named for it, you know . . ."

". . . so we'll just have to make do."

"Quite."

Her father was there, ostensibly, for tea, but really to talk incessantly about the new little Brody on the way. He had been visiting for a few days now, and Alice was weary and confused. He had been attentive and kind: he was trying to show how loyal he would remain. Alice could see that, and she was touched. On the other hand, he was endlessly constructing gruesome formulations for family unity after the birth of the baby.

"You know, I've been thinking, we'll all have to, ahem, get to know each other," he said, putting the photographs down. "I thought a sailing trip would be just the thing. A sailing trip. Two weeks along the coast. *Just the seven of us*."

"Let's take a walk," Alice said suddenly. She stood up.

Her father said, "It's raining."

Alice sat down.

"Your mother is looking well," Dad said. "I had a lovely lunch with her yesterday."

"You did?"

"Well, we had some business to discuss."

"An inflation clause on her alimony?" Alice said. "That's great, because, well, think of it—in all these years, well, it's shrunk to nothing . . ."

Her father looked uncomprehendingly at her. "Hmm? Clause? No, no. It was about some old bonds that have come due. Nothing important. We ate at the Yale Club. In the Ladies' Dining Room." Mr. Brody chuckled. "The Ladies' Dining Room." Then a peaceful look came over his face. "The Yale Club. Do you know what New York reminds me of, Alice? Most of New York?"

"A sewer or a jungle?" Alice said.

"Well, people do cross *against the light* here."

"I don't." If there was a red light, Alice simply turned in the direction of the green light and crossed the street there, and if it led her closer to her destination, so much the better. "I never do."

"Well," he said.

"In Canada they don't even have traffic lights, Dad."

"The minute I walked out the door of the Yale Club, I saw the misery of this place. The bag ladies. I was stopped, too."

"Really? By a bag lady?"

"No, it was a man. Terrible, disreputable-looking chap. No teeth. Gray hair, matted, hanging in his face. Stubble. Big dark glasses. And he had two ancient, scrawny old men with him, whom he introduced as Mafia soldiers. Only in New York!"

At the mention of the word "Mafia," Alice began to feel a little warm. She shifted in her chair.

"He was going on about this and that, a house he'd built, a woman. His wife, I think. I believe his wife was a lady of the night—a *prostitute*," he added when Alice looked confused. "Well, then the old boy grew a bit sinister. 'I know the score. Do you know the score? You have intercourse with her? While I'm trying to get her back, you have sexual intercourse with her? At lunchtime?' " Mr. Brody stopped for a minute to blush and clear his throat. "I *had* thought he was going to ask me directions."

Alice was sweating. She could feel the flush spreading from her face, her neck, down her back. She wiped her brow with her sleeve. She could not speak.

"Well, anyway, to make a long story short, he then began to insist that I show some—"

"Respect?" Alice asked. But it was impossible. It could not *be*. They had met; they had met at the wedding. She remembered. Louie had told Dad to dance with his mother.

"—show some compassion," Dad said.

But, Alice thought, what she remembered was a man with raven-black hair and snowy, capped teeth talking to a portly man with a huge mustache. Now Dad was rail-thin— he jogged mercilessly, and ate only bran, in preparation for fatherhood—and he had considerately shaved off the bristling mustache in anticipation of soft, newborn skin. And Louie was now gray and toothless, just like the man in Dad's story.

" 'Show some compassion,' he said. Then he threatened to break my kneecaps. To have the two little old men break them, actually. 'People get shot, you follow what I'm getting at? In the kneecaps, you understand me?' "

Alice groaned.

"Chin up, old girl. I've still got thc old knees," Dad reassured her. "The Big Apple! Wait till I tell Patricia! But, of course, you sophisticated city folk are used to this sort of thing, threats on the street, Mafia hit-men and all that."

Alice nodded. "Yes," she said. "Happens all the time."

✒ / Alice had decided that if her father insisted on masquerading as her peer instead of her daddy, she would oblige him. She would treat him in the pleasant, neutral manner she usually reserved for her neighbors in the elevator.

"But that's how you treat him already," Peter said.

"And when I send the kid a present, when it's born, I'll send it a proper, impersonal present. A distant-aunt present. A business-associate gift. I'll send it a silver spoon. A modern, unornamented silver spoon. No, no, I know! A check! I'll send it a check . . . for twenty-five dollars!"

Delighted with this plan, Alice sat down and thought for a moment about her mother. Brenda looked wonderful these days, which was encouraging. And she was cheerful. But the Louie problem was escalating, slowly and stupidly, like a jungle war. Louie called frequently, leaving messages on the answering machine like "My darling, speak to my heavy, tearful heart full of woe. Or you'll be sorry."

Brenda's tape was quite elaborate. It had been made by an English friend in a voice so good-humored and brisk it might have hopped from the pages of a Beatrix Potter book. Sometimes, a stranger would call on Louie's behalf, the sounds of a crowded bar in the background, and the two ambassadors would address each other.

"Hel-lo, I do apologize, but Dr. Brody is *not* at home just at present . . ."

"Barbara," the stranger would say to the tape, then Louie's voice could be heard saying, "No, no, *Brenda*."

"Brenda! Yeah, that's what I meant. So—I'm going to get you. I'm going to . . . have sex with you!"

Louie had begun calling Alice and Peter as well. Sometimes he would call to chat ("Your mommy's a whore. I worry about her, you follow?"), other times just to breathe heavily. Once Louie called Alice and said, "We loved you like a daughter." Once he called Peter and said, "Pete, keep her away from me."

"You stay away from her, that's all. You stay away."

"She's getting on my nerves. I know my rights, Pete. This little girl with a clipboard is not one of my rights. Look, man to man. I mean, where's privacy?"

Little girl with a clipboard. Peter repeated that happily to Alice. Yuki was still traipsing around after Louie Scifo. She had found a subject for her field study.

"Petey, Petey," Louie said, "in the name of friendship that is sacred . . ."

Peter told Louie that a social scientist in the field was a formidable thing.

One day Alice was looking out the window at a blue jay perched on a brownstone rooftop when she noticed her mother approaching below, in a huge down coat, with Louie darting dramatically from lamppost to tree trunk behind her. She pulled open the window and stuck her head out into the cold.

"Hi, guys!" she yelled, but they didn't hear her.

When Brenda came upstairs, she sat down and took off her boots, wet from slush. She was wearing Willie's socks. Alice could tell because the toes hung off the ends of her feet like stocking caps.

"I called a lawyer today," Brenda said. "Was that the right thing to do?"

"Absolutely," Alice said. Alice thought a proper, stern lawyer might be just the thing to set life straight.

"Mom, put something decent on," she said. "When you go to the office. To the lawyer's." She imagined a pleasant-looking, middle-aged man in a gray suit who loved opera.

"It's not a date, Alice," Brenda said.

"And lipstick," said her daughter.

Alice saw the lawyer herself a few days later. He came to Brenda's apartment to meet the family. Surely, there had never been a rounder, jollier counselor-at-law. His suit was a regulation blue pinstripe, but so rumpled and ill-fitting that whatever dignity it might have bestowed on the fat little man was lost. He smiled with dazzling white teeth. He wore a red motorcycle helmet. His name was Gianni Carson.

"Mr. Carson specializes in criminal law," Brenda said.

Alice stared at him in open disappointment. She had expected a tall narrow person with no helmet and less smile.

"Yes," Mr. Carson was saying. "Necrophiliacs, sheep-shaggers . . ."

His words had an almost independent energy, practically leaping from his mouth in their enthusiasm. He gasped with excitement, like the class overachiever. His helmet was off now, and Mr. Carson's hairstyle was revealed. He had no hair at all on top of his head. What he did have, on the sides and in the back, made up for that, though—it reached his shoulders, lank and brown, wisps of it floating in every direction. As he stood there, with his hair drifting around his head, his tie over his shoulder, and his shirttails visible below his jacket, he seemed to be standing in a sort of personal, permanent windstorm.

"Civil-liberties cases," he said. He looked at Alice's disgusted face. "AH HA HA," he began to laugh. "HA HA HA HA . . ."

It was the loudest laugh Alice had ever heard.

"*Ha ha ha*," he continued, winding down, tears in his eyes, then clamped his mouth shut and sat down on the couch. "I'm very unorthodox," he said quietly. "I pride myself on that, you know. But don't worry." His voice was getting louder now. "I'm a wonderful lawyer. I'm unorthodox, though. I'll admit it. *Ha ha ha!* Nobody can say I'm not!"

Then Mr. Carson rubbed his hands together and adopted a very serious expression. "First," he said, "we go for a restraining order. That means you go before a judge with your evidence and convince him to order Scifo to stay away. Supreme Court of New York. Now, I'm going to tell you something, not for general knowledge, about these judges." He leaned forward, his brow furrowed. "You know their robes? Underneath?" He leaned back, shaking his head. "Naked. Stark naked. *Ha! Ha ha! Ah ha ha* . . ." And he was shaking with laughter again, his face round and red. "Who else would have the audacity to judge but a degenerate? *Ha ha ha* . . ."

Alice noticed her mother was wearing her best suit.

"Admit it," Mr. Carson was saying, clapping his hands together. "I am unorthodox."

Then he jumped up, handed Brenda his red helmet,

and pulled her out the door. Alice followed them downstairs and watched them climb onto a large black motorcycle.

"Goodbye, Alice!" her mother called. She withdrew one arm from around Gianni Carson's enormous waist and waved it gaily. "Don't tell Grandma!" And she pointed to her coat, which Grandma had loaned her, with many reservations and precautions, before leaving for Florida. A calf-length mink, it sparkled in the winter sun, floating out behind the Harley-Davidson like a dark parachute.

✥ / Alice stood on the deck of the Staten Island ferry. The winter wind pressed her against the door to the cabin. She watched the gulls struggling to fly, never really making any progress. Inside, a man was playing a guitar and singing a song he called " 'Nam in the Evenin'." It had begun with the words "Flesh, flesh, black, white, and yellow, all turned red . . ." and Alice had come outside. She preferred it outside anyway. The bow of the ferry was small and empty. She could survey all around her. There, confined on the tiny semicircle of deck, with the wind blowing noisily, she felt comfortable.

She wondered if, on the shore of Staten Island, the blue Pinto would be waiting, if Louie would be there to escort her to Great Kills Pond to see the snowy owl.

"Audubon," he would say. "Great guy, great guy."

But it was Tuesday, wasn't it? Alice breathed in the cold air. It was Tuesday. She made her way carefully to the rail, held on tight, and watched the Statue of Liberty, barely visible in the fog. Staten Island awaited her, a happy enclave of restaurants with boats on their roofs, a haven. No Pintos in Staten Island today. Because Audubon was a great guy, and on Tuesdays, Louie followed Mom.

Alice got home that night just in time to change for dinner. They were going out with some friends, most of them baseball colleagues of Peter's, and Alice stood in the shower, dead tired, trying to remember when you were supposed to steal and what a perfect bunt situation was. She knew these things, she knew quite a bit about baseball now, but it bothered her that she could never remember them when she wanted to, did not have the ease, the ability to chat casually about baseball strategy the way Peter and his friends did.

"How come I don't know anything?" she asked Peter when she got out of the shower.

"I don't know," Peter said.

"I know *lots* of things."

"Is something bothering you, Alice?" Peter asked. He came over, looking concerned and absurd in his underpants.

Alice said, "I have a little shadow that goes in and out with me—"

"But he didn't bother you today. He was driving around *here*."

"—and what can be the use of him is more than I can see."

"Anyway, I thought Tuesday was your mother's day," Peter said.

Alice looked out the window and wondered if Louie would join them for dinner. Perhaps he would wait outside the restaurant, reading a newspaper, like a chauffeur. She had begun to experience this faint awareness of Louie all the time. He might drive by, might be stationed in the corner phone booth, might be anywhere at all. It wasn't only Alice, of course. He spent most days watching her mother. For a while, on Mondays, he had swung by Willie's, then downtown to Alice and Peter's, occasionally following one of them before returning to roost outside Brenda's window. Then Fridays became his day for Willie, Wednesdays for Alice and Peter. After a few weeks, that changed, too. He had a schedule, but it was as unreliable as a city bus schedule. Alice was never entirely sure he wouldn't cruise by just to break up the monotony, which she supposed was the reason he had branched out from Brenda surveillance in the first place, and the uncertainty kept her off balance.

"You know, I'd say we should take a vacation, just to get away, but I'm sure he'd come with us," she said.

"Yeah, the poor guy. Busy, busy, busy," said Peter. "Seven days a week."

"Mom, you're carrying a gigantic bag of dirty laundry," Alice said as she let her mother in one afternoon.

"It is *not* dirty!" said Brenda.

Brenda, it turned out, often carried a laundry bag of clean laundry with her. She hoped that Louie would think she was headed to the cleaners. Then, holding the big white bag, she would sneak past the cleaners and into the subway or her car.

A few days later, Brenda arrived at Alice and Peter's grasping the laundry bag with one arm and frantically searching all her pockets with her free hand. She had gotten into a taxi, she told them, but Louie had spotted her and followed. The driver was extremely sympathetic, darting through traffic to lose the tail with considerable drama and pride, after which he offered her the name of a friend. "He can, you know, *arrange* something," the driver said in a whisper. "You know, *something*."

Brenda had taken down the name ("Well, not to use," she told Alice. "Just to have. In an emergency") and then promptly lost it.

On her own visits to Brenda's apartment, Alice found similar indications that her mother had become completely preoccupied with the duties of being watched. She had a schedule of Louie-related chores that she assiduously attended to. "Close the blinds, draw the curtains AT ALL TIMES," said a piece of paper taped to the refrigerator. "Keep record of all Scifo phone calls—note DATE and TIME. Don't Forget to TRANSCRIBE CREEPY THREATS."

Her mother startled Alice with her devotion to these tasks. She would consult her list throughout the day, check the windows, scribble in a notebook, rewind the tape recorder, over and over again, like Joan Crawford dusting. Then she would click her watches, scoring her assiduity, and mark down her progress with crayons on a big graph taped to the wall.

"Look at this! A thing of beauty," Mr. Carson said one day, pointing to a notebook, laughing. When he laughed, he shook like Santa Claus, like a bowlful of jelly. It was Mr. Carson who had prescribed these measures. "I like my evidence neat. Makes a good impression. It's nice." His shoelaces were untied, and a button on his blue shirt had, understandably, popped. "Now, Alice, here's my legal strategy. Your mother buys a red dress. Short red dress. I pick her up in a Cadillac. Big silver Cadillac. I drop her off on Third Avenue. And then she stands there. *Ha ha ha* . . . She stands there. Get it? On the street! In a sexy red dress. *Haaaa!* It will drive him crazy. Crazy. It's unorthodox. Admit it. It is. *Ah ha ha ha* . . ."

Mr. Carson's plan, his real plan, was to build a case against Louie Scifo, patiently and meticulously, a case so strong it would never reach a hearing, a case so torrid Louie would be convinced by his lawyer to settle out of court. When Alice told him the whole thing seemed ridiculous to her and that her mother was becoming peculiar, he replied that they would not have a second chance. That if they failed in their first attempt to get a permanent restraining order, then all the evidence they had gathered would be null and void the next time around. They would have to start all over again. Every encounter with Louie, every word exchanged, every sighting of his car had to be documented. And not only by Brenda, but by Alice and Peter and Willie, too.

Alice was horrified. "I don't want to take notes," she said. "He'll be sitting out there thinking, Ha, ha, they're all inside wasting all their time taking notes on me sitting out here thinking ha, ha, they're taking notes."

Peter, however, to her surprise, expressed interest in the project. He admired Mr. Carson's approach. "Thorough. Precise. And I'm sick of this guy outside my window," he said.

Alice was sick of him, too, and Peter convinced her to help Mr. Carson. It was probably inevitable, she thought. And she was always on the lookout for Louie, anyway.

"Okay," she said.

"And then we'll hire a Hell's Angels bodyguard. I represent them. New York Metropolitan Chapter. Remember Altamont! No, no, we'll get the Hell's Angel to move in here and stand in front of the window. Naked. In the morning—yawning and scratching himself . . ."

Once, Louie disappeared for several days, and Brenda ventured outside to walk up and down her street just for the fun of it. She was cautious at first, her face shielded by her big white bag of laundry, but then she became bolder, leaving her laundry behind. She called Alice, as joyful as a child let out of school, to tell her.

But then, just as everyone had crept out of the cave and begun to blink in the sunlight, Louie returned, tanned and robust. He was back. He had taken a vacation.

"Without us," Peter said.

🐼 / Alice and Willie sat in a cab one cold windy night, bundled up and bumping into each other in their coats and hats and scarves.

"How is Pandadevi?" Alice asked.

Willie made a movement inside his parka that seemed to be a shrug.

"Willie, why don't you get married like a normal person?"

"Yeah, yeah, yeah."

"It's much better to be married."

"Why?" Willie asked.

"Well, I don't know. *I* like it better."

"Oh. Well, then, of course I'll marry immediately. But Pandadevi won't marry me. I'm racially inferior. She's not even supposed to go out with me. It's a sin or something."

"Anyway, I'm not talking about her," Alice said. "But Yuki, what about Yuki? She's smart, beautiful, a thorn in Louie's side, you would have lovely children. She would be a wonderful addition to the gene pool."

Willie turned and looked at her.

Alice said, "She's too good for you," and gazed haughtily out the window.

Willie and Alice were on their way to have dinner with their mother. These days, when they made this journey to Mom's, they always passed the same landmark—Louie Scifo, small and intense inside his parked car.

"If he's still there, if he's there tonight, I'm going to get out and have a little talk with him," Willie said.

At first, Willie had watched Louie Scifo as he watched everything—with infantile humor and little attention. He would hum the theme to *The Godfather* when they drove past Louie. He would salute. He would write messages on the palm of his hand and hold it to the window, like the nuclear spy captured by the Israelis.

But the month before, while he was attending a seminar on the Turkish proverb held at Princeton, Willie borrowed his mother's car for a week. On the first day, he had a blowout in the left lane of a crowded highway. The mechanic at the garage told him that the tire had been slashed, and a reign of tire terror followed. Tidy mounds of broken glass were found piled in front of each tire of the parked car, upturned nails arranged in different geometric patterns, nails actually pounded into the tires to form large capital Ls. Louie buzzed around him like a fly around a recumbent bull. Willie switched his tail, snorted a bit. But finally he had to get up and stamp around.

The cab pulled up to a red light. Straight ahead, across the wide avenue, stood Brenda's building. Outside the cab window stood Louie Scifo. He saw them and ran toward his car, parked in its usual place on the near corner—Louie's Corner, they had come to call it.

"This is too much," Willie said.

He sat beside Alice, very still, and then abruptly, like someone diving into a cold lake, he was out the door, slamming it behind him. Before Alice could follow him, the cab shot across the street with the green light, and frustrated and sputtering, Alice dug frantically in her bag, trying to pay, to do it quickly and get out of the cab. She stood, at last, on the sidewalk, and she realized she was shaking. She could see the pantomime unfolding on Louie's Corner, the movements that seemed slower and slower, the corner itself strangely distant: Willie raising his hand to the window and knocking again and again; Louie rolling the window down, motioning, pointing, shaking his fist, and then, quickly, rolling the window up again; Willie suddenly swinging one of his legs, noiselessly smashing his foot against the side of Louie's car; smashing it again in another place, and again in another, the steel toe of his hiking boot leaving large dents in the metal; Louie gesturing frantically from the reopened window, then opening the door; Willie skipping across the street toward Alice with a sheepish grin on his face; Louie pulling something from the trunk of his car and lifting it . . . a shotgun . . .

"Willie!" Alice screamed, as Louie raised the gun above the open trunk. *"He's got a . . .* shovel?"

Alice and Willie ran into Brenda's building, laughing and overwhelmed.

"Ha!" Willie said.

"What did he say to you?"

"He said, 'Your mother's a whore!' "

They had been frightened by a gun and it turned out to be a shovel. Willie had vandalized a car. Alice, at the last moment awakened from her daze of observation, had cheered him on, screaming, "Fuck you, *fuuuck yoouu!"* as she stood among the homebound lawyers waiting for the light to turn. Alice noticed how pink Willie's cheeks were. She wondered if her own cheeks were as flushed. She gave Willie a high-five.

"Ha!" he said again, grinning.

But after a few moments in the elevator, after they'd stopped laughing and their hearts had stopped pounding and they'd heard the commonplace creaking of the elevator cables, they looked at each other and then both looked away.

"Oh, dear," Alice said. She felt suddenly embarrassed, the way she felt after she got drunk and talked too much at a dinner party.

"Not cool, not cool," Willie said, shaking his head. "And with, with . . . witnesses."

And they rode up together in misery, for they realized that in Louie's outrageous game they were gawky, stumbling amateurs, hopelessly and forever outclassed.

"Don't tell Mom," Alice said. "Okay?"

"I could sell the car," Brenda said one day, looking at its two new, newly flat tires. "But I can't sell everything else, I can't sell my whole life. Well, I suppose I *could* move—like a Mafia squealer . . . I could move to Vancouver!"

In Westport, the house stood as Louie's surrogate, defiant in a show of solidarity with the man who had helped to build it: on the coldest night of the year, the pilot light in the gas furnace went out, and all the pipes in the house froze and burst. For the following two weeks, while the pipes and, ultimately, the entire heating system were being repaired, the tenants called Brenda every morning with an update and the plumber called every afternoon, babbling in dismay at what he'd found. "There's, there's no insu-

lation. On one entire side of the house. None. They just
. . . left it out, stopped. And the drains—the drains are all
mixed up. The toilet and the sinks. And the pipes, they go
every which way, and there are electrical wires twisted
around them, and . . ."

At first, Alice thought that Louie had found a tiny hole
in the house and stuck a long, long straw through it and
blown the pilot light out. But now she realized he didn't
have to blow it out. The house was programmed to plague
them. He had arranged everything long ago.

⚘ / There was a great deal of snow toward the end of March, but this did not discourage Louie Scifo. Alternate-side-of-the-street parking was suspended, and a fantastic white drift covered Louie's car, usually with him in it, until, with the advent of warmer weather, the snow slid lower and lower and finally lay, fully melted, a dirty, gleaming puddle on the ground.

In Westport, the house was flooded and the toilets ran over with foul sludge. It was spring.

Alice got up and left her apartment early each morning, walking along quiet streets of brownstones with their forsythia bushes almost ready to bloom. She passed garbage trucks and, sometimes, a few weary partygoers on their way home to bed as she headed for Central Park to look for birds to photograph, the early migrants, the hermit thrushes and white-throated sparrows and ruby-crowned kinglets. In these first spring days, the park was cool and fresh, and she would sit on one of the gray boulders and watch the sun break through the city's gray air. Then the ground suddenly sparkled with rich brown soil and bright blades of new grass.

The bare branches overhead cast black, clear shadows. Robins bounded across the lawns. Grackles shimmered in the sun. Alice saw a kestrel flying over the boating lake. Soon the joggers, the drawn, serious ones, would puff up and down the paths. Businessmen would march by with dogs trailing behind and folded newspapers held in front of them. Derelicts murmuring angry stories to imaginary companions; other bird-watchers like Alice—all would pass by. It was a bustling, cosmopolitan place, and yet the birds came, too, singing, scratching among the wet leaves of the year before. When one landed close to her, Alice would sit very still and stiff, feeling the cold from the rock beneath her, carefully taking her clear, unimaginative pictures of the small, fussy creature beside her. Don't put the bird in the middle of the frame. Focus on the eye. Stop down for detail. She would clutch the gunstock, an ornate wooden contraption that nestled into her shoulder, and try to hold the long lens still while she shot, rolls of film at a time, half of which might come out, with perhaps one shot to be used in the magazine. Click click click. And then the bird would stop, twist its head and blink its sharp eye, and then it would be gone, trailing a noisy flutter of air. Sometimes she sat and waited for the birds, and sometimes set off along the narrow mud paths in search of them. And she would remember how years ago, when she thought yellow warblers were escaped canaries and looked for them in the woods behind her house, she had walked so carefully in a vain attempt to emulate the silent, stealthy movements of Indian braves she read about in storybooks. She would put her toes down first, gently, then lower her heel in a slow, rolling movement of the foot, attempting to take every twig and dry leaf and pebble into account, but hearing snapping, crunching noises nevertheless, and seeing battalions of panicked insects retreating in every direction. Huge leafy heads of swamp cabbage grew in stinking clusters by the stream that cut through the Brodys' property. Dead branches draped with vines and fungus and frenetic carpenter ants lay, gray and decomposing, beneath the healthy trees to which they had once belonged. She would hear a pheasant's rasping honk, and then see it, large and incongruous above her, perched uncomfortably in a tree.

If Alice sat patiently and waited, an astonishing number of birds would come and show themselves: golden-crowned kinglets, red-bellied woodpeckers, a blue-gray gnatcatcher, veeries, ovenbirds, a brown creeper, a Louisiana water thrush, posing on damp trunks and narrow branches. And within a few weeks, the park would be overwhelmed with warblers and flycatchers. Today she brought her tripod and set it up in a promising place, a rocky outcropping near a little pond called the Gill, and waited. She heard birds singing all around her, she saw bits of motion in the trees, but all of it was out of range, and she waited some more, hoping one bird would perch in front of her lens long enough for her to press the shutter. Alice was grateful for Central Park, where the ornamental trees were small and the rocks were large: she could stand on a boulder and look a bird in the eye. On some days, there was even a remote chance that she might catch a hooded warbler or a pro-thonotary warbler. A well-designed park. In it, one was never forced to crane one's neck, as one was in Prospect Park, with its older, denser forest. Alice was sometimes required to photograph birds upstate, or to trek through Long Island marshes filled with mosquitoes and ticks as she looked for shorebirds. Or she would study maps and take buses and rattling trains to meet learned ornithologists and wild-eyed birders frantic to show her the newly discovered nesting sites of rails. But Alice much preferred the daily commute, the routine, of huge Central Park in the springtime, as busy as an office. It was so unlikely, she thought. All these birds stopping in, in the midst of the towers of Manhattan. And that someone should pay her to take photographs of them was almost as baffling. A magazine existed for the enjoyment and enlightenment of bird-watchers in New York, and to her eternal gratitude, Alice was employed to take pictures of whatever birds she could find who had chosen to pass through the Empire State.

Sometimes a rat would hurry by her in the park, and then Alice would go home. But today there was no rat. There was only Louie, with field glasses, crashing through the bushes to crouch behind her.

Instead of slowing down, growing weary and stale with the effort of tormenting Brenda and her family, Louie seemed to thrive, developing the gaunt resilience and stubborn, wild-eyed enthusiasm of a marathon runner. And perhaps that's what it's become to him, Alice thought—a marathon. Every morning he would show his face, expectant and sharp, at either Brenda's or Alice and Peter's, and the race would be on.

Alice got up, slipping on the boulder, startling herself with her own haste and fear. She began to walk quickly down a dirt path broken up by roots, and she could hear Louie's shoes scraping along behind her own. Her binoculars banged heavily against her chest. She clutched the tripod, its legs fully extended, and the top-heavy camera still attached to it. Run, Alice. Run with all your expensive equipment, she thought. Very clever. But she could not stop. She headed for the Belvedere castle. She had heard yesterday that someone had seen a palm warbler, the first of the year, and she hoped there would be other birders there, waiting for a second sighting. But it was still early, not yet seven, on a weekday, and she hadn't seen any birders yet. Still, she thought, there might be someone, some fool, some fool doing t'ai chi, perhaps.

Alice took the most direct route she knew, climbing up boulders, jumping from one to another, the camera cradled in her arm, the tripod trailing behind her. She was overcome with the same close, heavy panic she had felt as a child when suddenly, with no warning or cause, she would be afraid of the dark, afraid of its immensity, its inevitability, its simple presence. Behind her, Louie was whistling.

Smug little bastard, she thought. Whistling. While I'm scrambling around Central Park like a monkey. But she couldn't stop, could not even look back. The straps of her binoculars were tangled and twisted, the heavy bird guides in her jacket pockets thudded against her legs.

They'll think a mugger did it, she said to herself. For my camera and my binoculars. They'll never know it was him. With her free hand, she patted the camera protectively.

There was no one at the Belvedere castle. Louie continued to whistle behind her. Slowly, not knowing what else to do, she turned around, faced him, and he winked at her. He whistled loudly, lifting the binoculars that hung around his neck to his eyes, slowly moving them in an arc, up toward the sky, and then down again, until they were pointed at Alice.

"I'm out here looking at nature. Beautiful, just beautiful. I'm big on nature, you follow? Always have been. Always. *Always*," he said emphatically as if she had argued with him.

Alice walked down a few steps. Louie walked down a few steps. She sat on a rock. He sat on a rock just behind her. She sat there for several minutes, her chin in her hand, wondering what to do. The panic had stopped, but she was sure it would come back the minute she stood up again and resumed leading Louie Scifo and his whistle through the winding park paths. Still, she was grateful for the intermission.

Alice heard Louie light a cigarette, then stamp it out on the ground, then light another. She saw the palm warbler and took pictures of it perched on the stone wall beside her. So there, she thought. You cannot come between me and my birds. But the palm warbler flew away finally, and Alice was still sitting there. To break the tedium, she turned to Louie. "Smile!" she said, and lifted her camera.

"What?" Louie said. He dropped the binoculars he had been pointing at Alice. "Heh! This is an invasion of my privacy as a citizen."

And then, as a huge German shepherd bounded between them, followed by his frantic owner, a huge German shouting "Halt," Louie, with many worried glances at the camera, went away.

🏵   /   Alice left the park at Eighty-first Street and walked down Central Park West. The schoolchildren were everywhere, big ones striding along, little ones dawdling, pulling their parents back to look at crocuses growing around a tree, at the shattered glass of a car window glistening like pale green beads on the sidewalk. Alice was meeting her friend Caroline, the California actress, at a coffee shop. The entrance was in an old hotel, down a flight of steps. Alice had always liked it there—the coffee shop was set apart, protected almost. Today she was especially happy to walk down the steps into the hotel's dark, shabby lobby.

Alice waited, sipping her coffee, which was too hot. Caroline would be in town for a few weeks. Broke and bored, she had agreed to act as an East Coast emissary for a friend of hers who was a casting director and needed New York schoolgirls to be murdered in a low-budget horror film she was working on. Caroline knew the schools. She'd been to most of them in her checkered academic career.

Alice wondered how you chose a schoolgirl murder

victim. Did you go for sexy, precocious girls with curves and parted lips? Or for freckled, innocent, gangly ones?

Caroline came in finally and slid into the booth. "Sorry I'm so late. My mother and I were having words. Oh, she sends you her belated congratulations, by the way. She was particularly delighted to hear that you kept your name."

Alice remembered that the moment Caroline went to college, her mother, Mrs. Pond, cleaned out her room and rented it. Caroline was allowed to stay in the maid's room when she came home for vacations if she also paid rent. Mrs. Pond justified this, not on economic grounds—which she could not have done with a straight face even if she'd wanted to, since Caroline's father was still paying child support—but on moral grounds. Mrs. Pond could not allow the discredited rituals of bourgeois sentimentality in the historically male-dominated family to oppress her any longer, she said. Letting a perfectly good room lie fallow most of the year was regressive. Mrs. Pond had shaken off the shackles of her marriage to seek freedom and self-fulfillment. In real estate. She had been to many therapists and consciousness-raising groups, and her consciousness was now a prized possession. She insisted on being called Ms. Pond at the singles bars she frequented. She was a liberated broker.

"My mother is angry because I'm staying at a friend's apartment instead of being Caroline the Lodger. She said I should show her some respect."

"She did? She said that?"

"Mm-hmm."

Alice sat silently as Caroline ordered. She had always detested Mrs. Pond. Mrs. Pond would throw her arms around Alice and make a fuss about how happy she was to see her, then she would insult Caroline and compare her unfavorably, and unfairly, to Alice, until Alice found herself saying, No, no, my grades are terrible, I have no interests or ambitions, I'm unpleasant and boring and a disloyal daughter, sister, granddaughter, and friend, and I dress like someone going out to walk the dog. Mrs. Pond would then suggest that Alice consult one of her therapists. She liked to sit very close to people, even strangers, in order to whisper extended, self-pitying laments about her sacrifices and the world's long, paternalistic ignorance of her potential.

"Maybe she's really my stepmother," Caroline said.

"*I* have a stepmother."

Caroline paid no attention to her. She was eating a heavily buttered bialy. "Respect," she muttered. Then she laughed. "And she hates my boyfriend, whom she has not met, who is wonderful. I wish his name wasn't Mohammed. Still. I met him at a café in a soap opera. We sat across from each other. You could only see the back of my head, he had the camera angle. But he's awfully nice."

"Caroline, I have an idea and it makes me very happy and it will make you happy, too."

"Yeah?"

"We'll fix your mother up."

"Yeah?"

"With . . . Louie Scifo!"

Caroline was silent. She had been filled in on Louie Scifo, told he was not an agent, at least not a theatrical agent, although whether he was an agent of the CIA or the KGB or, say, the devil, Alice could not say with any real authority. Caroline closed her eyes, then opened them and stared at Alice. Then they both started laughing.

"Well, anyway, he's looking for a place to stay. Or at least he should be," Alice said.

"Oh, that's good. Yeah. We'll sick my mother on him. Mad Dog Pond."

They giggled some more, then paid the check and left. Alice wondered if Louie was out there waiting. Maybe he would follow Caroline. She could cast him in her movie as the sociopath in patent-leather shoes.

"Here," Caroline said, and she handed Alice a lavender business card that said, "Pond Properties. Reasonable Luxe Realty. Find Your Dwelling, Find Your Self."

"It's scented," Alice said.

"Yeah."

"I'm allergic," Alice said, sneezing. As they walked along the wide sidewalk, Alice noticed a blue Pinto parked up ahead. It was Louie's and it was empty.

"I'm allergic to perfume," she said again as she tucked the scented lavender card under one of Louie Scifo's windshield wipers.

April 25
Central Park

A little downy woodpecker, energetic but
deluded, pecked hopefully at my hand near the
bird feeders, then trailed after me, all day,
loyal as a dog.

1. 2 mourning doves
2. 1 tufted titmouse
3. 3 cardinals, 2 female
4. 6 robins
5. 1 blue jay
6. 1 red-tailed hawk
7. 2 chickadees
8. 3 flickers
9. 1 hermit thrush
10. 6 crows
11. 1 blue-gray gnatcatcher
12. 2 ruby-crowned kinglets
13. 1 winter wren (dabbling in the mud)
14. 1 house wren
15. 7 starlings

16. 2 black-and-white warblers
17. 1 blue-winged warbler
18. 3 yellow warblers
19. 32 myrtle warblers
20. 1 palm warbler
21. 1 yellowthroat
22. 1 worm-eating warbler
23. 12 white-throated sparrows
24. 6 Canada geese (flying overhead)
25. 1 house finch (singing)
26. 1 towhee (male)
27. 2 downy woodpeckers
28. 2 rose-breasted grosbeaks (males; usually don't see until early May)
29. red-bellied woodpeckers (several, heard only)
30. 1 red-headed woodpecker (a lone male that wintered south of Strawberry Fields: first time I've seen it with its breeding plumage; looks like a pigeon with a red head)

✿ /   The house in Westport was soaking in a grotesque brine of overflowed toilets and rising swamps. The tenants finally moved out in a damp rage. The plumbers, only recently finished replacing the frozen pipes, came back with their pumps.

"He's stopped up the drains with corks," Alice said.

But it was not true. The vent stack was stopped up with a dead squirrel.

"A squirrel, a squirrel," Brenda's neighbor Jack said when he called. He was overseeing the workmen and reporting back to Brenda. He seemed actually grateful that his neighbor's house was riddled with such interesting problems: his own house glowed with good health, a source of both pride and disappointment to someone who was only entirely happy when he could look after his property, when he could fix things, make things right. (Jack's most recent setback was his discovery that he need not laboriously paint his house each year to keep it fresh and white—only rub Clorox on the dingy parts, for they were mildew.) "A squirrel in the thing. Dead!" he said with obvious satisfaction.

Once the carcass had been removed, the toilets resumed normal activity. But the marshy wet that in years gone by had confined itself to the very edges of the property continued its languorous advance. It seeped and sloshed and bubbled. The floors in the house were oozing and swollen, the tubs full of black gum that had squeezed up, stinking, through the drains.

Every day there was a new report from Westport. When the floor in the bathroom was taken up, the carpenter did not find the layer of concrete he was accustomed to seeing on the ground floors of houses. On this ground floor, he found the ground. Dirt. Bare dirt. When the leaching drains outside were checked to see if perhaps they, too, were clogged with squirrels, it was discovered that the drains were open but were simply too shallow to be of any use. It was a peculiar arrangement, circular, neat, and entirely inefficient. The runoff ran off right back where it came from, and then seeped back up through the bare dirt floors to run off again.

When the roof began to leak, the shingles having been glued on instead of nailed, Brenda knew the time had come to go to Westport and save her house. She could not leave it to sink in its own drainage.

It was decided by the family that Brenda would not go alone. Grandma came back from Florida. Peter packed his computer into large, padded boxes. Alice packed her cameras and developing equipment. Then they all gathered up their rubber boots and the two cats and climbed into the car.

"The pipes are all facing uphill, Mrs. Brody," the plumber said when he greeted them. "They *drain* uphill." He stood beside a large hole in the lawn and an even larger yellow backhoe driven by the septic-tank specialist he was now working with. "Oh, and your cousin was here, looking for you, asking all about you, very concerned, very. Mr. Scifonowitz."

Spring was less advanced here than it was in New York, not by much, but the buds on the trees were smaller and more tender, the shoots of grass shorter, the breeze cooler. As they walked toward the house, they heard the sound of birds chirping and hammers banging.

Alice looked at the house, its brown shingles cushioned with moss, its cement walk lined with pale, misshapen mushrooms.

"Oh, that dirty Florida, even this is better," Grandma was saying.

A dehumidifier growled in a corner of the front hall, and while most of the floors were bumpy, warped, and cracked, they were at least dry. Low, fuzzy plant life had appeared on the exposed dirt floor of the bathroom. No one, not Brenda, not the plumber, not the carpenter, could bear to take up the floors in the other rooms. Perhaps those floors were the same underneath, dirt and gravel and dark pools of water, but perhaps not. If they were left alone, no one would have to know. And so the house was moist, fragile, and livable.

"Look at this interesting lichen," Brenda exclaimed happily, kneeling in a corner of the sitting room.

In the morning, Peter said he would walk to the store to get a newspaper. The rest of the family stared at him, puzzled.

"Take the car," Brenda said.

"No, it's a beautiful day, and it's only half a mile—that's ten blocks."

But no one walked in Westport. They jogged; they rode bikes: they exercised. If they wanted to get somewhere, to go from one place to another, they drove. No one in Westport walked, and the family smiled patronizingly at Peter.

Out he went, swinging his arms defiantly. Alice watched him march down the driveway. She considered the idea something of an urban affectation.

The first day he did it, Peter reported that he was stopped twice to see if he needed a lift to the service station for the tow truck. But this did not deter him. He continued to stride off every day to get the paper. Sometimes he would wear sweat pants, as a disguise.

One morning, Alice watched him walking down the driveway, but before he had quite gotten to the road, he stopped short, then turned around and called to her. She came out and saw what had stopped him. It was garbage, the Brodys' garbage, but it was not where the Brodys had put it. It lay strewn across the muddy pebbles of the driveway, hanging from bramble bushes, piled on the tiny lawn. It was garbage that had been put in the bin last night: aluminum foil, chicken bones, napkins, a milk carton, onion skins, a wine bottle from dinner; old newspapers and rotten fruit; bent nails, shingles, cracked pipes left by the carpenters and plumbers. But now the garbage was everywhere, dumped out of its plastic bags, which had been taken from their cans, which now stood empty inside the large wooden box used to keep out raccoons. The box's latch, which Alice herself had closed the night before, was open.

Alice walked farther, to the end of the driveway, and saw the mailbox. It had been torn from its post and lay in the bushes, open and distorted, like a bent tin can. The mail, all of it ripped open, had been ground into the mud.

"Hmph," said Grandma when the family was summoned to survey the wreckage. "And with all the ugliness in this lousy, filthy world."

The whole family was standing in the driveway nudging pebbles with their toes, like children waiting for the school bus. "I like beauty," Grandma was saying. "Beautiful, beautiful things. I must have beauty."

New garbage was there the next morning, and the next, until it became part of their routine and began almost to seem like some quaint ritual of Westport life Alice would sometimes remember in a nostalgic moment, like the amber-colored milk bottles lined up on the back stoop in winter, a frozen cylinder of milk pushing the cardboard cap above the thick glass neck of each one.

"We'll have to call the police again," Alice said to Peter. She was not at all hopeful about what they could do. "But at least they should know what's going on. Then, when we're all found, buried in pieces beneath the honeysuckle, they'll know who to blame."

They were sitting on the porch and Alice was almost grateful to Louie Scifo and the ramshackle house he had constructed for getting her out there on such a day. The air was cold but fresh and delicate with spring. A white-throated sparrow was singing, its song one low note, then three higher, exactly like the opening bar of a Vivaldi concerto Alice had played on her violin as a child, the only piece of music, in fact, she had ever mastered. She was especially fond of white-throated sparrows.

There was a stirring in the bushes and Alice's heart began to pound until she saw it was Brenda, pushing her way through to stand before them in her black bathing suit, tight white cap, and round-lensed goggles.

"Go next door and take a swim, Alice. It's good for you," she said.

"It's freezing cold, Mom. Mom? Let's call the police today, okay?"

"Oh. I guess so," Brenda said. She had knelt down to examine something in the wet grass. "Look. A little skeleton."

Alice got up and examined it. A chipmunk or a mouse. She wasn't sure which. Perhaps one of the cats had felt rejuvenated by the great outdoors and exhibited some proper instinctive cat behavior. Perhaps the red-tailed hawk she saw coasting by every now and then had dropped it here. She carried a spade full of dirt from the garden and poured it on the bones. When she and Willie were little, they had buried all their dead pets under a large white rock beneath a flowering cherry tree.

"That's nice, Alice," Brenda said.

Alice went inside, washed her hands, and called the Westport police. Within minutes, a police car had pulled into the driveway and a young policeman was stepping out.

"Hi, Mrs. Brody!" he said, holding out his hand to Brenda.

"Larry!" Brenda cried. "Little Larry. You're all grown up now. Willie!" she called. "Look who's come to visit."

Alice just recognized Larry, formerly a fat boy with glasses who always stood next to Willie in the class picture, and she said hello. "And, Mom, he didn't come to visit. He came to investigate."

Willie and Larry walked down to the twisted mailbox and mounds of garbage and stood talking awhile.

When they came back to the porch, Larry told them that he already knew Louie. He had been picked up a few years ago with a truckload of lumber and building supplies after just such a truckload had been reported stolen.

"I *found* it," he had told the police.

But there was nothing they could do about the garbage, Larry said apologetically, unless Louie was actually seen throwing it around, which, Alice thought, would be worth seeing for many reasons, though somehow she doubted she would have the chance.

One night, Louie came and rattled the barn's rickety Dutch doors. When the police arrived, he was, of course, gone. On another night, he quietly dismantled a cinder-block wall he had built, pulling the big gray blocks away one by one, then loudly smashing them, pulverizing them with a sledgehammer. Alice once again dialed the police. The policewoman who answered the phone at night was named Lois and had taken to calling Alice "Cookie."

Brenda turned on the outside light. "Oh, good," she said, surveying the damage. "I always thought that wall was ugly."

"You're dead," Louie would whisper into the phone. "Dead in a week."

During this time, Grandma cooked almost constantly—not the hearty, wholesome meals other people's grandmothers cooked, but bits of this and that, elaborate exhibits of complicated garnish, whole platters of radishes carved to resemble roses, carrot-and-turnip daisies, curled ribbons of scallions. Once she made Alice an entire aviary, with apple swans, a peacock of kiwi, and a watermelon pond with mint-leaf lily pads. She never ate any of these dishes, referring to them as works of magnificent art and offering them to her daughter and grandchildren with grave warnings not to let them slip beyond the family circle. Grandma never ate anything, as far as Alice could tell, except Dolly Madison vanilla ice cream and her own baked goods. She baked whenever she was not garnishing—bulging pies and cookies dripping with chocolate chips and cakes decorated with pink icing and animal crackers. She spent an entire day making creamy cheesecake, another making a lemon-meringue pie that stood nearly a foot high.

"Ah, fresh, fresh," she would murmur, breathing in the delicate scents of butter and chocolate, and then she would carefully fold the fresh creation in plastic wrap—when there were cookies or brownies, each one would be individually packaged—and then in aluminum foil, and then place the bundles in a plastic bag with a note scribbled on the back of a yellow stub from an old checkbook by way of identification. Then she would freeze them.

Grandma liked to accompany Peter on his morning walks as far as the deformed mailbox, where she would stand, breathe in the morning air, look at the mailbox, the debris, and the house itself, shake her head, and say, "For *this* she needed a Ph.D."

One morning, instead of garbage, there were huge patches of grass that had died overnight. The dry, brown grass spread itself out, not in the usual amorphous shapes of dying lawns, but in great, sweeping loops, as if a message had been scrawled there, in the crabgrass, in large script. At the end of the cryptic message, like a period, stood a red gasoline can. On a large piece of adhesive tape on its side was written, not in script, but in crooked block letters: VERY DANGEROUS POISON.

"Well," Brenda said when she saw the lawn. "At least we won't have to weed that! Now, come on, get your trowels." Brenda had informed them at breakfast that they would be weeding the little garden in the back. "I like it just the way it is, you know," she'd said, looking fondly at the budless rosebushes, the forest of dark mint plants, the three leaning blue irises, and the sprays of tiny daisy-like flowers just visible beneath the skunk cabbage and thistles. "But maybe I'll like it even better when we're done!"

Alice sat down at one end of the garden and waved to Peter at the other end. He waved back, plucked at a few weeds, then turned his face to the sun and closed his eyes. The sun was not hot, but it was seductive, still unfamiliar and exotic this early in the year. Alice pulled up a plant she hoped might be a weed.

"Good work," Brenda said, petting her head like a dog's. "And now our picnic. With lemonade!" And she went into the house.

Alice had been hearing a birdcall she could not quite identify. It grew louder now, and she couldn't stand the uncertainty any longer. She grabbed her binoculars and made her way into the woods. The bird's song started again, closer this time, just above her head. She looked and saw it was a Nashville warbler, a species she had never seen in Westport. The door slammed, and the bird flew off. Alice looked back toward the house. Brenda was standing there with a tray that held a big pitcher of pink lemonade. Alice could hear the sound of the ice tinkling against its sides. Brenda and Peter sat down on a wrought-iron bench and drank from tall glasses. Peter wiped his brow with his arm. There were three uprooted weeds in the wheelbarrow beside him. "Whew," he said.

Alice, reading the paper and drinking her coffee on the porch one morning, listening to the loud gurgles of the impressive new septic system, looked up to see Louie Scifo in the middle of the field, with a scythe. He was slashing at shoulder-high weeds, leaving behind flat and irregular patches, bald spots, on their neighbor's land. The neighbor, a blond-haired woman, was so quiet that for many years the only sign of life at the house had been a huge black hound, chained to a clothesline, who bayed at passersby and squirrels. The dog died when Alice was in high school, and the Brodys had then forgotten all about their neighbor.

At last, Alice thought, surprised at Louie's miscalculation. Trespassing. She called the police.

When the police arrived, their sirens blaring and lights flashing, Alice waited for Louie to disappear. But he did not move. He stood, in a white sweatshirt with a decal of a fuzzy creature and the words MONSTER MASH on it, and nonchalantly swung his sledgehammer at some rocks.

A policeman talked to him for a moment, then picked his way through the field toward the Brodys. "He, uh, lives there," said the policeman, clearly embarrassed.

"What nonsense," Brenda said. "Mrs. Margate lives there. There she is, see?" And she pointed at her neighbor, who was standing by a police car.

"Well, I know, but he lives there, too. Now. He's the caretaker."

"That was my sweatshirt," Willie said.

"It was *not*. It was *mine*," said Alice.

June 20
Westport

1. loggerhead shrike* (Life bird. Very, very
    rare here. Sitting on the telephone wires
    beside the school that isn't there,
    shrieking, which is where "shrike" came
    from, although it is also known as the
    butcherbird because it impales its victims
    on thorns and stores them there. Larders of
    dangling mouse cadavers, warbler remains,
    deceased bees, draped corpses of limp,
    long-gone snakes.)

🐾 / The room in Westport that Peter used as a study was lined on three sides with windows, but still it was dark, for every window was shrouded with a huge tangled growth of bushes and vines. Just beyond the bushes were trees: big, leafy maples and grand oaks. They leaned on each other like old married couples. Alice watched a squirrel disappear into the green above. Then she saw a downy woodpecker, its black-and-white body and top-heavy head with the splash of red in back. It traveled jauntily up a tall, tilted tree trunk, stopping frequently to bang its beak at the wood. Woodpecker skulls had been studied by people who designed motorcycle helmets. Maybe they should study Louie's skull, instead.

There were no windows on the back wall of the study: the house was built into a hill, and the back of the room was essentially underground. Alice looked at Peter working and she felt as if they were deep in a cavern, a cavern with dank floors and walls that seemed to be closing in on Peter a little more each day, shrinking slowly from the wet.

"Okay," she said, "let's get out of this moldy rathole. We're going to the beach."

"Too hot," Peter said. "Too Louie."

"Come on, get up, we'll take a walk on the beach, just the two of us, and eat a Popsicle and go swimming and collect shells and other romantic things."

"SJF seeks sensitive SJM, Box 192, New York Review—"

"You and I are going to the beach to have fun," Alice said firmly.

Brenda entered the room. "The beach?" she said. "Fun?" And she was off to tell the others.

Alice loved the beach in Westport. There was no surf; there were no dunes. It was not a glamorous place. But she liked the round smooth rocks, the crabs and minnows in the warm pools left behind by the tide. She liked the view of Long Island, even, far enough away to be pretty and indistinct.

They shouldered their burdens and heaved them toward the spot at the western end of the beach where they usually sat. Brenda set up two beach chairs, each with an umbrella attached to the arm. She then began digging the pole of another, bigger umbrella into the sand, then another. When she had finished, the four striped beach umbrellas had formed a bunker of shade. "There," Brenda said, putting on sunglasses and a wide-brimmed sun hat. She sat down and began smearing sunblock on her arms and legs.

Alice and Peter walked down to the water's edge. It was high tide. Alice saw a cormorant flying in the distance. Terns were diving into the water. She looked down at Peter's long toes and her own short, stubby ones and wondered what kind of children they would have.

"Picnic!" her mother called.

Alice was not hungry, and she left Brenda and Peter and Willie sitting in a circle beneath the umbrellas, peeling oranges and hard-boiled eggs, their backs to the sun and the blaring radios, like a wagon train pulled up for the night.

Alice looked at the sky. The color was deep and bright today, and the white clouds moved briskly by. She walked back to the water, tested it with her foot, then waded in. Seaweed sloshed around her calves. A rock, thrown by a little boy, skipped past her. Four skips. The water was warmer than usual and she dove in.

The salt water made her a better swimmer than she really was, and she shot along until she was tired, then turned and floated on her back, watching a sailboat race through bleary eyes, then looking toward the shore. She saw that she had gone a long way, almost to the other end of the beach. Her mother's beach umbrellas were far away, blue-and-white striped, orange and green, red and white, and an ugly brown-and-yellow one. She closed her eyes and began swimming slowly, serenely, back in the direction she had come. She felt alone when she swam, which she liked. No Louie, certainly. No anyone else, either, packed into the house, Mom scatterbrained and hideously cheerful, Peter sinking into a grumpy depression, Grandma an irrepressible, irrelevant background buzz. Willie, meanwhile, was working with a Turkish TV-documentary crew as a translator and had decided to become a television reporter in Turkey. He came to Westport on the weekends and brought a video camera with him. At night, the family would turn on the VCR, and they would watch on tape what they had seen all day: Louie mowing, Louie hacking trees, Louie drinking beer and smoking, Louie eating his lunch, Louie littering, Grandma giving a lesson in how to carve a radish, Louie digging a hole, Grandma telling a dirty joke in Yiddish, Alice laughing at it, Brenda hurriedly pulling a curler from her hair and smiling at the camera. Then they would see Peter pacing, which he did often, and they would hear the loud creak, creak, of the warped wood beneath his feet. Then Louie standing at the fence and waving.

There was also one interminable film of the Thanksgiving spider crawling through its luxurious home, a fish tank Willie had bought for it, and spinning a web. Willie, in spite of all his practice, was not a very good cameraman; he had a tendency to zoom dizzily toward his subjects, then jerk the camera with tremendous force to follow the slightest change in direction. He would proudly point to the spider's hairy leg, a dark angular blur on the screen, and discuss his cinematic technique: "Look, look! Oh, cool!" Then the tape would sputter and Grandma would appear on the screen in her imitation of a Jewish waiter, hunched over, bow-legged, and swinging her arms. "Lady," she would be saying in a heavy Yiddish accent, "dat's de vay I valk," the punch line to an off-color joke about matzoh balls. Then Willie would take himself off to film Louie tacking "No Trespassing" signs on Mrs. Margate's trees.

Alice swam happily through the green, salty water, thinking, Never mind, I'm by myself now. She heard the muted cries of the children playing on the sand, splashing in the water, and she opened her eyes and saw the blue sky and the beach on her right, seeming to speed past, and then, almost as an afterthought, she registered the gigantic dark-red jellyfish in front of her. It hit with a slippery thud.

The jellyfish slithered along the side of her body, leaving an itchy, stinging rash, and she waded out of the water cursing and trying not to cry. The lifeguard, a young man with thick white cream on his nose, red ears, and an otherwise perfect tan, poured baby powder on her, she wasn't sure why, which clung to her wet skin. As she walked back toward the umbrellas, half chalky white, she passed other people, walking from other lifeguards toward other stands of umbrellas, also covered in white powder.

"Hello," they would say, and then, like a code word, "Jellyfish."

⚜ / Peter was pacing, as usual, in front of his computer. Alice could see he was disgusted and weary, pale, as if he were wasting away inside that dreary room. His eyes were puffy and dim, for he had not slept the night before: the cat had woken Alice and Peter several times, demanding to be let into their room, then demanding to be let out again, rubbing its paws frantically and noisily against the door and meowing. Black Coat's meow was a resounding wail that had the additional disadvantage of sounding exactly like the word "meow." Black Coat was the only cat Alice had ever encountered that did indeed meow, like some sort of incarnation of abstract feline attributes, emitting huge, sinister cries in the night, *Mee-ow, meeee-ooww,* until Alice thought she would prefer to hear anything, a bear growling, the hiss of a poisonous snake inches from her face, rather than that distorted storybook noise.

Peter paced back and forth. Alice followed him, to annoy him. He glared at her over his shoulder.

"There's a cricket outside and it's driving me crazy," he said.

"It's a frog," Alice said.

Peter sat back down at the computer. Alice sat on his lap and kissed him a few times. "It's their mating call," she added. Then the phone rang.

It was probably her father, she thought, with information about the La Leche League. He called each week with full-scale accounts of the joys of pregnancy, describing the pre-natal classes, the breathing exercises, the recommended amounts of iron and potassium. Alice knew what Patricia would bring to the hospital in her suitcase. A nightgown, yes, but also a tennis ball. Or was it a basketball? And no lollipops, Dad had said. That was no longer considered wise.

"Hello?" Alice said.

"Your little friend will not live to see the morning," the familiar voice on the other end said. "Ever." And then Alice heard a loud, unmistakable *Mee-ow* in the background.

Louie and Black Coat called back several times to repeat the message.

"Well, it really is pretty low to abduct a cat," Peter said.

"So beautiful, so soft," Grandma said. "Like a hat."

"But I guess there's nothing we can do," Peter said. And Alice could tell what he was thinking: I'll be able to sleep tonight. And tomorrow night.

"He wouldn't hurt the cat, of course," said Brenda.

"Defenseless pussycat," Alice said, bursting into tears.

Peter looked ostentatiously at the scar on his wrist left by Black Coat's most recent attack.

"He could sell him, I guess," said Willie. "For experiments."

Louie called back again with this message: "Your poor little kitty has run away? But maybe he'll come back to his happy home. You see, there's some property, which belongs to me, in your toolshed, illegally in your toolshed that I built with my own sweat, namely my lawn mower. It could be returned to me, you understand?"

Peter and Alice, sitting sideways on his lap, and the ride-on power mower chugged down the driveway in the dark. Perhaps, Peter said, Black Coat would escape from Louie and dart across the road to be crushed by the roaring machine. Perhaps, thought Alice, Louie would dart across the road and meet the same fate. Or perhaps Peter and Alice would drive the lawn mower to the designated drop-off point, the bottom of the Margate driveway, where Louie and Black Coat would be waiting, schmoozing and chuckling at the gullibility of the humans.

The stink of gasoline and the clattering noise of the lawn mower surrounded them, separating them from the night. Stupid machine, Alice thought. Stupid cat. Stupid Peter and Alice riding the stupid machine to reclaim the stupid cat. They turned onto the road and soon saw Louie leaning against a tree, lighting a cigarette. Louie's face glowed orange and uneven, then dimmed.

Alice heard Black Coat as soon as they stopped the motor.

"*Mee-ooww,*" said the cat.

"Pete," said Louie from the gloom. "Alice," he said, formally, as if at a business meeting.

They said nothing.

Louie turned on a flashlight and smiled. Alice could see a large American Tourister suitcase on the ground. Deep, rich meows flowed from its interior. She thought how uncomfortable he must be, all alone in the luggage. "I don't like cats, myself," said Louie.

Peter tossed Louie the lawn mower's keys.

"It's dented! It's dented! No fair! No deal!"

"Okay," Peter said.

"Okay," Alice repeated. She wondered if Peter was serious, or just bargaining in some way.

Louie squatted down, shining his flashlight at the lawn mower's wheels and into its engine, like a man checking out a used car.

"W-e-e-e-ll," he said. "I could use a machine like that."

He stood thoughtfully scratching his head, appraising the lawn mower. "I could let you have this cat. But," he added as Alice walked toward the source of the meows, "the suitcase, that stays."

Alice and Peter stood with the open cat carrier waiting for Louie to produce Black Coat.

"I'm sorry, you follow? I can't give you this suitcase," Louie said as he unbuckled it. "I was going to throw it in, you understand me, for good faith. But no, it's impossible. I couldn't live with myself afterwards. How could I?" He pulled open the lid and then reached into the suitcase with both hands, like a doctor, only this doctor was delivering a spitting pile of black fur into the dark world. "Why, you . . . hey! . . . you little . . ."

The cat snarled and writhed, and Alice could see what was going to happen. Black Coat tore himself free and ran into the woods. Louie screamed with pain, swore he would sue, and puttered off on the lawn mower with his suitcase under one arm. Alice ran after the cat, leaving Peter alone with the empty cat box.

Alice stood in the woods, hoping to hear a loud mee-ow, but all she heard was Peter. "Here, kitty," he called as he walked slowly home. It was a halfhearted, almost inaudible call. "Here, kitty, kitty."

July 10
Westport

1. a lot of crows
2. too many starlings
3. more crows
4. a crowd of noisy, ugly house sparrows
5. 1 cardinal, dead

🙢 / Every day, Louie appeared in the meadow dressed in clothes Willie and Alice both claimed to have cast off in adolescence. He would ride ostentatiously on the power mower, or he would dig and chop and clip and saw, like any suburban gardener, until quitting time at five or six. But when Alice walked through the field one evening, trying to locate the nest of a common yellowthroat she'd been watching, she could see that Louie's landscaping, which had spilled over onto Brody property, had a unique design. In some places he cut small, round patches scooped out among the six-foot weeds; these were all connected to one another by a series of narrow paths. In other areas, stands of six-foot weeds and vines were left undisturbed within large, cropped areas strewn with hacked, swampy grass. And Alice realized that Louie had built a series of blinds.

One day Jack ran over, sweating and excited. "I saw him hiding while I was digging, you know, killing. Weeds. And I saw him, a viper in our thing. Bosom."

Some days Louie mowed a strip along the edge of

Margate territory, up and down, up and down, all day long, the same strip.

"To relax?" Jack said at first, hopefully, recognizing a potential colleague. But then he looked at the field as it fell away from the neatly mowed strip, at the mounds of sawed-off branches and brown stalks, at the pile of broken cement blocks Louie had trucked in for some reason, at the scattered beer bottles and cigarette packs, at the pools of mud that had gathered in the clearings. And he shook his head, as if to say that perhaps Louie had not relaxed quite enough.

Alice would watch Louie working and she would be overcome by a profound weariness. She would sit on the porch and the noise of Louie's drills and electric saws would fill the air around her, drowning out the birds, and she would imagine that it would always be like this, her whole family crammed in this house with the mildew and the bees and the man with binoculars next door. She would have her children here, raise them here, raise them on garnish and cake, and they would grow to be big and strong and one day one of them would buy a shotgun and he would walk up to the fence and he would put the gun against the temple of the strange man who lived there and he would . . . No. They would grow up big and strong and move away. And she would continue to sit here, alone, with only her mother, grandmother, and husband, day after day. She would learn to knit and garnish, herself, and she would grow old here, and one day she would walk over to the fence and with her last strength she would lift up the sledgehammer and she would swing it at Old Man Scifo, and it would hit his head with a dull thump and . . .

Alice would sit there in the sweet air and the grinding noise and she would see bullet holes in Louie's chest, blood seeping from them, darkening his shirt, *her* shirt, with 1

LOVE RINGO printed on it. She would feel Louie's jaw break beneath the impact of her fist. The sound of Louie's bones cracking filled her ears, visions of knives slowly, meticulously slicing Louie's flesh filled her imagination. At night, she would lie sleepless in the dark, waiting for even a faint sound, and then, whether she heard one or not, she would rush to the window, looking for Louie.

One day, as Alice sat on the porch in a particularly malevolent torpor, she saw Caroline's odious mother, Mrs. Pond, waving gaily from across the field and shouting her name. Alice stared, openmouthed, as Mrs. Pond bushwhacked her way through the ratty vegetation, calling, "Alice Brody! What a coincidence!"

Alice thought of Caroline and their plot. Louie had found the lavender business card. He'd found the card and called Mrs. Pond. He must have. Alice waved broadly to Mrs. Pond. Welcome, she thought. "Welcome!" she yelled. She noticed Mrs. Pond was carrying a briefcase bulging with papers. What was she doing here? Louie had probably invited her out for a back-yard barbecue, after which they would set fire to the Brodys' house and roast marshmallows on it, singing "Go Tell Aunt Rhody," while holding high-level consultations on a plot to take over Westport, Mrs. Pond acting as the front, the innocent real-estate agent, getting her foot in the door so Louie Scifo could slide through the crack to destroy the plumbing and then repair it, leaving a relative behind in every rec room to act as caretaker.

"God, look at this property," Mrs. Pond was saying. "It's a mess—scraggly. What are all those clumps of weeds? You know, you might ask Louie to do a little work for you. I mean, I don't know if he would, he's such a busy person, but he does do landscaping. He could certainly do something with this nasty-looking field."

This is heartwarming, Alice thought. She considered pointing out that Louie had already landscaped a good deal of the field, and that he hadn't even charged them. But she didn't want to prejudice Mrs. Pond in any way, so she held her tongue.

"Wonder what I'm doing here, hon?" said Mrs. Pond, who sometimes affected a Southern accent. "Just wanted Louie, Signore Scifo, your neighbor, to sign a few papers. He told me you recommended me when he called. You always did know quality, Alice, and you're loyal. Now, Caroline hasn't come up with one referral, not one client out of all those transient theatrical people she insists on fraternizing with. So here I am, I do it on my own, that's all. You know me—busy searching for meaning. And Scifo and I, we're doing a little business together, business with meaning. Scifo is particularly interested in Westport—investing, developing, becoming a real part of the community. This is my vocation, Alice."

"Mine, too," Alice said.

Mrs. Pond looked at her. "Well! Alice! Don't *you* look . . . filled out! Well, never mind that. The last time I saw you, you looked much too thin, ghastly, really. I didn't say anything, of course. It must have been difficult for you, Alice, growing up with such a beautiful mother. Don't you think condominiums have a place in Westport?"

And Mrs. Pond skipped back across the field. Alice watched her and her briefcase with delight. Louie's new business associate was a bad businesswoman, constantly losing money, and an ambitious and unscrupulous one as well.

"Bye, hon," Alice called happily after her.

※ / The Brodys had a cookout one evening and Willie brought his new friend, an open-faced girl with a blond ponytail and freckles on her nose. She wore no makeup and her voice was pleasant and plain. Her name was Molly and Alice thought she had never met someone so distinctly American until Molly said, "What the heck's a cookout?"

"She grew up in Turkey," Willie said.

"My father's a journalist. Oh, look! There's a man in the bushes with binoculars. Secret police."

Later, when they were drinking coffee in the spring twilight, Louie left the bushes, only to return seated on his lawn mower. Up and down along the strip he went. Up and down. And through the noise of the motor they thought they could hear a wailing noise, a word howled over and over again.

Watching Willie's video that night and turning up the volume, they realized what the word was: Brenda. Over and over. Brenda, Brenda, Brenda.

When Louie made his eleven-o'clock call that night, Alice answered the phone. She had been shaken by the episode earlier. It was not pleasant to think that someone you hated, someone you dreamed of murdering in various gruesome ways, was already suffering. It was she, Alice, and her family who were really suffering, and now that hideous shriek of psychic pain threatened to take some of the edge off their misery, to dwarf it. At the memory of Louie's bloodcurdling chant, dismay and guilt and pity came over Alice in successive waves, and she determined that it was her duty, as a human being, not to kill Louie, not to mash in his skull with cement blocks or chop him to pieces with the power mower, as she had spent the day planning in graphic daydreams, but to help him.

"Your mother is a whore," Louie said when she answered the phone. "A dead whore."

"Louie, I know we haven't always seen, um, eye to eye, but now I'm getting a little, you know, sort of worried or something, and maybe you should have someone to talk to, like a therapist, maybe, a psychiatrist . . ."

"Whore, whore, your mommy's a whore . . ."

"Someone you could explain things to, kind of talk things out . . ."

". . . a prostitute . . ."

". . . nothing to be ashamed of, of course, and who knows, after all . . ."

". . . with anybody . . . in cars . . ."

"Look," Alice said, trying to remain patient and understanding, trying to remember the desperate, mournful wail from the power mower, but angry and nearly screaming to be heard over Louie's singsong contributions to the conversation. "You have to do something or you're going to end up in the bin or, or . . . in *jail*."

"For what?" Louie Scifo said, his voice lifting with amusement and sarcasm. "For what?"

Alice hung up then, but Louie called back. Each time she hung up, he called back, and each time she answered the phone, somehow unable to let it ring.

"For what?" he kept saying. "For what?"

"Because you're scum," Alice finally screeched. "Scum, scum, scum."

Whenever Louie tried to speak, Alice drowned him out, screaming the word "scum" over and over.

"What are you, nuts?" Louie said when she stopped to take a breath. And he hung up.

But Alice called back this time. She called him back again and again and screeched, "Scum, you're scum, you're scum, scum, *scuuuum*," until Peter came and gently pulled her away from the phone.

Alice said, "Well, you certainly married into an aristocratic family. Dignified, cultured, gracious."

"You got mad."

"I got mad. That sinister toad is driving me mad. Mowing, mowing, mowing. He's going to mow in circles, smaller and smaller, like Jack, until, until, and nothing stops him, he never runs out of gas, or accidentally sledgehammers his toe, or falls in a manhole, or drowns, or anything. He just mows and creeps around. He's never called away on business, there are no funerals that require his attendance, he has no dentist appointments . . ."

Alice muttered on and on as Peter stroked her head. "He moves next door, *moves next door*, in Westport, my hometown, like a rat. My mother introduces him into Westport and he thrives like a rat, a white rat escaped from a lab, because he's found his ecological niche in a white split-level house *next door*, next door *to me*, and I don't even live here, not really . . ."

Alice was tired of waiting for Mr. Carson to decide he had enough evidence for a court hearing. This court hearing had begun to seem mythical, its promise the opiate of the Brodys. By the time there was one, she would probably be a stringy-haired recluse who spoke in tongues and Peter an embittered (but still eligible) divorcé. *Family Behind Bars.* And besides, there was never anything to eat in the house, only Grandma's frozen cakes. After making Alice climb up to the attic to bring down the silver and the good china, Grandma would set an elaborate table with fish forks and salad forks and dessert forks and bouillon spoons and napkins folded to look like tulips, and then there would be nothing to eat. People were always off to the supermarket. They drove there four or five times a day, but they always forgot the important things to eat, the coffee or the milk or the bread. There was a shuttle to Waldbaum's, but there was never anything to eat.

"There, there, Alice," Peter was saying. "Don't worry. I'll fix everything."

"Right," Alice said, but she was grateful to Peter for trying to reassure her.

Then the phone rang, and before she could stop herself, Alice had lunged at it and was screaming "Scum, scum" into the receiver, then saying, "Oh, Dad, hi. I thought you were someone else, I guess."

When she'd hung up, Alice went upstairs. Her mother had gathered armfuls of brambles and stalks and twisted prickly vines earlier in the day and now she was arranging them in oddly shaped bouquets throughout the house.

"Now, isn't that nice?" she said.

"Mom, they're crawling with ticks," Alice said. "We'll die of Lyme disease."

"Yes, dear," Mrs. Brody said absentmindedly.

"Who called before? Who was that?" Grandma asked Alice. "Your miserable father, he should rot in hell, what did he want, to give up such beauty and brains, a mental giant, for a farmer, an ignoramus, from the prairies." Alice's grandmother seemed the most comfortable with the situation in the house. Her complaints had become so rooted in her digestion, her aesthetic demands, and her low estimation of Alan Brody, so ritualized over the years, that she was reluctant to recognize new forms, to admit Louie into her canon. Louie bothered her only insofar as he blighted the landscape with rubbish or disrupted the family enough to upset Grandma's delicate stomach. Alice admired her.

"Dad called to say that Patricia's prickly heat has finally stopped."

"Prickly heat, morning sickness," Grandma said, adding several curses in Yiddish. "Those farmers are made of iron. But I, how I suffered with your mommy, *how* I suffered . . ."

Alice had listened to her father without paying too much attention. She did not think it fell within the realm of filial duty to care very deeply about Dad's wife's prickly heat. She was glad Patricia had suffered from prickly heat— it seemed only fair—but supposed on the other hand that Patricia couldn't realistically be expected to suffer from it forever.

As she listened to her grandmother, she thought of Louie Scifo. It was infuriating to be thinking of Louie Scifo. Tiresome, frustrating, time-consuming, infra dig. No thinking of Louie Scifo, she decided. Then she thought of Louie

Scifo some more. Think? Why shouldn't I think? I think I'll shave his belly with a rusty razor. I think I'll bind his head with a Boethian band. I think I'll smother him in silver nitrate, leaving just a hideous, discolored corpse.

What a wonderful idea! To *expose* him, literally, using silver nitrate, the miraculous powder of photography. Just a touch, here, there, and then the darkening spots, a pox on Louie. She could dust it on the garbage cans, Louie's faithful, ill-treated midnight companions. And then, when he arrived for the ritual flinging of litter, his claws would grasp silver nitrate, invisible silver nitrate, silver nitrate that he would not see as he crept back to sleep in his evil vault, that he would not notice until the next morning, when the first rays of dawn and the police would discover him, exposed to the light, in his bed—with guilty, blackened hands.

Alice laughed, and her grandmother, who was describing her nausea of fifty-odd years ago, frowned at her. Dirty, messy, but brilliant, Alice thought. She would probably turn black, too, but she didn't care. Louie Scifo would look out from the police car, bewildered, beaten, smudged. Never again would she see the corner of his jacket jutting out from a stand of weeds. Never again would she catch his eye in the rear-view mirror. She imagined his face as he saw his coal-dark skin; she imagined him helplessly rubbing the blotches and smears, Louie Macbeth.

✖ / Alice opened the door and stepped outside. She could see the stars, but there was no moon, and the dark was deep, still, and impenetrable. Good, she thought. Perfect. She'd left the door open behind her, and she wondered if Louie was watching at this very moment, as she stood in the light from the doorway.

"Black Coat," she called, trying to act naturally. The cat had never returned from his kidnapping, and taking into consideration the low morale at home, Alice could not entirely blame him. "Here, kitty, kitty."

She remembered standing on the back porch of the other house, the old house, staring into the darkness, calling the dog in for his dinner, looking across the lawn at the yellow lights in the Mandells' windows. She would strain her eyes, trying to see Jack or Nancy silhouetted there; then she would whistle for the dog, again and again, and when he did not come, she would step back into the house and open a can of dog food. At the sound of the electric can opener, the dog would come bounding into the house, panting, his tail wagging, his paws muddy, his long, wet hair dripping on Alice's bare feet as he rubbed against her. There were Irish setters romping through green fields on the can's label, but inside, it was pungent pink horse meat pressed together with dots of white fat. She would watch the round top as it separated from the can, held aloft by a magnet, and the dog food's smell would drift out, making her turn her head away. While the dog gulped down the cylinder of pink food, Alice would stand in the doorway again and hear the dull sound of car engines on the New England Thruway, a sound so much a part of life that she never even noticed it when it blended in with busier noises during the day.

Alice heard it now, though. She called the cat again, as she had called every night in the week since his abduction. There was no response, only the song of a mockingbird. It unnerved her to hear a bird sing at night.

At the end of the driveway, camouflaged by the dark, stood the enemy position, Alice's objective, a small rise, 172 feet from the front door (she had measured it that morning), on which two strategic installations stood waiting to be liberated—the garbage cans.

"Oh, well," Alice said loudly, standing in the light, as if she were on a stage. She raised her arms up and then dropped them in a gesture of defeat. "I guess Black Coat is gone forever." Then she went back into the house, closed the door behind her, and climbed out a window and hid behind a huge rhododendron. She was dressed in khaki pants with large pockets, an army green shirt, and the fishing vest she sometimes used for her camera equipment. She crawled out from the rhododendron and tiptoed awkwardly in her heavy hiking boots along the grassy edge of the driveway. She advanced slowly, sometimes seeking cover in the bordering woods, until the garbage cans, barricaded within their raccoon-proof box, stood—unpatrolled, she noted—on her right.

She breathed in the cool air and looked up at the stars. The mockingbird sang again. Alice made her approach. She opened the lid of the box slowly, so it wouldn't creak. Then, standing back a little, she reached over with the bottle of silver nitrate and sprinkled it on the tops of the two plastic bins. She closed the lid and poured the remainder of the chemical on the lid and latch.

"There," she said.

She had been preoccupied with this procedure, determined the operation should be executed with discipline and precision—and neatness, for she had to stay clean herself, untainted. But at the same time she dreamed pleasantly of the incriminating stains soon to adorn Louie Scifo. She dreamed and poured and stepped out of the way and dreamed some more, and so it wasn't until she had finished and stood in triumph with the empty bottle that she heard the rustle of branches behind her.

Alice looked into the darkness and saw no one, but she had no doubt about the noise. It was Louie. It was always Louie. He must have been there, watching her the whole time, stretched out on the cold, damp earth or hidden in a thicket of savage thorns. But the cold withdrew from him, the wet ignored him, the thorns turned away. He had watched unscathed, aloof, oblivious to every discomfort, too intent on his business of watching, and he had seen her and known that she was there, pouring, laying a trap for him, that she was pouring and gloating. He had watched her the whole time, and he had laughed.

Alice did not move. She listened to the crunching of gravel and twigs. When she looked around her, slowly turning her head, she saw only the dark night. She heard Louie but did not see him. Okay, she thought, then maybe he had not seen her, either.

Alice retreated a few steps, toward the house. But she heard a step just behind her. She walked some more, a little faster, telling herself Louie had not seen her, that he couldn't possibly have seen her in the dark, that not even Louie could do that, but she listened and knew she was being followed. And then, suddenly ashamed of her bottle of silver nitrate, frightened of the dark, of the distant thruway, of the mockingbird's song, she ran into the woods.

Alice stumbled through the trees. The mockingbird sang louder and louder as she got closer to it. She stopped for a moment to catch her breath, and her shadow stopped, too. She thought she could hear him panting.

Tired and disgusted, Alice sat down. Louie was there, and knew she was there, but if she didn't move, he wouldn't know exactly where, and he wouldn't be able to bother her. The house stood beyond the trees, its lights twinkling through the leaves. The garbage cans she had left behind were shrouded in darkness.

The mockingbird, very near now, kept up its song, rolling and excited, loud and resonant in the night. Alice shifted a little on the ground, the wet, earthy smells rising around her. And then she heard footsteps, smaller, lighter, than the ones she had heard earlier, but footsteps, she was sure. Louie treading more carefully, in an attempt to catch her off guard.

The footsteps crept closer to her; muttering dry leaves, the snap of a twig; and then the footsteps were there, right beside her, and something was rubbing against her boot.

Alice screamed. A huge light burst forth. Alice saw her cat, Black Coat, snarling as he rubbed against her leg. She saw Peter, crouched beside a tree, openmouthed, his face dirty, twigs and brown leaves protruding from his hair. She saw her mother, down by the garbage, turning her blackened hands and staring at them.

"Peter?" Alice said.

"Alice?" Peter said.

"Mom?" Alice called.

"Alice!" Brenda cried, raising both hands to her eyes to shield them from the light, leaving smudges on her face.

"Black Coat!" Alice screamed as the cat, prevented from catching and devouring the mockingbird, and seeking compensation, or perhaps revenge, sunk its teeth into Peter's ankle.

"Willie!" hollered Brenda. "Willie Brody, come out from behind that stupid camera this instant."

In the blaze of the light, Brenda danced and hopped, a picture of maternal fury. "For once," she screamed, "just for once, I wanted to take my garbage and put it in my garbage cans unobserved. That's all. But what do I find? My own son, spying, *spying*, on his mother. With a video camera. How dare you shine those lights at your own mother? Don't you 'Mom' me. What are you doing here? Are you crazy? Answer me, William Brody. And why am I all black?"

Willie hung back sulking, his tall body curled protectively around the video camera. "I was trying to help, that's all," he muttered. "Who asked you to sneak out in the dark. Why are you so dirty? How should I know you'd be emptying garbage at midnight. Boy, I'm not ever doing anything for this family again. Forget it. You won't have Willie to kick around anymore. I'm going back to New York. I'm going to Turkey. Why are you covered with soot?"

Alice and Peter remained silent and morose, unable to look each other in the eye, listening to Willie and Brenda yell explanations at each other as they all walked back to the house. Willie, tired of filming Louie triumphant, had snuck outside with his equipment, hoping to defeat Louie at last, to catch him in the act, and to get some practice for night filming of Turkish terrorist raids as well. He'd set up four lights on tripods, their wires connected to a big square battery. Brenda, on the other hand, feeling jumpy and confined, had decided several days before that to take out the garbage in solitude and peace would be the greatest luxury imaginable; and so, noticing that Louie opened and read her mail each day, she devised a plan wherein she sent herself a letter, a romantic letter setting up a rendezvous for that night at twelve o'clock at an address that was really the Danbury dump, forty-five minutes away. She had signed it, "Your own darling, You Know Who," and had reasoned that Louie would rush off at the allotted time to the allotted place so that *he* would know who, too. Brenda had apparently been right, for, even in the far-reaching glare of Willie's lights, Louie and his car were nowhere to be seen.

"And what's your excuse?" Brenda asked Peter.

"I thought Alice was Louie."

"You *what?*" Alice said.

"In the dark. I was following him. You. Instead of his following me. And you. Us."

"Meee-ow," said Black Coat.

Grandma, who stood watching them from the doorway, shook her head and said, "It happens."

**✻ / **There were days when Alice seemed to do nothing but jot down the times of Louie's phone calls and rearrange the dishes in the dishwasher. Sometimes she rearranged them so that more would fit in; sometimes she rearranged them by color. When the white bowls were lined up in the back of the dishwasher, the red enamel bowls in the front, and the flowered dessert plates in between, she would begin to rearrange with no real purpose at all, just moving things around, a cup from here swapped for a glass from there, which made room for a saucer or a pitcher. She would stand and ponder as if it were a chess move: saucer or pitcher, pitcher or saucer?

Alice had decided to boycott the outside, the land of Louie. The birds she was supposed to be photographing were also outside, with Louie, though, so Alice put out bird feeders on the porch to lure her subjects there. She set several cameras with different lenses up on tripods and occasionally walked by, took a look in each one, and snapped a few pictures.

"Ha!" she thought, peering out at the trees and the crisp blue sky. "So there."

One morning, as she was rearranging the dishes in the dishwasher by size, her mother rushed in from the porch. "Alice, there are two huge birds in a dead tree. I looked them up. They're very, very rare. Come quietly, now. They're . . . ivory-billed woodpeckers!"

"Mom, ivory-billed woodpeckers are extinct. There may be *one* in Cuba. And no one's even ever seen it."

"I *told* you they were rare," Brenda said. She pulled Alice toward the camera that had a telephoto lens. "Birding is exciting."

"Mom . . ."

"They are big and black and have red on them and long necks. I looked them up in that wonderful old book."

"It's completely out-of-date. It's forty years old."

"There was a beautiful drawing. Ivory-billed wood-peckers!"

"Mom, are their bills ivory?"

"I don't know, Alice. I don't have my glasses. Now hurry."

Alice looked through the camera and saw what she had expected, two pileated woodpeckers on a dead tree. As she remarked on the white wing patches in the painting and compared them to the black wings of the pileateds, which did look admittedly large and strange on the dead tree, as she tried to soothe her mother for discovering a bird that was somewhat uncommon rather than one that was extinct, Alice saw something else through the lens. She saw a shoe.

It was a patent-leather shoe, and it protruded from a wild rosebush. Alice jumped back, away from the camera, as if it was the shoe that had caught sight of her.

Will this persecution never end? she thought. Will he

never be bitten by a rabid squirrel? And then she looked at the shoe again. She looked carefully and saw the leg attached and a bit of Louie's head lurking above it. She moved the camera slightly until it focused on the shoe, the cross inside the circle just there, just on the shoe, like the sight of a gun on its target. "Bang," Alice said and clicked the shutter.

The next morning, she set out with sandwiches and hard-boiled eggs and little red boxes of raisins in her pockets, cameras hanging from her neck. She thought black-and-white was somehow more suitable to the day's subject matter than color. And she could use faster film, could capture her subject in lower light. She watched the sun come up over the oak trees, listened to the birds: cuckoos, orioles, warblers, and wrens, birds that she had never noticed as a child, had never dreamed would visit Westport along with all the robins and blue jays, sparrows and cardinals; and she waited for another undreamed-of visitor; she waited to catch sight of her prey. I will call this my Hidden Louie series, she thought, and pretended she was Eliot Porter off to take a picture of a dead horse in Arizona, although she felt more like Elmer Fudd.

Brenda had received papers from a lawyer with a Xerox of an old check for five thousand dollars she'd made out to Louie during the renovation of the barn. On the back was scrawled, "In partial payment of $28,410 I still owe to you, MY COMMON-LAW HUSBAND, for one (1) domicile, re-modeled, that you constructed," in Louie's handwriting, above a reasonable representation of Brenda's signature. There was a verbal agreement, the papers said, that upon the dissolution of their common-law marriage, Louie Scifo would receive half the value of the commonly held property in Westport, Connecticut, as well as annual payments of thirty-five thousand dollars a year until he remarried.

"Common-law marriage!" Brenda had cried, when she read the papers.

Brenda hired a Connecticut lawyer, a man named Thompson Zalman. While Gianni Carson pursued the case in New York City, Zalman would handle the palimony suit, which was filed in Connecticut, as well as Brenda's Connecticut harassment suit against Louie and the pursuit of a restraining order in Connecticut. A proper lawyer in proper pinstripes, he seemed slightly disgusted by the details of the case; at least, he did not appear to enjoy touching the correspondence from Louie's lawyer, always lifting it with two fingers and holding it away from him.

"Perhaps he's farsighted," said Brenda.

"Perhaps he's a big snob," said Alice. He had pink fingers that seemed to have been created solely to be scrubbed with a nailbrush. His immaculate hands and generally dapper appearance had at first inspired confidence in Alice, as well as a campaign to get her mother to start dieting. Alice imagined her mother beside this gentleman barrister, a Lincoln Center program in her hand, sauntering past the brightly lit fountain with all the other sleekly turned-out ladies. Her mother would drive not a Mercedes but, say, a Honda. A really good one. Well, maybe a Saab. She would fly to Switzerland or France and visit monasteries and mountain inns and come home and look radiant, just as her Westport friends did. Her husband, Thompson Zalman, would help her on and off with her coat, which would be a good coat, the kind of coat she used to wear. Alice thought this was a modest fantasy on behalf of her mother—straightforward nostalgia for the simple bourgeois life Alan Brody had carted off, along with the baby grand piano, to Canada.

But then Alice had brought Mr. Zalman a notebook, a chronicle of Louie's activities that Alice particularly liked. There were times, dates, places; a computer-drawn map (one of Peter's contributions) marking the terrain and each lair within it; computer graphs (also Peter's) tracking and comparing daily schedules of Louie's movements from one hideout to the next. To all of this was added Alice's collection of photographs of Louie crouching in the honeysuckle, peering through binoculars, smoking a cigarette high in a tulip tree. In order to get these candid photos, Alice had also hidden; she had, in fact, taken advantage of Louie's own network of blinds, scrambling out of one and into the next whenever he came too near. She was proud of the result, grainy impressionistic pictures, muffled and ghostly. She thought it was the best work she had ever done. There were dozens of them, all carefully labeled with captions like: "Louie looks on as Mom answers door, talks to Jehovah's Witness; 9:45 a.m. July 23."

"See?" she said to the lawyer. "He's watching us."

Mr. Zalman leafed through the notebook.

"Guerrilla Gardener," she added, handing him a blowup of Louie with several gardening machetes hanging from his belt, a coiled rope over his shoulder, a scythe in one hand and a stake in the other.

Mr. Zalman took the photo between his immaculate thumb and his immaculate forefinger and dangled it uncertainly in front of him.

"Thank you," he said, without conviction. And Alice realized that Mr. Zalman was disgusted by this "domestic case," that he did not like her photographs, he did not like her and did not like her family. But, Mr. Zalman, she wanted to say, we're not Louie. We're us.

"A messy business," she said instead, and decided she hated his fingers and his clean-shaven face and his crisp white shirts and blue suits. She thought her mother's gigantic Buick was just the right car, Brenda's coat practical, and any vacation an absurd and vulgar extravagance.

Mr. Carson was more appreciative of Alice and Peter's collaboration. When given the notebook, he admired not only its scope and precision but its layout and design as well. *"This* is the stuff of restraining orders," he said. "But where are the nudies? *Ah ha ha!* The cheesecake?"

"Too rich!" Grandma said. "I have *brownies* for dessert." She was serving miniature blintzes, referred to as "crepes suzettes," for dinner. "Oh, oh," she said. "They are magnificent perfection. You could commit suicide."

Mr. Carson accepted a plateful.

"Suicide," Grandma said proudly.

"Suicide," Mr. Carson agreed.

Grandma was dressed in a flowered-cotton housecoat. It was one of Grandma's principles to wear flowered-cotton housecoats. She also had a large wardrobe, of which she was very proud, and to which she was constantly adding. She tried on new clothes several times a day, modeled them, and then returned them to the closet. "Isn't your grandma chic?" she would say. "I'm just not like other grandmothers, poor things, what they wear. Oh, oh. None of those hideous fancy frills for me. Little old ladies. Ha. Some little old lady. Sleek and elegant, sleek and elegant—that's just my style." And it was true. Grandma did not dress like other grandmothers. Her clothes were perfect: stylish without being silly, elegant but not ostentatious. She would model them for Willie's video camera, one hand on her hip, the other at the back of her head. "There," she would say after a while. "That's enough. *Ex*-quisite. Was the camera on? Oh, you'll cherish that film. A record of a bygone era, when life was gracious and beautiful. Ach, you poor children, what I've lived to see, to see, to see. Ah, well, feel this belt, Alice. The softest, the finest Italian leather. Well, you know your grandma. Only the very finest. Top of the drawer." Then the clothes would be returned to the closet, to be taken out again only for the occasional trips to Forty-seventh Street her grandmother required to update her collection of gigantic jewelry and to keep up her spirits.

Grandma stood beside Mr. Carson as he ate, a spatula with more crepes suzettes poised eagerly beside his plate. Alice had never seen her grandmother offer food to a person not related at least by marriage, preferably by blood. But here was Grandma emptying plastic bags, defrosting, heating, serving up plate after plate to a complete outsider. The whole family was demoralized, even Grandma.

"This is an honor," Mr. Carson said to her.

"This is history," said Grandma.

"When do we discuss business?" Alice said. "I mean, this is war, the gloves are off, we're out for blood." She paused for dramatic effect, then said: "I have entered Louie Scifo's name on *every mailing list in existence.*"

Brenda looked at her, then broke into a great smile.

"Several times," Alice said. "Louis Scifo, Lou Scifo, L. Ouiescifo . . ."

Brenda periodically received brochures addressed to Louie Scifo announcing things like "Cross Your Fingers Holidays—*Just Outside* Sunny Atlantic City—You Bet!" and "The Sure Thing Report: You too can be a Winner, by following Our System, fool proof, TESTED BY EX-

PERTS, you can make a MILLION $—or more." Alice had found them inspirational.

"I've also called the EPA," Alice said. "I reported Louie for noise pollution and illegal dumping of toxic waste."

"You mean, he shouts and pours chemicals on the lawn?" Mr. Carson asked.

Alice smiled happily. That had been Peter's idea. Peter was extremely supportive of Alice's new campaign. Peter was a wonderful husband.

"Next, I thought we could sue for defamation of character. Why, he calls Mom a whore," she said. "The little shit. And, of course, indecent exposure."

Mr. Carson raised his eyebrows and stopped eating. "He does that?"

"Probably," Alice said.

And, she announced, it cheered her to think that the legal standard for determining negligence was what the reasonable man would or would not do. "That one will be a cinch."

"Lawsuits cost money," Mr. Carson said.

"But think of all the money we've *saved* because of Louie. No trips, no restaurants, no movies . . ."

That morning, Alice had woken up early and sat in bed with Peter's clipboard, listening to the birds and to the soft clacking of Peter's computer keys as they each tried to compile a list to show Mr. Carson. She heard a commotion and looked outside to see six blue jays attacking a bigger bird, some kind of goatsucker, probably a whippoorwill, although wishful thinking made her leave open the possibility of its being a chuck-will's-widow beyond its northernmost range. Ah, she thought. Clever birds. Mobbing, an exciting and sensible bird behavior, a preemptive group strike against an intruder. A miracle, she thought. A miracle of nature. She added the goatsucker, which she finally gave in and identified as a whippoorwill, to her bird list, then she went back to her other list. They could claim Louie had violated the RICO laws when he contracted to build the house, and could go after him for racketeering. They could sue him for assault and battery: his physical presence was a kind of assault; the fear that he would hurt them a kind of battery.

"And of course destruction of private property," Alice explained to Mr. Carson. "The mailbox, the tires, the glass door, the lawn . . ."

"Lost future earnings," said Peter, "actual costs . . ."

"Libel. Remember that stuff he wrote on Mom's check? That was *libel*. He claimed Mom owed him money, which she didn't. That check passing through the banks with that stuff on it. It's *published* to the banking concern. Could ruin her credit rating. Oh, and here's one you'll especially like—violation of civil liberties. His activities have deprived us of our basic freedoms."

Alice and Peter smiled proudly at Mr. Carson.

"This will tie him up in endless litigation," Mr. Carson said. Alice and Peter nodded. "But it will also tie *you* up in endless litigation."

"Yes," said Alice.

"I thought you wanted to get rid of Louie," Mr. Carson said. "You don't need to do this to get the restraining order. You people are insane."

"Exactly," Peter said. "We've already seen a psychiatrist. Well, we had to prove damages, elevate this stuff to a tort, right?"

Thompson Zalman had agreed to formally issue whatever complaints Alice and Peter could come up with. "We're sort of paying him by the yard," Alice told Mr. Carson. Then the letters between the lawyers would begin, more and more letters, accusations, denials, pleadings, costing Louie more and more money. If Louie could be a nuisance, they could be more of a nuisance. If they could not defeat him with grave justice, they could nip loudly at his heels with every absurd possibility of civil law.

Mr. Carson was frowning. He shook his head sadly when Grandma offered him a plate of radish roses.

"You can't win any of these suits," he said.

"Well, no, probably not," Peter said.

"It's unorthodox, though, isn't it?" Alice said. "You've got to admit, it's unorthodox."

"That's true," Mr. Carson said, brightening a bit. "That's true." He folded his fingers on his belly and sat quietly for a moment. "I'm *very* unorthodox, you know."

July 26
Westport

1. 1 rib cage, herring gull
2. 1 tail, blue jay

Alice drove about ten minutes until she got to an old red barn in the next town. The noise of the swallows who lived inside, far up in the rafters, was immense. Below them, a Pekinese with a yellow bow in its hair lay chained to a chair. When Alice walked in, the dog began yapping wildly, pulling at its chain.

"Hello, PeeWee," Alice said. The dog bared its white teeth, each one the size of a grain of rice, and ran forward until the chain yanked it back. "Hello, Mrs. Smithley."

Mrs. Smithley was the farmer's wife. She liked Alice because Alice liked vegetables, and always had, even as a child.

"PeeWee, sit," Mrs. Smithley called out, and the dog jumped, like a puppet, onto Mrs. Smithley's wide lap. Mrs. Smithley always sat on a yellow webbed chair, from which she handed out brown paper bags to her customers and weighed the vegetables. "Who's that fella in the car, Alice, gaping at you?"

"Oh, that's just Louie. He follows us."

"Does he want corn? Joe's bringing in corn."

"Well, I do," Alice said.

Mrs. Smithley fed PeeWee a dog treat and said her blood pressure was up. Then she told Alice never to get the gout.

"Okay," Alice said. She looked in the wooden bins to see if there were any string beans. Last week, she had walked out with Joe Smithley to the bean patch and helped him pick them, and she'd felt like a child on an outing. Visiting the Smithleys was always a little like a field trip. They had been there forever—they were both in their eighties—and Mr. Smithley's father had been there before them. They didn't own the twenty or so acres they farmed. Some rich, indulgent people did, and the Smithleys were allowed to farm the land until they wanted to stop, which clearly would not be until they died, both of them, in place, Mrs. Smithley with her feet up, a brown paper bag in her hand, Mr. Smithley behind the wheel of his ancient pickup truck, twine tied around the ankles of his overalls, a pith helmet on his head.

From the dark barn, Alice looked out at the cornfield. The cornfield had been the highlight of the rides she used to take on her horse. The flat dirt track that ran along the edge, a stone wall on one side, the tall stalks on the other, was where people took their horses to gallop, one of the few open stretches in the increasingly congested suburb.

Several other people had come in to wait for corn, women who carried little lidded baskets as purses and wore crisp Bermuda shorts. They discussed an upcoming flower show with Mrs. Smithley. Outside, Louie, looking bored, was gunning the motor of his car, sending exhaust fumes into the barn. In the distance, Alice could see the dust from Mr. Smithley's truck. She thought: Perhaps it will envelop Louie in a choking cloud and make him disappear.

The other ladies spotted the dust, too, and began tapping their boat shoes in excitement at corn, fresh, really fresh, just in from the field, but Alice was a little disappointed Mr. Smithley would be back so soon. For one thing, she loved the cool barn and the cheeping of the swallows and Mrs. Smithley with her hair held back by a child's pink plastic barrette. For another thing, she was engaged in a carefully planned skirmish against Louie: a volley of fiercely boring waits. She had already been to the Laundromat, which was unnecessary since there was a perfectly good washing machine and dryer in the house, but somehow that made it seem an even cleverer idea to Alice. Then she'd gone to the post office, not the little one near the beach, which was usually empty, but the big, crowded one downtown. There was plenty of unpleasant traffic to drive through, which was gratifying, and she was particularly pleased also because she could remember being left in the car when she was a child to wait for her mother in the post office's treeless parking lot, where she knew Louie would park and wait. It had been unbearably hot.

Ha ha ha, she'd thought, standing in the long line to buy stamps with a picture of Babe Ruth on them.

Alice politely fought over the ears with the other ladies, each one eyeing her neighbor, eyeing the ear she wanted, reaching quickly, but ready to withdraw if someone had the poor taste to reach for the same ear.

"You look at the silk, the color of the silk," said Mr. Smithley. "Light silk means younger corn."

"Never mind the silk, take the small ones," said Mrs. Smithley. "The small ones are the youngest. Obviously."

Alice laboriously opened each ear, stripping it down one side to inspect the size of the kernels. It was all so young and tender that it didn't really matter, but she wanted to take her time. She knew Louie must be squirming with impatience. Alice ran her finger along the gleaming-white kernels, cool and fragrant. She picked a tiny curled worm off the tip.

"Deer got some, too," Mr. Smithley said.

There were two skinny, rusted tractors, decades old and held together with string in some places, parked outside beneath some trees. In the spring Mr. Smithley would climb aboard one, Mrs. Smithley and her gout would somehow climb aboard the other, and they would plow their fields. Beyond the tractors was the chicken coop, where a dozen or so noisy red hens cackled and scratched. And then, farther back, in what used to be a series of horse pastures, were several massive new houses.

"Saw a coyote," Mr. Smithley said.

"Here?" Alice said. She thought coyotes lived in the West. "You mean a fox?"

Mr. Smithley shook his head. "Coyote," he said.

Alice heard a horn honking and glanced back at the driveway in front of the barn. It was Louie, looking angry and leaning on his horn. He held up his arm, glared at her, and began furiously tapping at his watch.

The next day, Alice gathered her family together on the porch for a meeting. "Reports?" she said. She already knew most of what had gone on yesterday while she was driving around with Louie in pursuit. But she believed these regular, formal strategy sessions were essential for morale. "Grandma?"

"Well, as you know, I did exactly what you desired, sweetheart, a plan carried out to perfection, executed with experience and skill, because, after all, that's just the way I am. About everything. I did my brownie wrapping—all of it, and remember, it was *two* batches—on the porch so Louie would have to watch me," Grandma said. "It was very, very tedious."

"Good," Alice said. "Annoy and Destroy. That's the strategy."

"I checked the mailbox while Louie was following General Alice here around town during troop maneuvers," Peter said when Alice nodded at him. "The subject received twelve pieces of junk mail, some of them repeats."

"Twelve?" Alice said. She clapped her hands with delight.

"Yeah, and then I watched him open them, after you two got back. He did not seem thrilled with any of it, not even the catalogue for polyurethane packing and mailing aids or the one for stylish, never-noticeable incontinence protective briefs. I also sat in the garden and listened to the Mets game on the Walkman and made loud, excited, tantalizing but unilluminating exclamations while he hid in the bushes."

"Good, good. Mom?" Alice said, waiting for her mother's report. "Mommy?"

"What?" Brenda said.

"What do you mean, what?"

"What?"

Her mother was not cooperating. Perhaps because her assignment was less glamorous than the others, Alice thought. Alice had reasoned that Louie was watching them in order to keep track of Brenda. Therefore, everyone should come out of the house and present him with things to watch, a display of boring, routine detail—everyone but Brenda. Her job was to hide.

"Mom, this is *fun*," Alice said.

"I guess so," Brenda said.

"As for the western front," Alice continued, "Willie is meeting with Mr. Carson about our New York campaign as we speak. And I will be returning this morning to the warm and friendly office of Thompson Zalman to discuss our various Connecticut lawsuits, to which we will be adding reckless endangerment, thanks to Grandma's quick reflexes and courageous disregard of physical danger when she pushed her foot through the rotten plank on the porch, which, of course, Louie built . . ."

"The pain!" Grandma said, and Alice thought how nicely her grandmother would do in court. Then she pressed the buttons on her golf scorers, the ones her mother had handed out last fall for her experiments. Alice had finally decided how to use hers. The left one would score Louie's victories, the one on her right wrist would score her own and her family's.

"That's not how you use them," Brenda told her. "You're supposed to modify behavior. Your own behavior."

"I am," Alice said.

Then everyone stood on the porch to see what Louie would pull out of the Margate mailbox that morning. With her telescope, usually used to identify shorebirds padding around in the distance at low tide, Alice could easily make out an impressive stack of white business envelopes, which Louie opened there in the driveway, tearing up some of the letters inside.

"More junk mail!" Alice exclaimed happily.

He stuffed the other letters in his pocket.

"More lawsuits!"

It was gray the next morning and Alice was kneeling behind a pile of dead branches. Louie had retaliated for the junk mail by pouring sugar into Brenda's gas tank the night before, but so what, Alice thought. She aimed her camera on its gunstock at the Pinto and whispered, "Rat-a-tat-tat."

Louie called most of Brenda's aunts and uncles in Florida and told them that as a friend, "a caring person," he was very, very worried about their niece, and the aunts and uncles became convinced that Brenda and her mother had cancer, and the children, too, probably, God forbid, a belief that no argument could shake. "You're not telling us," they would say plaintively when Brenda tried to explain.

Alice scored that a 5—five relatives had called Brenda—and clicked the golf scorer on her left wrist five times. Louie was ahead. But by the next day Alice's team was catching up. An appraiser from the town tax office appeared. She had received an anonymous call saying the house was under-appraised, she told them, "so I had to check it out, but, you know, looking at it, with all this rot and the leaky roof and the plumbing and the dead trees and all, I think this property has been over-appraised." Brenda's taxes went down.

"Fun!" Alice said.

Louie had also composed a list, forwarded to Brenda by his lawyer:

These personal garments and furnishing items that belong to me are required by me and must be returned, *to me*, without fail or any delay:

    lovely (three and a half carat) diamond ring complete with
        36 other diamonds
    glass paperweights (never used)
    two diamond watches (mint condition)
    sofa (*seven* feet long)
    two white plastic end tables
    one mechanical pencil
    two teleprompter cable TV control boxes (2)
    big frying pan
    personal items (new)
    crystal (glasses)
    all personal items
    clock radio (digital)
    glasses (crystal)
    blue-velvet suit, Nehru style
    electric construction tools (mine)

all other personal items
wall-to-wall carpet in apartment (blue in color)
dome-leaf diamond ring (custom-made)
personal clothing items, including but not limited to one
    blue-velvet suit . . .

The list went on for several pages and included tote bags Louie had given Alice and Willie as presents, a folding cot left behind with Brenda when some friends moved away from Westport, and several old blankets taken from the woman Louie had once lived with. The blankets had long since been sent, with Louie's knowledge, to a relief agency for victims of an Italian earthquake.

Brenda showed Alice an annotated copy of the list she was planning to send back to Louie's lawyer. In pencil, in a tiny hand, Brenda had scratched out her objections and comments, things like: "In his safe-deposit box," or "Gift from my mother," or simply, "Mine." Its appearance, the formal body of text with the penciled asides, reminded Alice of documents she had seen as a graduate student, medieval manuscript pages on which bored scribes had doodled and scribbled in the margins, leaving messages like "My feet are cold" to pass down through the centuries.

August 1
Westport

1. 67 cicada shells

🌹 / It was difficult to take Mr. Carson seriously, until Mr. Carson himself became serious. Then for
a moment he would sit down, hang his head, and give a
small, sad sigh, as if he were being reprimanded by a
starched nanny, looming strict and invisible above him.

"Okay, okay," Gianni Carson would say to his spectral
governess. "Okay." And he would lay aside his boisterous
jokes and thunderous laugh, closing the toy-chest lid with
a resigned thump.

"Tonight," he said to Brenda on one of these occasions.
He had ridden up to Westport on his motorcycle and was
now sitting in the garden. Alice, hidden in one of Louie's
grassy bunkers, snooped on them for a while, but came out
and put down her camera when she saw Brenda bring out
a pitcher of ice tea.

"Working hard, dear?" Brenda said to her. "I'm so
proud of you."

"Tonight," Mr. Carson said, "we'll finish this off."

"Oh, good," said Brenda, as if it were already settled,
just like that, and Louie a thing of the past.

"We'll go on a date."

"You and Louie?" Alice asked.

"Brenda and me. On a date. A date with destiny."

Alice considered saying, "Destiny Who?" But Mr. Carson looked too serious. "Can I come?" she said instead.

She felt a little left out. And what was this date about, anyway? If it was important, if it had something to do with Louie Scifo's demise, she wanted to be in on the kill. "I'll take pictures."

"I don't need pictures, Alice my friend. I've got . . . this!" And Mr. Carson dramatically pulled open his shirt to reveal a miniature recorder taped to his large waist.

When Brenda and Mr. Carson left the house that evening, they looked like a contented, prosperous couple. Mr. Carson was all tucked in and scrubbed down, and Brenda was wearing white pants and a navy-blue sweater, as if she were heading for the yacht club. Then she pulled on the red helmet and they climbed onto the motorcycle and left. They were bound for New York City, Mr. Carson's territory. "There's no place like New York," Brenda had said earlier. "It could be Rome, or *Paris*." Alice waved as she watched them leave. Then she waved to Louie, who followed close behind.

THE TAPE THAT GIANNI MADE

LS: Sir, sir, can I, you know, talk with you for a moment?

GC: Huh?

LS: I'm Louie. Louie Scifo. You're, uh, with a, you know, *friend* of mine.

GC: Oh, yeah?

LS: So, the, uh, lady could go get a table, sit down—I'm not, I'm not Hitler. Or anything.

BB: Is that all right . . . darling?

GC: Anything you say, dear.

LS: Okay, finish up, good, go, go. Now, sir, kindly excuse me. What is your name, you follow?

GC: Gianni.

LS: Okay, so, Jonathan, what is your last name?

GC: I don't even know you, pal.

LS: Hey, I introduced *myself*, you understand? With my last name. But okay, if you want to be like that, so cold, so unfriendly. I mean, who am I to dare to ask your name, just a stranger.

GC: Exactly.

LS: A stranger in need, you follow?

GC: Look, mister, I just came here to get some dinner.

LS: So okay, okay, buddy. Brenda—the lady, the lady in question—and myself. We've been living together. Nine years. *Fifteen* years. I see her out with a fella, you understand? Now that's what I'm saying.

GC: Excuse me, are you married to her?

LS: Well, no, not married. Not in so many words. Common law, you follow?

GC: You're living with her?

LS: Well, no, not living with her, No I'm not . . . Hey! Are *you* living with her?

GC: I just met her.

LS: Aha! That's what I mean!

GC: Um, Mr. Scifo—that is your name, isn't it?—Mr. Scifo, who is that girl over there? She seems to want to speak to you.

LS: What? That girl with the clipboard, the, uh, Oriental type of young lady? She's nothing, no one. Ignore her. Young lady, this is not China. Am I right? Beat it, you follow? Okay, so, then all the furnishings in that apartment belong to me, all of them. Seventy-five percent. The house. The money that I, that I loaned to put into the house. Are you married? No? Oh. So, I just want to explain myself, that I'm very involved with her, and I'd like to get her back, and you know, that I don't like any interference.

GC: Are you threatening me?

LS: *Threatening* you? Nooooo, nooooo . . . You're innocent. An innocent bystander, you understand what I mean? But *now*, now you *know* the situation. It's up to you to think about it. In other words, in other words, what I'm trying to say, you follow me?, that it's like a love triangle.

GC: You followed us here to say that? To threaten me?

LS: I was *not* following you—I just happened to *see* you. I have, uh, *friends*, yeah, some, some very dear, dear friends in the neighborhood. And I've seen you before. *With her.* And, well, I am very much in love with this individual. And I want you to *understand*. In other words, I don't want you to get involved, in other words, in the sense where maybe you might think that it's, uh, it's a great, a great *opening* for you.

GC: I asked her if she was seeing anyone, and she said no.

LS: You, a stranger, asked that to her? Well I *happen* to be her boyfriend.

GC: Well, that's not what she said.

LS: Well, yeah, but, you know, she broke off from me. In other words, we had just come back from Florida, you understand? I took her to Florida, you understand, and then back in New York all of a sudden, it's a complete shock to me, all of a sudden it's a break-off. You follow me? Are you a, uh, married man? Divorced, right? Where'd you meet her? Heh, now, look, I'm trying to be nice. I *happen* to be *jealous* . . . *I'm* not here to harass *you* . . . Listen, do you *know* my last name? Scifo. *Italian* name. I'm what you might call connected.

GC: You're threatening me.

LS: No, no, I'm *saying*. I have loads of friends that, that are *concerned*. I am sick about the situation. You know, I'm trying to say, while you build up her morale, you understand what I'm trying to say? Then I have no *chance*, you follow what I mean?

GC: Look, this is probably upsetting Brenda and—

LS: *Her?* Well, Jonathan, don't upset *me*. Now bear it in mind, if you think that there's any, uh, involvement with her, for you, that I'm around. There's going to be interference, because *I am around*. And there's furnishings involved, too.

GC: You're threatening to annoy me if I continue to see Brenda?

LS: Look, you have to understand one thing, Jonathan. I'm going to tell you one thing. *(Whispered) She's going through the change of life*. And that is probably why all this here upsetting situation . . . You understand? I'm man-to-man with you. In other words, it's a ticklish situation. You're not the first one. There was another man. Another man. That was involved with her. That actually slept with her. At the Yale Club. All right? But that man got the word. And he stayed away. My friends *talked* to him. Because they knew how upsetting I was. How *upset* I was. Because, see, Jonathan, I feel this way—if it was a trial separation and then a final separation, then there's understanding, you know what I'm trying to say?

GC: But you weren't married.

LS: Jonathan, Jonathan, don't be a lawyer. Okay? Don't act like a lawyer. Seventeen years of living with her—it's *com-*

mon law marriage. Okay? So don't, don't be like an attorney. In other words, try to bear . . . Don't get aggressive. Try to bear with my feelings, okay?

GC: Your friends scared this man away?

LS: Noooooo. No, no, no. They *talked* to him. In my behalf.

GC: But this man cared for her and—

LS: No, he *didn't* care for her. It was just a, a, a *fling*! In other words, he didn't care for her. Don't you understand? They talked to him in my behalf and he understood. He understood. You see, he understood. Jonathan, let me tell you something—it's a *triangle love affair*. In other words, you're *in the middle*.

(Silence for a moment)

LS: Jonathan? I am very deeply in love with her. At this point, I don't know *what* I'll do . . .

GC: You're threatening me again.

LS: You see, Jonathan, Jonathan, you don't let me finish. Threat. You don't let me finish the sentence. In other words, you're interrupting. Okay? At this point I don't know what I would do—whether I would accept it and stay clear or whether I would be a nuisance and try and win her back. You follow me? Okay. Now the point is, you're an innocent bystander. You've heard of these things where, where, a guy is jealous and he creates problems and so forth. I want you to have compassion.

GC: Look, I think very highly of Brenda—

LS: How do you think very highly of her? You just met her.

GC: Oh, for heaven's sake.

LS: Jonathan, Jonathan, you're being very abrupt, Jonathan. You want to punch me in the mouth, Jonathan? Is that it? Because that's the way you're talking. I'm being a gentleman here. I'm being a gentleman and talking to you nice. And, and, you're telling me, *in a flat manner*, you're telling me that you're ready to hit me. It's the *way* you said, "Oh, for heaven's sake," Jonathan. Very abrupt. Like you want to hit me, Jonathan. Which I wish you would. I wish you would, Jonathan. I really wish you would. I tell you what, Jonathan. One phone call, Jonathan. I've got connections, all right? She's a woman I want back. Eight years, Jonathan, eight or ten years. You just had sex with her. Over a decade! Years of breaking my ass. Putting out money. Building a house with my own hands. A dozen years, Jonathan. Nearly. You think you're going to scare me?

GC: Come on.

LS: You're *not* trying to scare me, Jonathan? You certainly *are*, Jonathan. You're not even, you're, you're, you're not even man enough to tell me your last name! How long do you think it would take me to find out? One phone call, Jonathan. I was being a gentleman. Don't you understand that? I was being a gentleman and I said, "What's your last name?" "None of your business." I mean, you don't talk to me like that. Jonathan, remember, you don't talk to me like that. I came to you as a brokenhearted person. I *don't* threaten. That's *finding out*. The phone call is *finding out*. Why should I threaten you? I told you, you're an innocent bystander. Really. You got sucked into this just like she sucked somebody else in. All right, you met her. She's gonna give you a whole line of baloney. Okay? And she's gonna try for you to go on her side because probably you had sex with her—Jonathan, Jonathan, that's a *statement*. Because when you said, "That's none of your business," you know what I mean? That puts a bug in my head. Don't you understand what I'm saying? That puts a bug in my head. You want to talk to her, go ahead. She's seventy-five percent reliable. Seventy-five percent. Go ahead, go ahead . . . Talk with her, go out with her, have sex with her. I spoke to her psychiatrist. You understand? She's going through the change of life. Psychiatric problems. The truth. Listen, I've seen a doctor of psychiatry. I *am* a doctor of psychiatry. I consulted with a colleague, distinguished, you follow? Because what happened was, that with my following her, and my sleeping in the car, and my spying on her . . . I collapsed. And I ended up in the hospital.

GC: I'm, uh, sorry to hear that . . .

Alice put on her party dress. Her funeral dress, actually. She did not have a blouse with a big bow like Patty Hearst's, which she regretted. But the dress was a modest, somber, unremarkable garment, and it seemed just the thing. Peter put on his wedding suit, Grandma got out of her housecoat into a chic but respectable gray dress, and Brenda wore a suit bought especially for the occasion. They were going to court.

They had two court dates—the first, this one in New York, the other in Connecticut later that week. The tape had been the last piece of evidence Gianni Carson felt he needed, and he was already in court when they got there, waiting for them, rubbing his hands in happy impatience.

They sat in the echoing courtroom. Lawyers shuffled around with yellow pads and big, dark-bound books. Their clients sat, some in little whispering clusters, some alone, motionless and silent. Alice had never been inside a courtroom before, and she was surprised at the activity in the large, airless room. Hushed echoes of nervous conversation, angry jokes; clicking footsteps; someone getting up, someone else sitting down, people squeezing in and out of the long pews. She had expected to see rows of silent citizens, like the audience in a theater. Instead, the milling crowd paid little attention to the judge, who never used his gavel or talked above a whisper.

Alice heard a scramble behind her, the scuffle of feet, a loud voice saying, "Handicapped, handicapped." She turned around to see Louie Scifo entering the courtroom through the heavy wooden doors. He did so with some difficulty, then walked slowly down the center aisle. He was on crutches, and he wore a big white neck brace.

Mr. Carson came in and out of the room, whispering things to Brenda, leafing through notebooks, swinging the big doors.

Louie was summoned out by his lawyer at one point. Alice watched him on his crutches. No blouses with bows for him. He laboriously made his way back up the aisle, his groans almost inaudible.

"The brace, the neck brace." Mr. Carson chuckled. "Oh, it's wonderful. The law is wonderful, wonderful . . ."

Louie's lawyer had been presented with the transcript of the tape and the careful notebooks logging Louie's movements. He was reading them now.

Alice sat on the hard bench and waited. Her mother and grandmother were heatedly discussing a slight Grandma had received from her sister-in-law.

"Mother, it was *fifty* years ago," Brenda said finally.

Alice realized that the judge must be hearing their case, although she herself could hear nothing. Mr. Carson and Louie's lawyer were now standing in front, leaning over the bench talking to the judge. Alice had carefully prepared her testimony. She had decided to cry at certain points of it, which she knew she would probably do anyway. She cried when she was angry. Now, though, she was feeling some stage fright. She remembered seeing an episode on *Divorce*

Court when she was a child. The husband claimed that the wife hit him in the head, or vice versa, and then the kids were called to the stand and broke down under cross-examination to admit that actually they had left a rake on the lawn—they had been *about* to put it away, as asked by their parents several times—and Dad had stepped on it with his heel, the handle banged him on the back of the head, and there you had it. The parents reconciled. What if she, Alice, broke down under cross-examination, said a rake had accidently done all the mischief? What if the children *hadn't* left a rake there at all, all those years ago, and, like Alice now, had simply cracked under pressure, had been willing to say anything to get off the witness stand? What if Mom and Louie ended up reconciling in the courtroom? And Dad, too?

"The judge is looking the stuff over," Mr. Carson said, when he returned. "We'll come back again next week."

Alice's disappointment was somewhat softened by her relief at not taking the stand.

As they left the courthouse, they saw Yuki and her clipboard.

"You have victory?" she asked sadly.

🦋 / The idea of a world without Louie still seemed far off, a frail, shimmering vision in the distance, like a mirage or a childish fantasy of heaven. Alice could not quite make it out, even now, as they drove from West-port to Bridgeport for the long-awaited hearing. At last, she thought. But she felt disconnected. Familiar street signs surprised her.

Once in the courthouse, though, she felt better. The building was small and had recently been painted in sooth-ing pastel colors and outfitted with pleasant boxy white chairs. She could have been in elementary school, and she had liked elementary school. Besides, the crowd of people waiting outside the courtroom were her people, her family. They chatted and drank coffee, as giddy and expectant as guests at a wedding awaiting the bride. Alice and Peter had their photographs and charts, Willie his videos. Grandma brought her injured ankle (it had only been slightly bruised to begin with and was now healed, but still she could com-plain quite convincingly of the pain). Even Aunt Beverly had come.

They waited to be called in, watching Thompson Zalman scribble things in a leather-bound notepad with a slender gold pen. Alice looked around her comfortably. This time, if she had to testify, she would. Everyone would now get to see her Connecticut photographs—*Louie Does Westport!*—which had, unfortunately, not been admissible in New York State. She had brought her camera with her to record this event, too, thinking it would go nicely at the end of the final volume of the notebooks.

She looked around for something to shoot. The most obvious thing was Louie. But Louie, she realized, was not there.

"Where is he?" she asked Willie.

"I don't know," Willie said. He peered into the courtroom, then shook his head. Louie was not there, either.

Once, Mr. Zalman approached. "Mrs. Brody, kindly follow me," he said and ushered her into the courtroom, which caused some excitement among her entourage. But when she came out she said the judge only wanted to know where Mr. Scifo was.

Mr. Scifo? Alice thought. *Mr.?* As in *Mr.* Mephistopheles?

Louie's lawyer was bustling to and from the pay phone, into and out of the courtroom, dabbing at his red face with a handkerchief. He had no idea where Louie could be.

Alice stood holding her camera and felt the anger of the past year rising up inside her until her ears were ringing. This time, Louie Scifo, Mr. Louie Scifo, had *not* followed them.

"No sense of behavior, of *etiquette*," said Grandma.

Aunt Beverly looked grim. She had received several of Louie's phone calls, and despite everything everyone told her, she was determined that Brenda was on the threshold of death, and that Alice, Peter, Willie, and Grandma were treading close behind. "AIDS," she kept whispering to herself. "Tsk, tsk. AIDS . . ."

Finally, after several hours, an annoyed judge issued a subpoena. Louie was cited for contempt of court. It was not what they had come for, but a subpoena! Alice took a picture of the judge as he waited for the elevator. Perhaps Louie would go to jail!

✎ / It was midsummer now in Westport, the air hot and heavy, the frogs and crickets forming a noisy ring around the house, the bees swarming in the walls, living out their intense lives like loud neighbors. The stream at the bottom of the hill dribbled quietly by. The muddy water of the pond was almost invisible beneath a thick green covering of algae. Alice woke up in the morning and felt as if she were existing in another, heavier medium, in water or molten lead. The humid air pressed against her, jealous of the space she took up, greedy to expand and push her out. The birds were shrieking, hurling their songs back and forth from branch to branch, hollering threats and warnings and territorial jingoism. The sky outside was nearly white.

"I'm nauseous," Alice said to Peter. He was already awake, examining a complicated computer graph depicting the monthly patterns of Louie's harassment. He had named it a tide-watch graph, and used blue ripples instead of bars. The sight of the statistical waves made Alice dizzy. "I'm nauseous."

"Nauseated," Peter said. "You're nauseated." But Alice knew she was pregnant. Riding home in the car from the courthouse yesterday, she had to hold on to the armrest and stare out the window, straight ahead, the way her mother had taught her to do for nausea when they drove through the Pennsylvania hills to visit Grandma and Grandpa. "We're here because we're here," they would sing when they finally drove up the steep driveway to the stone house. Her grandmother would tell her the sharp points on the Victorian wrought-iron fence were to disembowel burglars. Her grandfather would take her to the shoe store run by three obese brothers, their heads oddly normal atop their bulk, their feet tiny below. Alice thought Scranton was the most glamorous city in the world.

Alice's gynecologist said he could see her the next day, and she and Peter took the train in that night. They went out to dinner at an Indian restaurant but the smell made Alice feel awful, and they left. They came back to their apartment, which looked very substantial to Alice, heavy and large, after her mother's airy little house. Alice collapsed on the couch. With her head in Peter's lap, she listened to the record he had put on, feeling secure and nearly asleep, until startled by a sudden thudding of timpani and brass. Peter grinned down at her. "Berlioz. 'The March to the Scaffold,' " he said. "Just for you, darling."

Alice retreated to the bedroom, got into bed, and thought how much she hated to go to the doctor, any doctor. Memories of the year she'd spent in the hospital became so fresh in a doctor's office. When she lay on the examining table, she could feel the walls moving in, shrinking her world to a place where people in white served her and distressed her, bringing meals on textured plastic trays, pushing long needles into her veins. She would then feel her muscles and spirit slackening, preparing her for prolonged illness, for her new ecological niche.

She had been on her back in the hospital for so many months that, since then, she had learned to appreciate sheets and pillows and every sort of bed as she would a summer cottage: one didn't live there, one retreated there now and again. One made the little nest as pretty as possible and breathed in the fragrance of freshly laundered linens with profound appreciation and gratitude. It was under the covers, half asleep, that Alice sometimes felt most alive, reeling with joy that she didn't have to stay there.

But at the doctor's, on a table, there was only Alice, in a paper gown, on a length of shiny paper that crinkled as she moved; and the confusion she felt at devolving from an effective, vertical person to a horizontal creature of fear and self-pity would sweep over her, forcing tears— of fear and self-pity—from her eyes.

"The test is positive," the doctor said.

Alice sighed with relief. She wasn't pregnant. She wasn't ready to be pregnant. It was probably Dad's fault, but there it was—she wasn't ready. There should be a decent interval between Dad's baby and her own. She and Peter had been hoping to have a baby, until Alice heard her father's news and decided to put it off. She did not want to discuss her morning sickness with a pregnant stepmother. She really didn't. When Alice had heard that Patricia was pregnant, she had consoled herself with the thought that now Patricia would become pallid and dumpy, unable to fit into a single tweed suit. But if Alice was pregnant, she would be fat and gray-faced, too. She would have to wear stupid-looking maternity clothes, dresses that not only made you look like you had a huge stomach, because you

did, but made you look like you were one of Richard
Nixon's daughters, which of course you weren't and nothing could induce you to be. But when you were pregnant, you had no control anymore. It was like being sick.
Richard Nixon's daughters. "Look, Mommy, towels!"
one of them had said on national television, examining
her wedding gifts. Although maybe it was Lynda Byrd
Johnson.

"The test is positive," the doctor said. "Congratulations, Alice."

Alice realized that "positive" meant that she was pregnant. She tried not to cry. This was the miracle of life. But
her thoughts kept veering toward Patricia and Dad. And,
too, whenever she imagined a child being born, she pictured
her artificial hips—the smooth metal ball and the smooth
plastic socket. One would go "Pop." The other would go
"Pop": "Pop, pop," a tragically crippled young mother. But
no, she told herself. You are not sick. This is not a relapse.
The doctors have always told you that having a baby would
be fine. You will not go to the hospital for a year. You will
go for a few days. And you will come home with a sweet
little baby.

"I'll need drugs," she told the doctor. "Drugs. And
what about a cesarean? No, actually drugs will be fine."
They would give her a shot. Her hips would not pop. She
would not writhe in pain like the woman giving birth on
public television.

Alice smiled wanly at Peter in the waiting room. She
made the thumbs-up sign, wondering if he would take it to
mean she was pregnant or was not pregnant. He made a
funny face, hugged her very tight, and began humming the
Berlioz.

They went back to Westport the next day. Willie came with them on the train.

"Willie," Alice said to her brother. "Your sibling-to-be is going to be an aunt."

"Huh?" he said.

Brenda and Grandma picked them up at the station and Alice told them before she had even closed the car door. Fueled by an overwhelming sense of guilt because she had worried about what she would wear even as the miracle of conception had been announced to her, Alice wanted to tell everyone, quickly. And her dismay regarding her pregnant stepmother and even her fears over her hips, though they remained, seemed callow to her, only slightly less callow than her fashion concerns.

"My Harry should only be here," her grandmother said.

Brenda suggested they have a celebration party. And by the time they were driving up their road, Alice felt much better.

"I'm going to take a walk," she said. "Let me off at the school. The ex-school."

Suddenly nostalgic, and quite confident that Louie was in hiding somewhere out of the state, Alice walked past the school-less field and up a road that had once been a swampy path leading to a pond. Hidden deep in the woods, the pond used to be disturbed by no one but a few muddy neighborhood children, some frogs, and a great blue heron. The pond had been drained and several houses built there, but Alice still saw a heron once in a while, flying above her, its great gray wings sweeping up and down, momentarily blocking out the sun. Alice walked along, frightening the chipmunks, sending them hurtling back into gaps in stone walls. The leaves on the trees looked a little weary. They'd lost the earnest green of the spring. Alice felt tired. She turned around and walked back home.

She saw Black Coat sitting by the bent mailbox, panting, his pink tongue just visible in the black fur. Beyond him was her mother's house, deep in the shade, fronted by jungle-size red flowers, the impatiens Brenda had planted over the septic tank. The house looked cool and small and pleasant, better than it had looked to Alice all spring or summer. Alice glanced over at the field and she stood for a moment, staring, as she realized why. The paths that Louie had beaten down, the scruffy clearings and hacked tree trunks, the bald spots and weedy tunnels, had all burst into bloom.

What had once been a thorny tangle of thistles and bracken was now a garden. Wildflowers that had never been able to grow in the dense brush had now rushed to cover the cleared field. Lush vines had draped themselves over fallen trees. Tunnels were transformed into romantic bowers. Pink and white morning glories, growing over arched dead branches, formed arbors over Louie's paths, themselves now blooming with veronica. Everywhere, black-eyed Susans and daisies and pinks and beautiful blue cornflowers stood bright and thick among the airy Queen Anne's lace. Given sun and space, the flowers that had always been squeezed and shaded by close, towering weeds had burst into bloom, turning piles of rubbish into gentle hillocks. The house stood, modest and shady, surrounded by ancient trees and bright new flowers.

"Mom!" Alice said, running into the house. "Look what happened to the field!"

"You know, Louie *told* me he was a master landscaper," Brenda said.

Alice spent a pleasant evening in the new garden. She prowled through the network of trails, breathing in the scent of the flowers, feeling their delicate petals, trying physically to understand that Louie was not there, had not been there always, and need not be there forever into the future. The bees circled and hovered, heavy round bees that looked too large, too ungainly, too poorly designed to ever be able to fly, swooping effortlessly from flower to flower. A hummingbird passed close by Alice's face.

Peter came out and walked with her for a while and listened to the evening birdcalls.

"What is that one?" he asked.

"A flicker."

"That one?"

Alice listened carefully, and then she heard the quiet, breathy buzz of a blue-winged warbler.

"What about that screechy arpeggio, from over there?"

They stayed outside, walking and listening in the flowering meadow, until the mosquitoes rose up in force, at which point Alice and Peter moved inside and thought up stupid names, like Algernon and Allegra, for their child.

When the phone rang, Alice answered it happily, drowsily. Maybe it was Louie offering articles of surrender.

"Alice, it's Daddy."

Alice had reconciled herself to maternity dresses and physical pain, but still she found she could not quite bring herself to tell Dad she was pregnant. He might tell her how Patricia felt when she found out or, worse, how *he* felt when he heard the news. He would lecture her on Lamaze classes and recommend books. She couldn't bear it.

"Oh, hi, Dad," she said as casually as she could.

Dad cleared his throat. Then there was the strangling sound that meant he was crying.

Alice waited, embarrassed, then said, "So, Dad, what's new?"

"Little Rachel," Dad said finally, through his tears. "Your *sister!*"

When the birth of Dad's baby was announced to the household at large, Peter made a face, Brenda looked stunned, Grandma said, "Poor ugly little child," and Willie announced he was becoming celibate. "I mean, this is it. This is, well, it's, well, disgusting. And selfish. And, and, it makes a person, well, reconsider. I mean, it's barbaric. Don't they have birth control up there? This is not the nineteenth century. Is this how people behave in Canada? In Turkey, people don't behave like this. They'd be thrown in a rat-infested prison for the rest of their lives. Well, I don't want to live in a rat-infested prison. Uh-uh. And did I ask for a sister, a half-sister? Did anyone ask for one? Did Dad ask my opinion? People are incredibly selfish, especially Dad. I don't ever want a child of mine to have to say what I'm saying about Dad. So I just won't have any. I will devote myself to my work. No more girls. Sex is dangerous. It's stupid. Big waste of time and energy. Fit only for the likes of Dad. Ugh. It's embarrassing, a little baby. Hasn't Dad read any Freud? Didn't he know this would upset me? Mom wouldn't do this to me, would you, Mom? Of course not. Men are pigs. I'm staying away from women. Dad has ruined my life." And he stomped off to bed.

Alice found Willie's anger and disgust rather touching. It had never occurred to her that he would take the birth of Dad's baby so hard, that he, too, would feel betrayed that there was a child to take his place, and envious and piqued that his father beat him to the punch. When Willie began his complaint tonight, she watched him and she remembered the way he always looked when they talked about Dad—sad and lost and very young. And she realized how hurt he was, not so much by this baby, which, after all, was only a baby, a faraway baby, perhaps even a lovely baby, but how hurt he still was by Dad's departure so many years ago. He had never forgiven Dad. She had never forgiven Dad. Alice had a happy thought: Dad would be sure to do something stupid while bringing up Baby Rachel. And then *she* would never forgive Dad, too.

Alice started toward Willie's room, eager to console him with this reflection, when she suddenly thought of the baby she herself was carrying. Well, it would grow up to be a baby, and then a child and then a teenager and then an adult. And somewhere along the line, Alice would do something stupid, and the baby would never forgive *her*.

"Shit," said Alice.

🦋 / *"The family sits pensively as they drive toward their historic mission,"* Willie boomed into his microphone in the back seat, where he sat with Grandma. He was making a documentary called *Run, Louie, Run*.

"Mmm! Such *talent*," Grandma said.

For weeks, the court had been unsuccessful in locating Louie Scifo. Finally, Brenda was asked if she had any idea where he might be, and she thought of his parents' house in Queens. When she was told the process server would try the address first thing in the morning, Alice and Peter nodded at each other. They knew what they had to do.

But Brenda refused to join them, claiming it was a waste of time.

"No, no, it's beyond time," Alice explained, "an extraordinary gap in the fourth dimension, an endless, satisfying, ineffable metamoment. We leave at dawn."

". . . for there, on a quiet tree-lined street, in a neighborhood known for its quiet tree-lined streets . . ." Willie continued.

Grandma sighed proudly. "Oh, that dirty dog," she

added, "he should rot, that skinny, homely bitch of a crook, what he did to my Brenda."

Alice wondered if Grandma was talking about Louie or her father. Dad was coming to visit soon, wasn't he? He was bringing the infant to Connecticut to make his family spiritually uncomfortable, then taking it to a small Nantucket inn to make complete strangers physically uncomfortable.

". . . but this is not an ordinary day, even here, in this ordinary but unlikely spot, for finally, to this close but tattered American family, for whom fear and suspicion have become daily companions, a new beginning is waiting, a sense of freedom and liberty, just around this modest brick corner . . ."

Peter parked the car down the block and across the street from Louie's parents' house, right behind Louie's blue Pinto.

"Bingo," he said.

It was a quiet street, except for the planes roaring by now and again, almost suburban, with its frame and brick houses, little lawns and rosebushes. One yard was decorated with Christmas lights and model windmills. Three children sat motionless on a stoop, each wearing a Walkman.

Grandma unpacked the refreshments: a fanciful assortment of food knickknacks. The radio was playing something from *La Forza del Destino*, which Peter once said should be translated as *Tough Shit*.

"That Paparazzi, he's so big and fat, how can he sing with that belly?" Grandma said.

"Um, this is a *baritone*," Peter pointed out. "Leonard Warren. He was singing this the night he dropped dead on stage."

"Poor thing."

Alice wondered whether Grandma meant Warren or Pavarotti.

"Oy, yoy. Just like poor Elvis."

Still not sure, Alice turned her attention back to Louie. His parents' red-brick, two-family house had small, lace-curtained windows and a flourishing vegetable patch in the front yard. Nothing was stirring.

"Thank God, thank God your grandpa, so generous, so considerate all his life, left your mommy this wonderful, spacious car," Grandma said. Alice could hear the whir of Willie's camera. "Now, see, Willie, how *comfortable* we are," Grandma continued.

Alice took out her binoculars. She saw some house sparrows and a grackle. A plane slowly lifted itself into the sky. Maybe Louie was on it and would be hijacked, brutally murdered, and thrown, with callous indifference, onto the burning tarmac of a Middle Eastern airport, she thought.

"Flocks of migrating birds sometimes smash into planes and get torn up by the jet engines," she said aloud.

A police car cruised by, the cops looking them over. Alice pointed to a house finch that sang a loud, beautifully phrased song from one of the scraggly trees. The hot sun radiated from the windshield onto her face and neck. She felt this way at the beach, nothing to do, nothing to think about, baking in the sun, waiting. She hated the beach, she decided. She turned the radio off. The children with the Walkmen had gone inside. No one was on the street. Alice could hear what she realized was Willie's soft sleep breathing from the back, as well as occasional mutters of appreciation as Grandma admired herself and her jewelry in a hand mirror. Alice wondered if she would get a tan through the windshield. Then she saw movement, far off, and looked into her binoculars again. It was a motorcycle

approaching. An enormous man drove it. There was someone sitting behind him, too, clinging to his gigantic waist.

"It's Mom!" Alice said. "Mom and Gianni Carson!"

She wondered what had lured her mother there. At
breakfast, Alice had even tried characterizing the expedition
as a picnic. Brenda had paused, obviously tempted. But
then she said, "Alice, you're just teasing me," gathered up
her gardening tools, and took them outside, where she
stretched out on a lounge chair and read yesterday's paper.

"*Here* they are!" Gianni Carson cried as he pulled up
beside the car.

Brenda, smiling, looked from one of them to the next.
"Guess what?" she said.

"You changed your mind and came?" Alice said.

Her mother shook her head.

Alice noticed that her mother was wearing a new helmet—not the red one, which Mr. Carson had on, but a
brilliant blue helmet on which *Brendala* was written in gold
script.

"You got your very own motorcycle helmet?" she said.

Grandma had begun feeding Mr. Carson sandwiches
through the car window. They were shaped like hearts and
diamonds and spades and clubs. Brenda shook her head
again.

"Mom, we give up," Willie said.

"No process server today—that's what we came to tell
you. It's a miracle! Louie signed the voluntary restraining
order. He signed! He got scared of the subpoena. Last night!
He signed, he signed. The wicked witch is dead. Poor
thing."

This was not right, to make peace behind General
Alice's back, to make peace at all, for that matter. She
deserved to see a process server, to see Louie in court, Louie

Scifo in jail. What kind of war ended without a final, glorious battle? Where were the bodies, the smoking cannon? And what happened now? What about all her notebooks and charts, all her plans? Would life be empty without them, would she become depressed and violent, a pathetic, burnt-out vet suffering from Post-Louiescifo Syndrome? God, was she suffering from it already?

"Of course, I did tell his lawyer yesterday that Louie could have all his frying pans and broken clocks," Brenda added. "And now *we* have one thousand feet. He can't come within one thousand feet of me or anyone in my family or my house or my apartment. A thousand feet! I just found out."

"But . . ." Alice said.

"Well, Alice, some cookware—it was a small price to pay."

"We packed everything up so nicely," Mr. Carson said. "Took us all morning, catching all those moths to put in with the Nehru suit, frying that old fish in the pan."

"Mmm, mm, I've never liked fish, not the tenderest, most *ex*-quisite filet of Dover sole," Grandma was saying.

"Willie, put your goddamn camera away, have respect for your mother," Brenda said.

"Fish," Alice said. She sat, distracted, looking at her mother. I like fish, she thought. She began to cry.

"There, there," Brenda said, "never mind. Tomorrow's another day."

"*In a sudden, surprise move that stunned everyone involved in this complex game of legal cat-and-mouse,*" Willie said, "*the defendant, Louie Scifo, has come forward from the obscurity of his Queens, New York, hideout and pledged cooperation with law-enforcement agencies in two states, according to reliable sources close to the case.*"

We sat in the car forever, still and stupid and hot, for nothing, like reptiles on a rock, Alice thought.

"He can't get away with this," she said. "We'll, we'll *sue* him."

Brenda climbed off the bike, shed her blue helmet, and kissed her children, her mother, and Peter through the windows.

"Goodbye!" she said. "We're off. Gianni and I are taking a cross-country trip. A motorcycle tour of America! Las Vegas, the Grand Canyon, Death Valley, up the coast to Big Sur. And Scranton, naturally. I'm so excited! Now, there's cold chicken in the refrigerator, and I took out one of Grandma's cakes so you can celebrate. And there's fresh corn from the farmer's. I'll miss you children so much. And Mother, too. I'm so lucky—I've seen so much of you all this summer. And now, an adventure! We decided this morning, when we heard the good news. Gianni's so unorthodox. Goodbye! I'll call. Why, we can go to Vancouver. Shall we visit Dad and see the child? Well, perhaps not. Goodbye, goodbye!" And as Alice and the others waved, in some confusion, Brenda and Gianni Carson were gone, only the roar of the motorcycle left behind.

"*Motorcycles—freewheelin' adventure or coffins on the go? When we return, we'll discuss the pros and cons . . .*"

"Willie, shut up," Alice said.

"To ride on that monster, I don't know, I don't know, here she's got a beautiful, roomy automobile, practically a limousine . . ." Grandma muttered, shaking her head.

Peter and Alice looked at each other. Peter shrugged his shoulders.

Alice got out of the car. The shorebirds were migrating

south, she thought, and Jamaica Bay was not too far away. Perhaps she should take her family bird-watching. She looked around, hoping for a flock of egrets or plovers. She saw, instead, two small old people, a man in a black suit and hat and a woman with a lace apron over her dress, running down the middle of the street. "Wait! Wait!" the couple were calling. "Hello! Hello!"

Alice looked at Louie's mother and father and wondered why they were running down a city street on a hot day carrying a tray of cookies and plastic party glasses and a bottle of sherry and why, too, they had thought it necessary to spawn such an unpleasant and annoying son.

"To celebrate!" Louie's father said, out of breath, handing round the glasses.

Celebrate? she thought. It wasn't *their* mother who'd been released from persecution. Was Louie so pleased to get his frying pan? She didn't want Louie to be pleased. About anything. Ever.

"The whole family! Here you are on this wonderful day," said the little old man.

"Oh, no, thank you," said Grandma daintily when Mrs. Scifo offered her a cookie from the tray. "Oh, I never eat sweets. Well, just one. For the celebration."

"What celebration?" Alice started to ask, but Louie's father interrupted her with a gleeful cry.

"Here they come!"

Parading slowly, ceremoniously down the street, trailed by a collection of chattering people, came a small man in a white suit and a tall woman, also in white, wearing a veil.

"Ta dum de dum." Louie's father seemed to be singing the wedding march. "Ta dum de dum . . ."

"The happy couple!" said Louie's mother.

"Petey, Petey, Petey!" said Louie Scifo, now beside the car in his dazzling suit, leaning in the window and pointing a finger up at the woman beside him. "William! Granny! And, of course, Alice," he added, straightening up and facing Alice over the roof of the car. "May I have the pleasure, the honor, to introduce you to my rosy future, a credit to the lovely female sex, the lucky, lucky person of my dreams, my . . . wife!"

The bride threw back her veil.

"Mrs. Pond!" Alice cried.

"Mrs. Scifo!" Louie finished. "The second," he added, looking at his mother.

"The third," Alice said loyally, thinking of his dead wife, her family's benefactress. She stared at the couple, gawked, moving into the street to get a closer look. Mrs. Pond. Mrs. Pond was wearing her mother's "very large" diamond ring—the one Louie had demanded back in his letter even though Brenda had returned it long before. Mrs. Pond was married to Louie Scifo. Mrs. Pond was Mrs. Scifo. "Mrs. Pond," Alice said again.

"Yes, I think I will use Pond," Mrs. Pond said, importantly smoothing the sides of her white dress—a white business-lady suit, actually. "Here in America, Baronessa de Scifo would be de trop, I suppose. Such darling, modest people, dropping the title."

"Yeah," Alice said.

"I'm so happy I could share this with you, Alice. You don't get out much, do you, dear? Socially."

Alice smiled.

"But how *are* you, dear? Really?" Baronessa Pond whispered. "Peter didn't lose his job or anything, did he? His occupation is so . . . uncertain."

"I love weddings," Alice said.

". . . and here's Caroline, my little bridesmaid . . ." Mrs. Pond was saying.

Caroline glared at her mother and at Louie. Then she glared at Alice.

"Don't even speak to me," she said. "Don't even *try* to apologize."

"I didn't know they'd get *married*," Alice said.

Willie got out of the car to film the festivities.

"*A touch of tradition, a tie to the Old Country, this joyous reception in the street has, for a brief moment, transformed this Queens, New York, gutter into Renaissance Siena, a colorful piazza, a nuptial Palio . . .*"

Alice realized that a receiving line had formed.

"We saw you," said Louie as he pumped her hand. "From the window there. I happened to recognize the car, you understand what I'm saying? I said to Mrs. Scifo, the new Mrs. Scifo, I said, 'The Brodys!' You understand me, Alice? We came to you. We want to share with you. We want to be with you . . . Where's Mommy?"

"What is your reaction?" Willie kept asking everyone, shoving his microphone, and the video camera it was attached to, into their faces. Grandma was out of the car, too, chatting with Louie's mother. Alice looked in at Peter, still behind the wheel, his shirt plastered to his chest, his eyes closed.

A cab pulled up and honked loudly. The wedding party, gathered in the middle of the street, pressed up against Brenda's Buick to let it pass.

"I love weddings," Alice said again, her chin on the roof just beside Ms. Pond-Scifo's chin.

The cab slowly inched past them.

"This is *not* the Triborough Bridge, my good man," cried a voice inside. A baby bleated.

Alice stiffened. What is the date? she wondered in sudden horror. Is the date the twenty-first? Because if the date is the twenty-first . . . She turned and saw, in the back seat of the crawling taxi, a man and a woman and a bundle of pink blankets.

"Driver!" said the man, who was, she admitted to herself with both resignation and wonder, definitely Alan Brody, her father. He was leaning forward, banging on the plastic divider. "Driver! This will not do!"

"There, there, don't cry," said the woman in a motherly voice that belonged, there was no getting around it, to Patricia Hum Brody. "Although certainly this novel and arduous journey must be somewhat overwhelming to someone of your limited experience."

Maybe they will just drive away, Alice thought. And not see me.

"What is your reaction?" Willie asked suddenly, shoving his video camera in through the cab's open window.

"Driver! Stop! This *will* do, after all."

"Dad? Patricia! Hello. I didn't know you were coming to Louie's wedding. Of course, I didn't know we were coming. I didn't know he was getting married. What is your reaction anyway?" He paused, then said, "Hello, kid," and waved, rather feebly, at the blankets in the cab.

"Alice!" Alan Brody cried.

"Welcome to Queens, Dad."

"Alice," he said tenderly. "It's fate. 'My fate cries out . . .' " He got out of the cab carrying the bundle of blankets, then inserted it in a denim halter that hung from his shoulders. Alice saw a small wrinkled face. She heard another bleat.

"Rachel!" she said. "Patricia!" she said to the pale,

drawn woman smiling bravely from inside the taxi. "What an unexpected pleasure. And isn't she beautiful."

Patricia, obviously dazed, her eyes darting from Alice and Willie to Alan Brody and the baby to the wedding guests sipping sherry, said "How do you do?" several times.

The driver was unloading the trunk. Dad clutched a baby backpack, a large carton of disposable diapers, and a folded nylon-and-aluminum Port-A-Crib. The baby pouch, the only piece of paraphernalia on active duty, still hung on his chest, like a medal. Alice could not take her eyes off it. Dad suddenly gulped, put the stuff down on the sidewalk, and burst into tears. "Tempus fugit, Alice," he said, trying to hug her without suffocating Rachel the Infant, who could barely be seen, just the very top of her little head. (She is bald! Alice noticed.) "Tempus fugit. That's what my father told me when you were a baby, the very first time he saw you. That's what I'm passing on to you today."

Alice sensed there was something wrong with the analogy, but she just nodded.

"You'll drive us, Alice. This driver is impossible. Lost, insolent, almost certainly a Communist and possibly a habitual drug abuser as well."

"Dad!"

But the driver, lifting out a stroller, a car seat, and a baby bath, appeared to understand no English. "Yes, Triborough Bridges. Excellent, excellent," he kept saying in a heavy Eastern European accent.

Patricia climbed out of the taxi and looked around.

"What colorful local festivities," she said. "Perhaps we're interrupting."

"It's fate, that's all. 'Who can control his fate?' "

"Fate can be discourteous, too, Alan," Patricia said, somewhat sternly.

Gee, Alice thought. She looked at Patricia with a rush of tenderness.

"Now, Alice, have we trespassed in terms of social propriety?" Patricia asked. "Please be frank."

"Naah," Alice said. Not only had Patricia questioned Dad, an endearing act in and of itself, but her politeness suddenly struck Alice as a pure and delicate thing, an embrace of life, a moral statement as earnest and unchanging as the laws of nature. Her manners and conversation were not petty, relentless, hostile assaults, as Alice had always thought. They were profound, instinctive, lavish expressions of the endless search for unity and peace, for eternity.

"Aren't you tired?" Alice said. After all that searching and whatnot. "Take a load off your feet." She opened the door to the Buick and Patricia got in with a sigh.

"Your father needed to reaffirm his heritage, I know, and to expose Rachel to her American birthright in the historical atmosphere of Nantucket Island. Dual nationality is demanding. But I *am* tired. Post-partum fatigue . . ."

Alice heard the baby bleating again.

"Feeding time!" Dad cried jovially. He handed Rachel in through the window, then accepted a sherry from Louie's father. "Righto. Some spirits would do nicely just now, thank you," he said.

Patricia, the baby at her breast, was soon fast asleep. The baby has no hair, Alice thought again, and in spite of her new appreciation of her stepmother, she entertained a fleeting hope that it would never grow any.

"Peter," she whispered in his ear, her head through the open window. "Peter." She shook him lightly, but he did not wake up. "You're pretending to be asleep," she said.

"No, I'm not."

Alice turned back to the bride. Mrs. Pond, her elongated body encased in white, towered high above Louie. Perhaps it was for this event that he'd wanted the velvet Nehru suit so badly.

Mrs. Pond had resumed talking to Alice, and as she talked, Alice experienced a feeling of cool refreshing contentment. A subpoena? Never mind. Louie had been served Mrs. Pond.

"I think you make a perfect couple," Alice said.

"Now," said Louie, "a toast. A toast to the Brodys, what a lovely surprise, a beautiful, beautiful people, and congratulations to them on the birth of the beautiful, beautiful little girl . . ."

She is kind of cute, in a bald sort of way, Alice thought, looking at the little face resting on Patricia's shoulder. Of course, she *is* related to *me*.

"And to you, Mr. Scifo," Dad said, holding up his glass, "on this your final day of peace and freedom, ahem, last day of loneliness I of course meant to say, ha ha . . ." He began to sing "I'm Getting Married in the Morning" in his best cockney accent.

"Want to meet my sister?" Alice said as Caroline walked past, but Caroline just continued on her way.

Alice watched as the older Mr. Scifo tied a pair of boots to Louie's car. They were Alice's boots. Willie, the man of celibacy, began flirting with Caroline, who seemed to cheer up a bit. A gray cat climbed onto the roof of the Pinto and stretched out there. Now Grandma was talking into Willie's microphone with a thick Irish brogue: ". . . where am I gonna find an orchestra to play at three o'clock in the mornin'," the punch line to a joke about the rhythm method. It was late in the afternoon, but the heat was unbearable, close and insistent. Dad presented Louie with a giant jug of Glenfiddich. ("Duty-free. I got it for Peter, but I know he'd want you to have it on such a magical day.") Willie had his arm around Caroline. Two starlings whistled shrilly at each other from the trees.

Peter still sat in the car, a yellow legal pad now propped up against the steering wheel. Alice got in and sat beside him.

"Dad gave Louie a big bottle of scotch he brought for you."

"This is very interesting, Alice," he said, tapping his pencil on the pad. "Look . . ."

"Peter, it's all over," she said. For a moment, she felt lost. Like a soap-opera character who comes out of a coma. She had woken up after months and months, pregnant, in Queens, with an infant half-sister, at a wedding in the street. She put her head on Peter's shoulder. "It's all over."

"Right. Now. I figure that Louie, over the previous ten-month season, has completed, on the average, four successful plays a day, disrupting and annoying Brenda and the family a total of twelve thousand times," Peter replied. Taking this as a perfect score, for Peter could not imagine anyone breaking this record, Louie's CRS, Chaos Rendered Score, was 12,000 with a 1.000 average, he said. Working certain outside factors into his formula, such as Louie's propensity for striking at night and on holidays, the end of his status as a neighbor, his marriage, the existence of the voluntary restraining order, and the possibility of time healing all wounds; assigning each of these factors a numerical value and making various adjustments along the way, Peter hoped to calculate, roughly, a projection of Louie Interference Behavior for the following year.

"The numbers *are* a little misleading here, I admit,"

Peter told Alice. "For example. Louie's projected CRS is incredibly low—a mere 40. So, the quality of the chaos rendered has to be mathematically accounted for. Now, when you consider that each projected instance of chaos rendered occurs on a holiday—Thanksgiving, birthday, Memorial Day, Yom Kippur, whatever—you realize that it has maximum chaos value. My figures—and they're absurdly rough at the moment, just preliminary figures—my figures suggest interference behavior four times a day, but in key situations, so you really have to assign a kind of reverberation factor, of, say, 100 to each instance, which brings the total value up to 4,000, or an average of .333. But when you consider that the original base score total of 12,000 also includes holiday scoring, I don't know, maybe I'm not . . ."

"Alice," Louie said, suddenly beside her, sitting in the car, his mouth close to her ear. He put his arm around her, squeezing her. She could feel his pinkie ring digging into her shoulder. "Alice," he said. "The little lady and myself. We're married, you follow what I'm saying? True. Truly. I want you to understand that, Alice. Don't feel bad. I worry about you, Alice, you understand? I worry about Mommy, Alice. I feel for her. Take care of Mommy, Alice. Mommy's very hurt, see, and that's why we're having this little talk. Father-daughter kind of thing, you follow? Mommy needs you now, Alice. Go to her, Alice, go to her."

"She's away," Alice said. "She went away."

Peter was scribbling and muttering to himself. Louie had returned to the street to toast himself and his bride. Alan Brody joined his wife and baby in the back seat. "Long day," he said, then fell asleep, too. Sleep, sleep, my lovelies, Alice thought. Sleep. For, when you wake, you will be given insufficient portions of ostentatiously spicy ethnic food on large plates in a room stripped of acoustic tiles, remanded to an off-Broadway play, then transported to a lively salsa night club frequented by people of color . . . *on the subway.* She cackled like a witch, but none of them even stirred. The baby's hands were folded into tiny pink fists. Alice noticed that both her father and Patricia had identical white stains on their right shoulders. She took their picture. She took Peter's picture. Then, with her camera, Alice got out of the car. She aimed the camera at Louie and Mrs. Pond. "That's it, that's it, that's *it*," she said, but she did not press the shutter. She felt faint from the heat and sat on the hood and closed her eyes.

"Someday I want to get to that de Scifo villa in Sicily," Mrs. Pond was saying. "I'm waiting for the property values to go up. And then: co-op or condo, condo or co-op? Do you like the sound of La Baronessa Terrace? But first, there's so much here in our own America. We will honeymoon at home—we're driving cross-country!"

"In a car?" Grandma asked.

"Vegas, La (that's what they call L.A.), Frisco. I think we might go all the way to *Vancouver*, although it's not American, not strictly, but there's plenty of scenic real-estate opportunity . . ."

Alice opened her eyes. The glare filled her vision, and there was only white before her, a silvery-white blur and the damp heavy air. She was dizzy and the hood of the car burned beneath her hands as she tried to steady herself. The new Mrs. Scifo was droning in the background, as rhythmic, as unvaried, as the bees in the house. Willie was saying, "Oh, no, *feature* films—that's what I've always been interested in. And rock videos, of course . . ." Perhaps Louie and his bride could house-sit for Dad and Patricia and Dad's baby. Alice heard an accordion launch into "Ha-vah Nagilah." The starlings, inspired perhaps, began whistling in earnest now, up and down the block, dozens of them. Starlings were wonderful mimics. Alice had heard of starlings that were trained to speak, like parrots. These starlings hooted and squealed. "Ha-vah na-ra-na-nah . . ." sang the accordion. Alice blinked against the colorless glare. She breathed deeply. Slowly, the pale blur took shape. A lot of people. Clapping. It was the wedding party, arranged in a semicircle, facing her, close together, their elbows touching, swaying back and forth, clapping to the music from a cassette player that stood, beside the bottle of sherry, on the roof of the Pinto. In the center of this undulating group was Louie Scifo, the scourge of the Brodys, the man who strolled tirelessly up and down the boulevards of Brenda's life, the eternal suitor on his insane promenade, swinging his cane, lifting his hat to Brenda and her family even in their dreams. But now Louie was a married man beneath a pallid, sweltering sky, surrounded by his family, friends, and enemies and the calls of an agitated flock of birds. Alice could see them, the starlings, perched in the trees, dark spots of iridescence glittering like spills of oil. Louie, in his white suit, loomed larger and larger. He was approaching her, holding out his hand. He was taking her hand. Alice was sliding off the car, onto her feet. Heat shimmered from the pavement. The tape player vied with the squealing birds. Overhead, a lone cormorant, long and black, flew toward the sea. With great ceremony, Louie lifted Alice's hand aloft, as if they were to begin a minuet.

"Dance with your mother," Alice said. "Dance with your mother."

And then Alice stood and stared in weary disbelief, for Louie Scifo did exactly as she said.

PLUME   **Ⓓ SIGNET**

THE DELICIOUSLY WITTY
NOVELS OF CATHLEEN SCHINE

☐ **RAMEAU'S NIECE** This delightful literary romp spoofs the cultural elite, taking contemporary fiction to new levels of comedy. Margaret Nathan is the brilliant though mortifyingly forgetful author of an unlikely bestseller celebrated as much by feminists as deconstructionists. She seems blessed until she finds herself seduced by an eighteenth-century lascivious novel she has discovered. "Witty, erotic, hilarious."—*People*   (271614—$10.95)

☐ **TO THE BIRDHOUSE** The good news is that Alice, the inimitable heroine of *Alice in Bed*, is very much up and around. The bad news? Alice, along with the rest of the Brody clan, must rid her mother of a boyfriend from hell. Never has the course of false love followed so fouled-up a path as when Alice and friends set up road-blocks to this reptilian Romeo on a highway of hilarity that runs from the wild West of Manhattan to the wilds of Westport. "Funny . . . joyful . . . wonderful."—*New York Times Book Review*   (276624—$10.95)

☐ **ALICE IN BED** Alice is a sexy, bright, beautiful, liberated post-adolescent, and the bed she occupies is a hospital bed, where she is visited by a succession of doctors, good, bad, enormously indifferent to her pain but in several cases extremely responsive to her charms. Fortunately, Alice is far more than a stricken sexy sickie. She is wise beyond her years, witty past all propriety, and as fresh and funny a heroine as has ever graced the pages of a novel. "A buoyant first novel . . . hilarious!"—*Newsweek*   (276756—$10.95)

AND FROM SIGNET . . .

☐ **THE LOVE LETTER** National Bestseller! Helen MacFarquhar is perfectly happy raising her eleven-year-old daughter, running her own bookstore, and having pleasing passing affairs with sensibly selected lovers. Certainly she should have enough self-control to resist a twenty-year-old college student who works for her, no matter how attractive and attracted he is. Does she? Or does she not? "Perfect!"—*New York Times*   (188470—$6.99)

Prices slightly higher in Canada.